THE NEW PROPHECY

# WARRIORS
## MIDNIGHT

# WARRIORS

# WARRIORS:
# THE NEW PROPHECY

THE NEW PROPHECY

# WARRIORS

## MIDNIGHT

# ERIN
# HUNTER

HARPERCOLLINS*PUBLISHERS*

Midnight

Copyright © 2005 by Working Partners Limited

Series created by Working Partners Limited

All rights reserved. No part of this book may be used or reproduced in any
manner whatsoever without written permission except in the case of brief
quotations embodied in critical articles and reviews. Printed in the United
States of America. For information address HarperCollins Children's
Books, a division of HarperCollins Publishers, 1350 Avenue of the
Americas, New York, NY 10019.

www.harperchildrens.com

Library of Congress Cataloging-in-Publication Data

Hunter, Erin.

Midnight / Erin Hunter.—1st ed.

p.   cm.

Summary: Called by StarClan to fufill a new prophecy, a group of
young cats sets out on a long and dangerous journey, knowing only that
trouble threatens the forest, as the adventures of the warrior clans
continue.

ISBN 0-06-074449-9 — ISBN 0-06-074450-2 (lib. bdg.)

[1. Cats—Fiction.   2. Fantasy.]   I. Title.   II. Series.

PZ7.H916626Mi   2005                                    2004016135

[Fic]—dc22

Typography by Karin Paprocki

7  8  9  10

❖

First Edition

*For Chris, Janet, and Louisa Haslum*

*Special thanks to Cherith Baldry*

# ALLEGIANCES

## THUNDERCLAN

**LEADER**
: **FIRESTAR**—ginger tom with a flame-colored pelt

**DEPUTY**
: **GRAYSTRIPE**—long-haired gray tom

**MEDICINE CAT**
: **CINDERPELT**—dark gray she-cat
  **APPRENTICE, LEAFPAW**

**WARRIORS**
: (toms, and she-cats without kits)

  **MOUSEFUR**—small dusky brown she-cat
  **APPRENTICE, SPIDERPAW**

  **DUSTPELT**—dark brown tabby tom
  **APPRENTICE, SQUIRRELPAW**

  **SANDSTORM**—pale ginger she-cat
  **APPRENTICE, SORRELPAW**

  **CLOUDTAIL**—long-haired white tom

  **BRACKENFUR**—golden brown tabby tom
  **APPRENTICE, WHITEPAW**

  **THORNCLAW**—golden brown tabby tom
  **APPRENTICE, SHREWPAW**

  **BRIGHTHEART**—white she-cat with ginger patches

  **BRAMBLECLAW**—dark brown tabby tom with amber eyes

  **ASHFUR**—pale gray (with darker flecks) tom, dark blue eyes

  **RAINWHISKER**—dark gray tom with blue eyes

  **SOOTFUR**—lighter gray tom with amber eyes

**APPRENTICES** (more than six moons old, in training to become warriors)

**SORRELPAW**—tortoiseshell and white she-cat with amber eyes

**SQUIRRELPAW**—dark ginger she-cat with green eyes

**LEAFPAW**—light brown tabby she-cat with amber eyes and white paws

**SPIDERPAW**—long-limbed black tom with brown underbelly and amber eyes

**SHREWPAW**—small dark brown tom with amber eyes

**WHITEPAW**—white she-cat with green eyes

**QUEENS** (she-cats expecting or nursing kits)

**GOLDENFLOWER**—pale ginger coat, the oldest nursery queen

**FERNCLOUD**—pale gray (with darker flecks) she-cat, green eyes

**ELDERS** (former warriors and queens, now retired)

**FROSTFUR**—beautiful white she-cat with blue eyes

**DAPPLETAIL**—once-pretty tortoiseshell she-cat, the oldest cat in ThunderClan

**SPECKLETAIL**—pale tabby she-cat

**LONGTAIL**—pale tabby tom with dark black stripes, retired early due to failing sight

# SHADOWCLAN

**LEADER**  **BLACKSTAR**—large white tom with huge jet black paws

**DEPUTY**  **RUSSETFUR**—dark ginger she-cat

**MEDICINE CAT**  **LITTLECLOUD**—very small tabby tom

**WARRIORS**  **OAKFUR**—small brown tom
**APPRENTICE, SMOKEPAW**

**TAWNYPELT**—tortoiseshell she-cat with green eyes

**CEDARHEART**—dark gray tom

**ROWANCLAW**—ginger she-cat
**APPRENTICE, TALONPAW**

**TALLPOPPY**—long-legged light brown tabby she-cat

**ELDERS**  **RUNNINGNOSE**—small gray-and-white tom, formerly the medicine cat

# WINDCLAN

**LEADER**  **TALLSTAR**—elderly black-and-white tom with a very long tail

**DEPUTY**

**MUDCLAW**—mottled dark brown tom
**APPRENTICE, CROWPAW**—dark smoky gray, almost black, tom with blue eyes

**MEDICINE CAT**

**BARKFACE**—short-tailed brown tom

**WARRIORS**

**ONEWHISKER**—brown tabby tom

**WEBFOOT**—dark gray tabby tom

**TORNEAR**—tabby tom

**WHITETAIL**—small white she-cat

**ELDERS**

**MORNINGFLOWER**—tortoiseshell she-cat

## RIVERCLAN

**LEADER**

**LEOPARDSTAR**—unusually spotted golden tabby she-cat

**DEPUTY**

**MISTYFOOT**—gray she-cat with blue eyes

**MEDICINE CAT**

**MUDFUR**—long-haired light brown tom
**APPRENTICE, MOTHWING**—beautiful golden tabby she-cat with amber eyes

**WARRIORS**

**BLACKCLAW**—smoky black tom

**HEAVYSTEP**—thickset tabby tom

**STORMFUR**—dark gray tom with amber eyes

**FEATHERTAIL**—light gray she-cat with blue eyes

**HAWKFROST**—broad-shouldered dark brown tom

**MOSSPELT**—tortoiseshell she-cat

**QUEENS**      **DAWNFLOWER**—pale gray she-cat

**ELDERS**      **SHADEPELT**—very dark gray she-cat

**LOUDBELLY**—dark brown tom

## CATS OUTSIDE CLANS

**BARLEY**—black-and-white tom that lives on a farm close to the forest

**RAVENPAW**—sleek black cat that lives on the farm with Barley

**PURDY**—elderly tabby tom that lives in woods near the sea

HIGHSTONES

BARLEY'S FARM

WINDCLAN CAMP

FOURTREES

FALLS

OWL-TREE

RIVER

SUNNING-ROCKS

RIVERCLAN CAMP

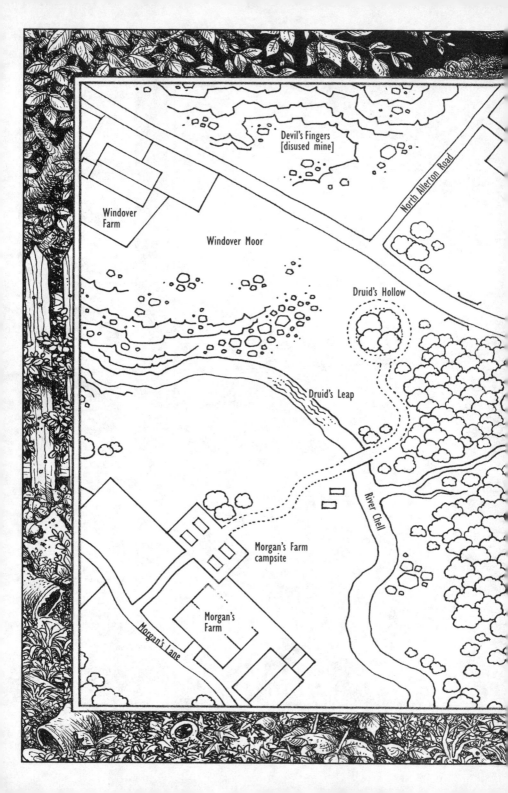

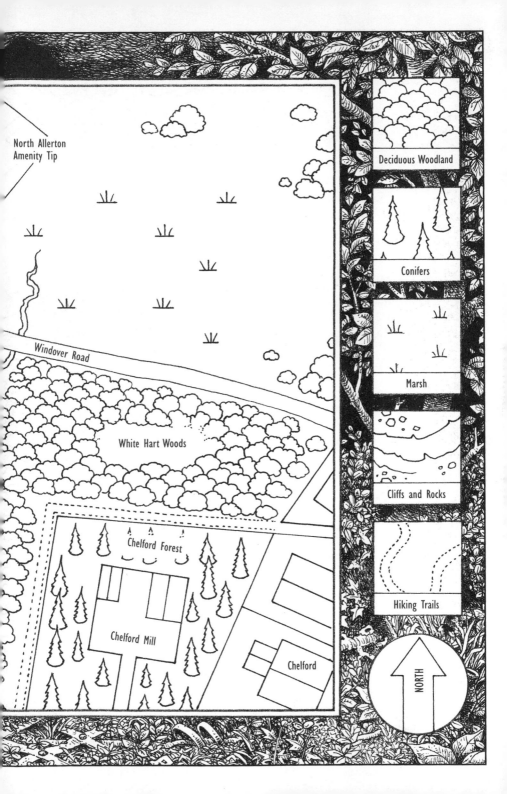

North Allerton
Amenity Tip

Windover Road

White Hart Woods

Chelford Forest

Chelford Mill

Chelford

Deciduous Woodland

Conifers

Marsh

Cliffs and Rocks

Hiking Trails

NORTH

# PROLOGUE

❧

*Night lay upon the forest. There* was no moon, but the stars of Silverpelt shed their frosty glitter over the trees. At the bottom of a rocky hollow, a pool reflected the starshine. The air was heavy with the scents of late greenleaf.

Wind sighed softly through the trees and ruffled the quiet surface of the pool. At the top of the hollow, the fronds of bracken parted to reveal a cat; her bluish gray fur glimmered as she stepped delicately from rock to rock, down to the water's edge.

Sitting on a flat stone that jutted out over the pool, she raised her head to look around. As if at a signal, more cats began to appear, slipping into the hollow from every direction. They padded down to sit as close to the water as they could, until the lower slopes were filled with lithe shapes gazing down into the pool.

The cat who had appeared first rose to her paws. "A new prophecy has come!" she meowed. "A doom that will change everything has been foretold in the stars."

On the opposite side of the pool, another cat bowed his tawny, bracken-colored head. "I have seen this too. There will be doubt, and a great challenge," he agreed.

"Darkness, air, water, and sky will come together, and shake the forest to its roots," the first cat went on. "Nothing will be as it is now, nor as it has been before."

"A great storm is coming," meowed another voice, and the word *storm* was taken up, repeated and passed around the circle until it seemed that thunder rumbled through the ranks of watching cats.

As the murmur died away a lean cat with a glossy black pelt spoke from near the water's edge. "Can nothing change what is about to happen? Not even the courage and spirit of the greatest warrior?"

"The doom will come," the blue-gray cat replied. "But if the Clans meet it like warriors, they may survive." Lifting her head, she let her luminous gaze travel around the hollow. "You have all seen what must befall," she meowed. "And you know what must be done. Four cats must be chosen to hold the fate of their Clans in their paws. Are you ready to make your choices before all of StarClan?"

As she finished speaking, the surface of the pool shivered, though there was no wind to disturb it, then was still again.

The bracken-colored tom rose to his paws, starlight turning the fur on his broad shoulders to silver. "I will begin," he meowed. He glanced sideways to meet the gaze of a light-colored tabby with a twisted jaw. "Crookedstar, do I have your permission to speak for RiverClan?" The tabby bowed his head in agreement, and the first cat went on, "Then I invite you all to see and approve my choice."

He stared down into the water, as motionless as the rocks around him. A pale gray blur appeared on the surface of the pool, and all the cats craned forward to see it more clearly.

"That one?" murmured the blue-gray cat, staring at the shape in the water. "Are you sure, Oakheart?"

The tip of the bracken-colored tom's tail flicked back and forth. "I thought that choice would please you, Bluestar," he meowed, amusement in his tone. "Do you not think she was well mentored?"

"She was excellently mentored." Bluestar's neck fur rose as if he had said something to challenge her, then lay flat again. "Does the rest of StarClan agree?" she asked.

A murmur of assent rose from the watching cats, and the pale gray shape thinned and vanished from the water, leaving it clear and empty again.

Now the black cat stood up and padded to the very edge of the pool. "Here is my choice," he announced. "See and approve it."

This time the shape in the pool was tawny-colored and lean, with strong, well-muscled shoulders. Bluestar gazed down at the image for some moments before nodding. "She has strength and courage," she agreed.

"But Nightstar—does she have loyalty?" called another cat.

The black cat's head whipped around and his claws dug into the ground in front of him. "Are you calling her disloyal?"

"If I do, there's reason for it." The answer was shot back. "She was not born in ShadowClan, was she?"

"Then that could make her a good choice," Bluestar

meowed calmly. "If the Clans cannot work together now, they will all be destroyed. Maybe it will take cats with a paw in two Clans to understand what has to be done." She paused for a moment, but no other objections were forthcoming. "Do StarClan approve?"

There was some hesitation, but it was not too long before soft meows of agreement came from all the assembled cats. The surface of the pool rippled briefly, and when it stilled again the tawny shape had gone.

Another black cat got up and approached the water's edge, limping on one stubby, twisted paw. "My turn, I think," he rasped. "See and approve my choice."

The gray-black shape that formed in the pool was hard to see against the reflection of the night sky, and the cats peered at it for some time before anyone spoke.

"*What?*" the bracken-colored cat exclaimed at last. "That's an apprentice!"

"I had noticed, thank you, Oakheart," the black tom meowed dryly.

"Deadfoot, you can't send an apprentice into danger such as this," another cat called from the back of the crowd.

"Apprentice he may be," Deadfoot retorted, "but he has courage and skill to match many warriors. One day he might make a fine leader of WindClan."

"One day is not now," Bluestar pointed out. "And the qualities of a leader are not necessarily those that the Clans need to save them now. Do you wish to make another choice?"

Deadfoot's tail lashed furiously and his neck fur bristled as he glared at Bluestar. "*This* is my choice," he insisted. "Do you—or any other cat—dare to say he is not worthy?"

"What do you say?" Her gaze went around the circle. "Do StarClan approve? Remember that every Clan will be lost if one of our chosen cats should weaken or fail."

Instead of a murmur of approval, the cats muttered at each other in small groups, casting uneasy glances at the shape in the pool and at the cat beside it. Deadfoot stared back with fury in his eyes, his fur fluffed up so that he looked twice his size. He was obviously ready to take on any cat who challenged him.

At length the muttering died away and Bluestar asked once again, "Does the Clan approve?" The assent came, but it was low and reluctant, and a few cats did not speak at all. Deadfoot let out an ill-tempered growl as he turned and limped back to his place.

When the water was clear again Oakheart meowed, "You have not yet made your choice for ThunderClan, Bluestar."

"No—but I am ready now," she replied. "See and approve my choice." She gazed down proudly as a dark tabby shape formed in the depths of the pool.

Oakheart stared at it, and stretched his jaws wide in a soundless mew of laughter. "*That* one! Bluestar, you never cease to surprise me."

"Why?" Bluestar's tone showed she was nettled. "He is a noble young cat, fit for the challenges this prophecy will bring."

Oakheart's ears twitched. "Did I say he was not?"

Bluestar held his gaze, not looking at the other cats as she demanded, "Does the Clan approve?" When the agreement came, strong and certain, she gave Oakheart a contemptuous flick of her tail and looked away.

"Cats of StarClan," she meowed, raising her voice. "Your choices have been made. Soon the journey must begin, to meet the terrible storm that will be released on the forest. Go to your Clans, and make sure each cat is ready."

She paused, and her eyes blazed with a fierce silver light. "We can choose a warrior to save each Clan, but beyond that we cannot help them. May the spirits of all our warrior ancestors go with these cats, wherever the stars may lead them."

CHAPTER 1

*Leaves rustled as the young tabby* cat slid through a gap between two bushes, his jaws wide open to drink in the scent of prey. On this warm night in late greenleaf, the forest was full of the scuffles of tiny creatures. Movements twitched endlessly at the edge of his vision, but when he turned his head he could see nothing but thick clumps of fern and bramble, dappled with moonlight.

Suddenly he stepped out into a wide clearing and gazed around in confusion. He could not remember being in this part of the forest before. Smooth-cropped grass, glowing silver in a cold wash of moonlight, stretched in front of him as far as a softly rounded rock where another cat was sitting. Starlight sparkled in her fur, and her eyes were two small moons.

The young tabby's bewilderment increased as he recognized her. "Bluestar?" he meowed, his voice shrill with disbelief.

He had been an apprentice when the great leader of ThunderClan had died, four seasons ago, leaping into the gorge with a pack of blood-hungry dogs after her. Like all her

7

Clan, he had grieved for her and honored her for the way she had given up her life to save them. He had never thought to see her again, and he realized for the first time that he must be dreaming.

"Come closer, young warrior," Bluestar meowed. "I have a message for you."

Shivering with awe, the tabby tom crept across the shining stretch of turf until he crouched below the rock and could look up into Bluestar's eyes.

"I'm listening, Bluestar," he mewed.

"A time of trouble is coming to the forest," she told him. "A new prophecy must be fulfilled if the Clans are to survive. You have been chosen to meet with three other cats at the new moon, and you must listen to what midnight tells you."

"What do you mean?" The young cat felt a prickle of dread, cold as snowmelt, creep down his spine. "What kind of trouble? And how can midnight tell us anything?"

"All will be made clear to you," Bluestar replied.

Her voice faded, echoing strangely as if she were speaking from a cavern far beneath the earth. The moonlight also began to grow dim, leaving thick black shadows to creep out of the trees around them.

"No, wait!" the tabby cat cried out. "Don't go!"

He let out a terrified yowl, thrashing his paws and tail, as darkness rose up and engulfed him. Something poked him in the side and his eyes flew open to see Graystripe, the ThunderClan deputy, standing over him with one paw raised to prod him again. He was scuffling among the moss in the warriors' den, with the golden sunlight leaking through the branches above his head.

"Brambleclaw, you crazy furball!" the deputy meowed. "What's all the noise about? You'll scare off all the prey from here to Fourtrees."

"Sorry." Brambleclaw sat up and began picking scraps of moss from his dark fur. "I was just dreaming."

"Dreaming!" grunted a new voice.

Brambleclaw turned his head to see the white warrior Cloudtail heave himself out of a mossy nest nearby and give a long stretch. "Honestly, you're as bad as Firestar," Cloudtail went on. "When he slept in here he was always muttering and twitching in his sleep. A cat couldn't get a good night's rest for all the prey in the forest."

Brambleclaw twitched his ears to hear how disrespectfully the white warrior spoke about the Clan leader. Then he reminded himself that this was Cloudtail, Firestar's kin and former apprentice, well known for his barbed tongue and ready scorn. His impudent talk didn't stop him from being a loyal warrior to his Clan.

Cloudtail gave his long-furred white coat a shake and slipped out of the den, flicking the end of his tail at Brambleclaw in a friendly way to take the sting out of his words as he went by.

"Come on, you lot," meowed Graystripe. "It's time you were moving." He picked his way through the moss on the floor of the den to prod Ashfur awake. "Hunting patrols will be going out soon. Brackenfur is organizing them."

"Right," Brambleclaw mewed. His vision of Bluestar was

fading, though her ominous message echoed in his ears. Could it really be true that there was a new prophecy from StarClan? It seemed fairly unlikely. For a start, Brambleclaw could not imagine why she would choose to give it to him, of all the cats in ThunderClan. Medicine cats frequently received signs from StarClan, and ThunderClan's leader, Firestar, had often been guided by his dreams. But they were not for ordinary warriors. Trying to blame his wild imaginings on too much fresh-kill the night before, Brambleclaw gave his shoulder one last lick and followed Cloudtail out through the trailing branches.

The sun was barely up above the hedge of thorns that surrounded the camp, but the day was already warm. Sunlight lay like honey on the bare earth in the center of the clearing. Sorrelpaw, the oldest of the apprentices, lay stretched out beside the ferns that sheltered the apprentices' den, sharing tongues with her den mates Spiderpaw and Shrewpaw.

Cloudtail had gone over to the nettle patch where the warriors ate and was already gulping down a starling. Brambleclaw noticed that the pile of fresh-kill was very low; as Graystripe had said, the Clan needed to hunt right away. He was about to go and join the white warrior when Sorrelpaw sprang up and came bounding across the clearing toward him.

"It's today!" she announced excitedly.

Brambleclaw blinked. "What is?"

"My warrior ceremony!" With a little *mrrow* of happiness, the tortoiseshell she-cat hurled herself at Brambleclaw;

the unexpected attack bowled him over and they wrestled together on the dusty ground, just as they used to when they were kits together in the nursery.

Sorrelpaw's hind paws battered Brambleclaw in the belly, and he thanked StarClan that her claws were sheathed. There was no doubt that she would make a strong and dangerous warrior, one that every cat would respect.

"All right, all right, that's enough." Brambleclaw cuffed Sorrelpaw gently over one ear and scrambled up. "If you're going to be a warrior, you'll have to stop behaving like a kit."

"A kit?" Sorrelpaw meowed indignantly. She sat in front of him, her fur sticking up in clumps and covered with dust. "Me? Never! I've waited a long time for this, Brambleclaw."

"I know. You deserve it."

Sorrelpaw had ventured too close to the Thunderpath while she was chasing a squirrel in newleaf. A Twoleg monster had struck her a glancing blow, injuring her shoulder. While she lay in Cinderpelt's den for three long, uncomfortable moons, under the gentle care of the medicine cat, her brothers, Sootfur and Rainwhisker, had become warriors. Sorrelpaw had been determined to follow them as soon as Cinderpelt declared her fit enough to begin training again; Brambleclaw had watched how hard she had worked with her mentor, Sandstorm, until her shoulder was as good as new. She had never shown any bitterness at being forced to train for several moons longer than the usual apprenticeship. She really deserved her warrior ceremony.

"I've just taken fresh-kill to Ferncloud," she meowed to

Brambleclaw. "Her kits are beautiful! Have you seen them yet?"

"No, not yet," Brambleclaw replied. Ferncloud's second litter of kits had been born only the day before.

"Go now," Sorrelpaw urged him. "You've just enough time before we hunt." She sprang up and danced a few steps sideways, as if all her energy had to go somewhere.

Brambleclaw set off for the nursery, which was hidden in the depths of a bramble thicket near the center of the camp. He squeezed through the narrow entrance, wincing as thorns scraped against his broad shoulders. Inside it was warm and quiet. Ferncloud was lying on her side in a deep nest of moss. Her green eyes glowed as she gazed at the three tiny kits curled up snugly in the curve of her body: one was pale gray like her, the other two brown tabbies like their father, Dustpelt. He was in the nursery too, crouched beside Ferncloud with his paws tucked under him, occasionally rasping his tongue affectionately over her ear.

"Hi, there, Brambleclaw," he meowed as the younger warrior appeared. "Come to see the new kits?" He looked ready to burst with pride, quite different from his usual prickly, detached air.

"They're beautiful," Brambleclaw mewed, touching noses with Ferncloud in greeting. "Have you chosen names for them yet?"

Ferncloud shook her head, blinking drowsily up at him. "Not yet."

"There's time enough for that." Goldenflower, the oldest

ThunderClan queen and Brambleclaw's own mother, spoke from her mossy bed. She had no kits of her own to nurse, but she had decided to stay in the nursery and share the care of the new arrivals instead of taking up her warrior duties again; she was nearing the time when she would go to join the elders in their den, and was the first to admit that her hearing and eyesight were no longer sharp enough to keep up with the best hunting patrols. "They're strong, healthy kits, that's what matters, and Ferncloud has plenty of milk."

Brambleclaw respectfully dipped his head to her. "She's lucky to have you to help look after them."

"Well, I didn't do too bad a job with you," Goldenflower purred proudly.

"There's something you could do for me," Dustpelt meowed to Brambleclaw as he was leaving.

"Sure, if I can."

"Keep an eye on Squirrelpaw, would you? I want to spend a day or two with Ferncloud, while the kits are still so small, but Squirrelpaw shouldn't be left without a mentor for too long."

*Squirrelpaw!* Brambleclaw groaned inwardly. Firestar's daughter, eight moons old, recently apprenticed—and the biggest nuisance in ThunderClan.

"It'll be good practice for when you have an apprentice of your own," Dustpelt added, as if he sensed his Clan mate's reluctance.

Brambleclaw knew that Dustpelt was right. He hoped that Firestar would choose him to be a mentor before much longer, with an apprentice of his own to train in the warrior code, but he also hoped that his apprentice would not be some smart-aleck ginger she-cat who thought she knew it all. He was well aware that Squirrelpaw would not take kindly to orders coming from him.

"Okay, Dustpelt," he meowed. "I'll do my best."

When Brambleclaw emerged from the nursery he saw that more cats had appeared in the clearing. Brightheart, a pretty white she-cat with ginger patches on her fur like fallen leaves, had just chosen a piece of fresh-kill from the remains of the pile and was taking it across to where Cloudtail still sat by the nettle patch. The uninjured side of her face was turned to Brambleclaw, so that he could almost forget the disfiguring wounds she had received when the dog pack roamed the forest. One side of her face was seamed with scars, and her ear had been shredded; there was only a gouge mark where her eye should be. Even though she survived the vicious attack, the Clan had feared that she would never be a warrior. It was Cloudtail who had trained with her and worked out ways of making up for her blindness on that side, even turning it into a strength, so that now she could fight and hunt as well as any cat.

Cloudtail greeted her with a flick of his tail and she sat beside him to eat.

"Brambleclaw! There you are!"

Brambleclaw turned and saw a long-legged ginger warrior heading toward him from the direction of the warriors' den. He padded over to meet him. "Hi, Brackenfur. Graystripe said you're organizing hunting patrols."

"That's right," Brackenfur meowed. "Will you go out with Squirrelpaw this morning, please?"

He angled his ears toward the apprentices' den, and Brambleclaw noticed for the first time that Squirrelpaw was half-concealed in the shade of the ferns. She sat tall, her tail curled around her paws, her green eyes following a bright-winged butterfly. When Brackenfur beckoned her with his tail, she got up and strolled across the clearing, her tail straight up and her dark ginger fur gleaming in the sunlight.

"Hunting patrol," Brackenfur explained briefly. "Dustpelt is busy, so you can go with Brambleclaw. Can you find another cat to go with you?"

Without waiting for an answer, he hurried off toward Sandstorm and Sorrelpaw.

Squirrelpaw yawned and stretched. "Well," she meowed. "Where shall we go?"

"I thought Sunningrocks," Brambleclaw began. "Then we can—"

"Sunningrocks?" Squirrelpaw interrupted, her eyes stretching wide in disbelief. "Are you mouse-brained? On a day as hot as this, all the prey will be hiding down cracks. We won't catch so much as a whisker."

"It's still early," Brambleclaw replied crossly. "The prey will be out for a while yet."

Squirrelpaw let out a heavy sigh. "Honestly, Brambleclaw, you always think you know better than anyone else."

"Well, I *am* a warrior," Brambleclaw pointed out, and knew instantly it was the wrong thing to say.

Squirrelpaw bowed her head in deep and exaggerated respect. "Yes, O Great One," she meowed. "I shall do exactly what you say. And when we come back empty-pawed, maybe you'll admit that I was right."

"Well, then," Brambleclaw mewed, "if you're so clever, where do you think we should hunt?"

"Up toward Fourtrees, by the stream," Squirrelpaw replied promptly. "That's a much better place."

Brambleclaw was even more annoyed when he realized that she might be right. In spite of the endless hot days that had lasted all greenleaf, the stream there still ran cool and deep, with thick clumps of reeds where prey could hide. He hesitated, wondering how he could change his mind without losing face in front of the apprentice.

"Squirrelpaw." A new voice rescued him, and Brambleclaw realized that Sandstorm, Squirrelpaw's mother, had padded over to join them. "Stop ruffling Brambleclaw's fur. You chatter as much as a nest of jackdaws." Her annoyed green gaze turned on Brambleclaw and she added, "And you're just as bad. The pair of you are always squabbling; you can't be trusted to hunt together if you can't even get out of the clearing without scaring half the prey between here and Fourtrees."

"Sorry," Brambleclaw muttered, embarrassment sweeping through his fur from ears to tail-tip.

"You're a warrior; you should know better. Go and ask Cloudtail if you can hunt with him. And as for you," Sandstorm meowed to her daughter, "you can come and hunt with me and Sorrelpaw. Brackenfur won't mind. And you'll do as you're told, or I'll know the reason why."

Without looking back, she headed straight for the gorse tunnel that led out of the camp. Squirrelpaw stood still for a moment, a sulky look in her green eyes, and scuffed the ground with her forepaws.

Sorrelpaw came up and gave her a friendly nudge. "Come on," she urged. "This is my last hunt as an apprentice. Let's make it a good one."

Reluctantly Squirrelpaw nodded, and the two cats set off together after Sandstorm; the dark ginger apprentice shot a last glare at Brambleclaw as she passed him.

Brambleclaw shrugged. Squirrelpaw would get more experienced mentoring from Sandstorm than she would from him, so he wasn't letting Dustpelt down even though the warrior had asked him to keep an eye on her. And he wouldn't have to listen all morning to her annoying chatter, so he wasn't sure why he felt slightly disappointed at being set on a different patrol.

Pushing off the feeling, he bounded over to the nettle patch where Cloudtail and Brightheart were finishing their prey. Their single kit, Whitepaw, had just padded across to join them; as Brambleclaw came up he heard her say, "Are you going hunting? *Please* can I come with you?"

Cloudtail flicked his tail. "No." Whitepaw had begun to look disappointed when he added, "Brackenfur said he'd take you. He is your mentor, after all."

"He told me he's really proud of you," Brightheart purred.

Whitepaw brightened up. "Great! I'll go find him."

Cloudtail gave her an affectionate cuff over the ear with one paw before she dashed off, her tail waving excitedly.

Brambleclaw hoped that didn't mean that Cloudtail and Brightheart wanted to go out alone. "Do you mind if I join you?" he asked.

"Sure, you can come," Cloudtail replied. He jumped up and nodded to Brightheart, then the three cats trotted together across the clearing toward the gorse tunnel.

Just before he headed into the close-growing thorns, Brambleclaw glanced over his shoulder at the quiet activity going on in the camp. Every cat looked well fed, sleek furred, and confident that their territory was safe. Bluestar's message came back to echo in his mind. Could it be true that some great trouble was coming upon the forest? Brambleclaw felt his fur prickle with foreboding. He decided that he would not tell any cat about the dream. That seemed like the only way he could convince himself that it meant nothing, and there was no new prophecy coming to disrupt life in the forest as they knew it.

The sun was setting in a ball of fire, turning the tops of the trees to flame and sending long shadows across the clearing. Brambleclaw stretched and sighed with satisfaction. He was tired after the long day's hunting, but his stomach was comfortably full. All the Clan had fed too, and there was an ample pile of fresh-kill. Greenleaf had been longer and hotter than any cat could remember, but the forest was still full of prey, and there was plenty of water in the stream close to Fourtrees.

*A good day*, Brambleclaw thought contentedly. *This is how life should be.*

The rest of the Clan was beginning to slip out into the clearing and gather around the Highrock, and Brambleclaw realized it was time for Sorrelpaw's warrior ceremony. He padded closer to the Highrock and sat down close to Ferncloud's brother, Ashfur, who gave him a friendly nod. Graystripe was already sitting at the base of the rock, looking as proud as if his own apprentice were about to be made a warrior. Graystripe had fathered two kits, but they had grown up in RiverClan, where their mother had been born. He had no kits in ThunderClan, but liked to keep an eye on the progress of all the young cats.

As Brambleclaw watched, the deputy was joined by Cinderpelt, the medicine cat, and her apprentice, Leafpaw, Squirrelpaw's sister. She looked nothing like Squirrelpaw; she was smaller and slighter, with pale tabby fur and a white chest and paws. The sisters were not much alike in character either. When Leafpaw sat down and tipped her head to one side to listen to what her mentor and the deputy were saying to each other, Brambleclaw wondered, not for the first time, how she managed to be so quiet and attentive when her sister Squirrelpaw never stopped talking.

At last Firestar, the Clan leader, appeared from his den at the other side of the Highrock. He was a strong, lithe warrior, his pelt blazing like flame in the light of the setting sun. After pausing for a word with Graystripe, he bunched his muscles and leaped to the top of the Highrock, from where he could look down on the Clan.

"Cats of ThunderClan!" he announced. "Let all those cats old enough to catch their own prey join here beneath the Highrock for a Clan meeting."

Most of the cats were there already, but as Firestar's voice echoed around the clearing the last of the Clan members slid out from their dens and trotted over to join the others.

Last of all came Sorrelpaw with her mentor, Sandstorm. Her tortoiseshell fur was freshly groomed, her white chest and paws shining like snow. Her amber eyes gleamed with pride and suppressed excitement as she paced across the clearing. Beside her, Sandstorm looked just as proud; Brambleclaw knew how much the ginger she-cat had suffered when she had seen her apprentice lying injured on the Thunderpath. They had both needed courage and perseverance to reach this ceremony.

Firestar sprang down from the Highrock to meet the apprentice and her mentor. "Sandstorm," he began, using the formal words that had been handed down through all the Clans, "are you satisfied that this apprentice is ready to become a warrior of ThunderClan?"

Sandstorm inclined her head. "She will be a warrior the Clan can be proud of," she replied.

Firestar raised his eyes to where the first stars of Silverpelt were beginning to appear in the evening sky. "I, Firestar, leader of ThunderClan, call upon my warrior ancestors to look down upon this apprentice." The Clan was hushed as his voice rang out across the clearing. "She has trained hard to understand the ways of your noble code, and I commend her to you as a warrior in her turn." He turned to Sorrelpaw, locking his gaze with hers. "Sorrelpaw, do you promise to uphold the warrior code and to protect and defend this Clan, even at the cost of your life?"

Remembering how he had felt at this moment in his own warrior ceremony, Brambleclaw watched Sorrelpaw's whole body quiver with anticipation as she lifted her chin and replied clearly, "I do."

"Then by the powers of StarClan I give you your warrior name. Sorrelpaw, from this moment you will be known as Sorreltail. StarClan honors your courage and your patience, and we welcome you as a full warrior of ThunderClan."

Stepping forward, Firestar rested his muzzle on top of Sorreltail's head. In return she gave his shoulder a respectful lick before backing away.

The rest of the warriors gathered around her, welcoming her and calling her by her new name. "Sorreltail! Sorreltail!" Her brothers, Sootfur and Rainwhisker, were among the first, their eyes gleaming with pride that their sister had finally joined them as a warrior.

Firestar waited until the noise had died down. "Sorreltail, according to tradition you must keep vigil in silence tonight, and watch over the camp."

"While the rest of us get a good night's sleep," Cloudtail added.

The Clan leader flashed him a warning glance but said nothing as the cats parted to let Sorreltail take up her position in the middle of the clearing. She sat with her tail curled around her paws and her gaze fixed on the darkening sky, where the light of Silverpelt grew steadily stronger.

With the ceremony over, the rest of the cats slipped away into the shadows. Brambleclaw stretched and yawned, looking forward to his comfortable nest in the warriors' den, but content to stay in the clearing for a while to enjoy the warm evening. He could not see any signs that other cats had shared his disturbing dream; and yet Bluestar had suggested that three other cats would be involved in the new prophecy. Brambleclaw felt a purr rising into his throat, half-amused by how quickly he had believed that a cat from StarClan had visited him in his dreams. That would teach him to gulp down fresh-kill just before he went to sleep.

"Brambleclaw." Firestar padded over and settled down beside him. "Cloudtail says you hunted well today."

"Thank you, Firestar."

The leader's gaze was fixed on his daughters, Leafpaw and Squirrelpaw, who were heading toward the pile of fresh-kill.

"Do you miss Tawnypelt?" Firestar meowed unexpectedly.

Brambleclaw blinked in surprise. Tawnypelt was his sister; the former ThunderClan deputy, Tigerstar, had fathered them before he had been banished from the Clan for trying to seize power from Bluestar, who was leader then. Later Tigerstar had made himself leader of ShadowClan, only to be killed by a rogue cat in a failed attempt to extend his power over the whole forest. Tawnypelt had always felt that ThunderClan blamed her for her father's crimes, and she had made the decision to join ShadowClan shortly after he became that Clan's leader.

"Yes," Brambleclaw replied. "Yes, Firestar, I miss her every day."

"I didn't understand how you might feel about her. Not until I saw how close those two are." Firestar nodded toward the two sister apprentices, who were choosing prey from the pile.

"Firestar, you're not being fair to yourself," Brambleclaw insisted uncomfortably. "After all, you miss your sister, don't you?" he dared to add.

Firestar had begun life as a kittypet before he joined ThunderClan, and his sister, Princess, still lived with Twolegs. Firestar visited her from time to time, and Brambleclaw knew very well how important they were to each other. Princess had given Firestar her firstborn kit to raise as a warrior—and that was Cloudtail, Brightheart's loyal friend.

The Clan leader tilted his head to one side, thinking. "Of course I miss Princess," he meowed at last. "But she's a kittypet. She could never live this kind of life. You must wish that Tawnypelt had stayed here in ThunderClan."

"I guess I do," Brambleclaw admitted. "But she's happier where she is."

"That's true." Firestar nodded. "The most important thing is that you've both found a Clan where you can be loyal."

A warm feeling crept through Brambleclaw. Once Firestar had doubted his loyalty because he looked so much like his father, Tigerstar, with the same muscular body and dark tabby pelt, the same amber eyes.

Brambleclaw suddenly wondered if a truly loyal Clan cat would mention the disturbing dream and Bluestar's warning that great trouble was coming to the forest. He was trying to find the words to start when Firestar stood up, dipped his head briefly in farewell, and padded over to where Sandstorm was sitting with Graystripe near the Highrock.

Brambleclaw almost followed him, but then he reminded himself that if StarClan really wanted to send a prophecy of great danger, they would not give it to one of the youngest, least experienced warriors in the Clan. They would tell the medicine cat, or perhaps the Clan leader himself. And obviously Firestar and Cinderpelt had not received an omen, or they would be telling the Clan what to do about it. No, Brambleclaw told himself again, there was nothing whatsoever to worry about.

# CHAPTER 2

❧

*The sun had not yet risen* when Brambleclaw set out with the dawn patrol. Even in the few days since Sorreltail's warrior ceremony, the leaves had begun to turn to gold and the first chill of leaf-fall lay on the forest, though it still hadn't rained for longer than a moon. The young warrior shivered as long grasses, heavy with dew, brushed against his fur. Cobwebs spread a gray film over the bushes, and the air was filled with damp, leafy scents. The twittering of waking birds began to drown out the soft padding of the cats' paws.

Brightheart's brother, Thornclaw, who was in the lead, paused to look back at Brambleclaw and Ashfur. "Firestar wants us to check Snakerocks," he meowed. "Watch out for adders. There are more of them since the weather has been so hot."

Brambleclaw instinctively unsheathed his claws. The adders would be hidden in cracks now, but as soon as the sun came up the warmth would tempt them out again. One bite from those poisoned jaws could kill a warrior before a medicine cat could do anything to help.

Before they had gone very far Brambleclaw began to hear

faint sounds behind him, as if something were moving around in the undergrowth. He paused, glancing back in the hope of an easy bit of prey. At first he could see nothing; then he noticed the fronds of a thick clump of fern waving about, though there was no breeze. He sniffed the air, opening his jaws to drink it in, before letting the breath out again with a sigh.

"Come out, Squirrelpaw," he meowed.

There was a moment's silence. Then the bracken waved again and the stems parted as the dark ginger she-cat came out into the open. Her green eyes glared defiance.

"What's going on?" Thornclaw padded up to Brambleclaw, with Ashfur just behind him.

Brambleclaw indicated the apprentice with a flick of his tail. "I heard something behind us," he explained. "She must have followed us from the camp."

"Don't talk about me as if I weren't here!" Squirrelpaw protested hotly.

"You shouldn't be here!" Brambleclaw retorted; somehow Squirrelpaw had only to open her mouth for him to feel that his fur was being rubbed the wrong way.

"Stop bickering, the pair of you," Thornclaw growled. "You're not kits anymore. Squirrelpaw, tell us what you're doing. Did some cat send you with a message?"

"She wouldn't have been skulking in the bracken if they had," Brambleclaw couldn't resist pointing out.

"No, they didn't," Squirrelpaw meowed with a resentful glance at Brambleclaw. Her paws scuffled in the grass. "I wanted to come with you, that's all. I haven't been on a patrol for *ages*."

"And you weren't told to come on this one," Thornclaw replied. "Does Dustpelt know you're here?"

"No," Squirrelpaw admitted. "He promised last night we'd do some training, but every cat knows he spends all day in the nursery with Ferncloud and their kits."

"Not anymore," Ashfur mewed. "Not since the kits opened their eyes. Squirrelpaw, I think you might be in trouble if Dustpelt goes looking for you."

"You'd better go back to camp right away," Thornclaw decided.

Anger flared up in Squirrelpaw's eyes, and she took a step forward that brought her nose-to-nose with Thornclaw. "You're not my mentor, so don't order me around!"

Thornclaw's nostrils flared minutely as he let out a patient sigh, and Brambleclaw admired his self-control. If Squirrelpaw had spoken to *him* like that, he would have been tempted to rake his claws over her ear.

Even Squirrelpaw seemed to realize she had gone too far. "I'm sorry, Thornclaw," she meowed. "But it's true I *haven't* been on patrol for days. *Please* can I come?"

Thornclaw exchanged a glance with Ashfur and Brambleclaw. "All right," he mewed. "But don't blame me if Dustpelt turns you into crowfood when we get back."

Squirrelpaw gave a little skip of excitement. "Thank you, Thornclaw! Where are we going? Are we looking for anything special? Is there going to be trouble?"

Thornclaw swished his tail across her mouth to silence her. "Snakerocks," he replied. "And it's up to us to make sure there won't be trouble."

"Watch out for adders, though," Brambleclaw added.

"I know that!" Squirrelpaw flashed back at him.

"And we do it *quietly*," Thornclaw ordered her. "I don't want to hear another squeak out of you unless there's something I need to know."

Squirrelpaw opened her mouth to reply, then took in what he had said and nodded vigorously.

The patrol set off again. Brambleclaw had to admit that now she had gotten her own way, Squirrelpaw was behaving sensibly, slipping quietly along behind the leader and staying alert for every sound and movement in the undergrowth.

The sun was well risen by the time the four cats emerged from the trees and saw the smooth, rounded shapes of Snakerocks in front of them. A dark hole gaped at the foot of one of them; it was the cave where the dog pack had hidden. Brambleclaw shuddered, remembering that Tigerstar, his own father, had tried to lead the savage animals to the ThunderClan camp in deadly revenge against his former Clan mates.

Squirrelpaw noticed his expression. "Scared of adders?" she taunted him.

"Yes," Brambleclaw replied. "And so should you be."

"Whatever." She shrugged. "They're probably more scared of us."

Before Brambleclaw could stop her, she bounded forward into the clearing, obviously meaning to poke her nose into the hole.

"Stop!" Thornclaw's voice brought her skidding to a halt. "Hasn't Dustpelt told you that we don't go dashing in anywhere before we're sure of what we're going to find?"

Squirrelpaw looked embarrassed. "Of course he has."

"Well, then, act like you might have listened to him once or twice." Thornclaw padded up beside the apprentice. "Have a good sniff," he suggested. "See if you can scent anything."

The young she-cat stood with her head raised, drawing the morning air into her mouth. "Mouse," she meowed brightly after a moment. "Can we hunt, Thornclaw?"

"Later," the warrior replied. "Now concentrate."

Squirrelpaw tasted the air again. "The Thunderpath, just over there"—she waved her tail—"and a Twoleg with a dog. But that's stale," she added. "I'd guess they were here yesterday."

"Very good." Thornclaw sounded impressed, and Squirrelpaw curled her tail up in delight.

"There's something else," she went on. "A horrible scent . . . I don't think I've smelled it before."

Brambleclaw raised his head and sniffed. He quickly identified the scents Squirrelpaw had mentioned, and the new, unfamiliar one. "Badger," he meowed.

Thornclaw nodded. "That's right. It looks as if it's moved into the cave where the dogs were."

Ashfur groaned. "Just our luck!"

"Why?" Squirrelpaw asked. "What are badgers like? Are they a problem?"

"Are they ever!" Brambleclaw growled. "They're no good to any cat, and they'd kill you as soon as look at you."

Squirrelpaw's eyes widened, though she looked more impressed than frightened.

Ashfur cautiously approached the dark cave mouth, sniffed, and peered inside. "It's dark as a fox's heart in there," he reported, "but I don't think the badger is at home."

While he was speaking Brambleclaw suddenly caught the scent again, much stronger this time, washing over him from somewhere behind them. He leaped around to see a pointed, striped face appear from behind the trunk of a nearby tree, its huge pads crushing the grass, its muzzle snuffling along the ground.

"Look out!" he yowled, every hair on his pelt bristling in fear. He had never been this close to a badger before. Whirling around, he dashed out into the clearing. "Squirrelpaw, *run!*"

As soon as Brambleclaw gave the alarm, Ashfur dived into the undergrowth, while Thornclaw bounded toward the safety of the trees. But Squirrelpaw stayed where she was, her gaze fixed on the huge creature.

"This way, Squirrelpaw!" Thornclaw called, starting to come back.

The apprentice still hesitated; Brambleclaw barreled into her, thrusting her toward the trees. "I said run!"

Her green eyes, blazing with fear and excitement, met his for a heartbeat. The badger was lumbering forward, its small eyes glittering as it scented cats intruding onto its territory. Squirrelpaw pelted toward the edge of the clearing and launched herself up the nearest tree. Reaching a low branch she dug in her claws and crouched there, her ginger fur fluffed out.

Brambleclaw clawed his way up beside her. Down below the badger was blundering back and forth, as if it could not tell where the cats had gone. Its black-and-white head swung threateningly from side to side. Brambleclaw knew that it could not see very well; usually badgers only came out after dark, and this one would be on its way back to the cave after a night's feeding on worms and grubs.

"Would it eat us?" Squirrelpaw asked breathlessly.

"No," Brambleclaw replied, trying to slow his pounding heart. "Even a fox kills to eat, but a badger will kill you just for getting in its way. We're not prey to them, but they won't tolerate any trespassers on their territory. Why did you hang about down there instead of running like we told you?"

"I've never seen a badger before, and I wanted to. Dustpelt says we should get all the experience we can."

"Does that include the experience of having your fur ripped off?" Brambleclaw asked dryly, but for once Squirrelpaw didn't reply.

While he was speaking Brambleclaw hadn't taken his eyes off the creature below. He breathed a sigh of relief as it gave up the search and padded over to the cave mouth, where it squeezed itself inside and was gone.

Thornclaw leaped down from the tree where he had taken refuge. "That was closer than I'd like," he meowed as Brambleclaw and Squirrelpaw scrambled down to join him. "Where's Ashfur?"

"Here." Ashfur's pale gray head popped out of a tangle of briars. "Do you think that badger is the same one that killed

Willowpelt last leaf-bare?"

"Maybe," Thornclaw replied. "Cloudtail and Mousefur drove it away from the camp, but we never found out where it went."

A pang of sadness went through Brambleclaw as he remembered the silver-gray she-cat. Willowpelt was the mother of Sorreltail, Sootfur, and Rainwhisker, but she had not lived to see her kits become warriors.

"So what are we going to do about it?" Squirrelpaw asked eagerly. "Shall we go in there and kill it? There are four of us, and only one badger. How hard could it be?"

Brambleclaw winced, while Thornclaw closed his eyes and waited a moment before speaking. "Squirrelpaw, you *never* go into a badger's den. Or a fox's, for that matter. They'll attack right away, there isn't enough room to maneuver, and you can't see what you're doing."

"But—"

"*No.* We'll head back to camp and report it. Firestar will decide what to do."

Without waiting for Squirrelpaw to argue any more, he set off in the direction they had come. Ashfur fell in behind him, but Squirrelpaw paused at the edge of the clearing. "We could have dealt with it," she grumbled, glancing back longingly at the dark mouth of the cave. "I could have lured it out, and then—"

"And then it would have killed you with one swipe of its paw, and we'd *still* have to go back and report it," Brambleclaw meowed discouragingly. "What do you think we would have said? 'Sorry, Firestar, but we accidentally let a badger get your daughter'? He would have our fur off. Badgers are bad news, and that's that."

"Well, you wouldn't catch Firestar leaving a badger in ThunderClan territory without doing anything." Squirrelpaw swung her tail up defiantly and plunged into the undergrowth to catch up with Thornclaw and Ashfur.

Brambleclaw raised his eyes, murmured, "Great StarClan!" and followed.

When he emerged from the gorse tunnel into the clearing, the first cat he saw was Dustpelt. The brown tabby warrior was pacing up and down outside the apprentices' den, his tail lashing from side to side. Two of the other apprentices, Spiderpaw and Whitepaw, were crouched in the shade of the ferns, watching him apprehensively.

As soon as Dustpelt spotted Squirrelpaw, he marched across the clearing toward her.

"Uh-oh," Squirrelpaw muttered.

"Well?" the tabby warrior's voice was icy. Brambleclaw winced, knowing how short-tempered he was; the only cat who had never felt the rough side of his tongue was Ferncloud. "What have you got to say for yourself?"

Squirrelpaw met his glare bravely, but there was a quaver in her voice as she replied, "I went on patrol, Dustpelt."

"Oh, on patrol! I *see*. And which cat ordered you to go? Graystripe? Firestar?"

"No cat ordered me. But I thought—"

"No, you didn't think." Dustpelt's voice was scathing. "I told you we would train today. Mousefur and Brackenfur took their apprentices to the training hollow to practice their fighting moves. We could have gone with them, but we didn't, because you weren't here. Do you realize that every cat has been searching the camp for you?"

Squirrelpaw shook her head, scuffling the ground with her front paws.

"When no cat could find you, Firestar took out a patrol to try following your scent. Did you see anything of him?"

Another shake of the head. Brambleclaw realized that following a scent in the heavy dew that morning would have been next to impossible.

"Your Clan leader has better things to do than chase after apprentices who can't do as they're told," Dustpelt went on. "Thornclaw, why did you let her go with you?"

"I'm sorry, Dustpelt," Thornclaw apologized. "I thought she'd be safer with us than wandering around the forest by herself."

Dustpelt snorted. "That's true."

"We could still go and do the training," Squirrelpaw suggested.

"Oh, no. No more training for you until you learn what being an apprentice really means." Dustpelt paused for a heartbeat. "You can spend the rest of the day looking after the elders. Make sure they have enough fresh-kill. Change their bedding. Go over their pelts for ticks." He blinked. "I'm sure Cinderpelt has plenty of mouse bile for you."

Squirrelpaw's eyes flew wide in dismay. "Oh, yuck!"

"Well, what are you waiting for?"

The young apprentice stared at him for a moment longer,

as if she couldn't believe he really meant it. When there was no change in her mentor's hard stare, she whisked around and flounced across the clearing toward the elders' den.

"If Firestar's out looking for Squirrelpaw, we'll have to wait for him to get back before we can report the badger," Thornclaw observed.

"Badger? What badger?" asked Dustpelt.

While Thornclaw and Ashfur began to describe what they had seen at Snakerocks, Brambleclaw bounded across the clearing and caught up with Squirrelpaw just outside the elders' den.

"What do you want?" she spat.

"Don't be angry," Brambleclaw mewed. He couldn't help feeling sorry for her, even though she had deserved some sort of punishment for leaving the camp without any cat knowing where she was going. "I'll help you with the elders, if you like."

Squirrelpaw opened her mouth as if she were about to make a rude retort, and then clearly thought better of it. "Okay, thanks," she muttered ungraciously.

"You go and get the mouse bile, and I'll make a start on the bedding."

Squirrelpaw's eyes opened wide in a winning expression. "You wouldn't rather get the mouse bile, would you?"

"No, I wouldn't. Dustpelt especially told you to do that. Don't you think he'll check?"

Squirrelpaw shrugged. "No harm in trying." With a flick of her tail, she stalked off to find Cinderpelt.

Brambleclaw headed for the elders' den, which was in a patch of grass sheltered by a fallen tree. The tree was a burned-out shell; Brambleclaw could still scent the acrid tang from the fire that had swept through the camp more than four seasons ago, when he was only a kit. But the grass had grown up again around the tree trunk, thick and luxuriant, making a comfortable home for the elderly cats whose service to the Clan was done.

When he pushed his way through the grasses he found the elders sunning themselves in the small, flattened clearing. Dappletail, the oldest cat in ThunderClan, was curled up asleep, her patchy tortoiseshell pelt rising and falling with each breath. Frostfur, a still beautiful white queen, was dabbing lazily at a beetle in the grass. Speckletail and Longtail were crouched together as if they were in the middle of a good gossip. Brambleclaw felt the familiar jolt of sympathy when he looked at Longtail; the pale tabby tom was still a young warrior, but his eyesight had begun to fail so that he could no longer fight or hunt for himself.

"Hi, there, Brambleclaw." Longtail's head swung around as Brambleclaw entered the clearing, his jaws parted to take in the newcomer's scent. "What can we do for you?"

"I've come to help Squirrelpaw," Brambleclaw explained. "Dustpelt sent her to look after you today."

Speckletail broke into rasping laughter. "I heard she went missing. The whole camp was in an uproar, looking for her. But I knew she'd just have gone off by herself."

"She tagged onto the dawn patrol," Brambleclaw meowed.

Before he could say any more, there was the sound of another cat pushing through the grasses, and Squirrelpaw appeared. She had a twig clamped in her jaws; hanging from it was a ball of moss soaked in mouse bile. Brambleclaw wrinkled his nose at the bitter scent.

"Right, who's got ticks?" Squirrelpaw mumbled around the twig.

"You're supposed to look for them yourself," Brambleclaw pointed out.

Squirrelpaw shot him a glare.

"You can start with me," Frostfur offered. "I'm sure there's one on my shoulder, just where I can't get at it."

Squirrelpaw padded over to the she-cat, parting her white fur with a forepaw and grunting when she discovered the tick. She dabbed at it with the damp moss until it dropped off; ticks obviously found mouse bile as disgusting as cats did, thought Brambleclaw.

"Don't worry, youngster," Speckletail mewed as Squirrelpaw went on searching Frostfur's pelt. "Your father was punished many a time when he was an apprentice. Even after he became a warrior. I never knew such a cat for getting into trouble, and look at him now!"

Squirrelpaw swung around to look at the elder, her green eyes sparkling, obviously begging for a tale.

"Well, now." Speckletail settled herself more comfortably in her grassy nest. "There was the time when Firestar and Graystripe were caught feeding RiverClan with prey from our own territory. . . ."

Brambleclaw had heard the story before, so he began to collect the elders' used bedding, rolling the moss together until he had gathered it up in a ball. When he took it out into the clearing he spotted Firestar emerging from the gorse tunnel, with

Sandstorm and Cloudtail behind him. Thornclaw was hurrying across to meet them from the other side of the clearing.

"Thank StarClan Squirrelpaw's safe," Firestar was mewing as Brambleclaw came into earshot. "One of these days she'll get into real trouble."

"She's in real trouble now," Sandstorm growled. "Just wait till I get my paws on her!"

"Dustpelt already did." Thornclaw gave a *mrrow* of amusement. "He sent her to help the elders for the rest of the day."

Firestar nodded. "Good."

"And there's something else," Thornclaw went on. "We found a badger up at Snakerocks, living in the cave where the dogs used to be."

"We think it might be the one that killed Willowpelt," Brambleclaw put in, setting his ball of moss down. "We've not seen any trace of a badger anywhere else in the forest."

Cloudtail let out a growl. "Oh, I *hope* it is. I'd give anything to get my claws on that brute."

Firestar swung around to face him. "You'll do nothing of the kind without orders. I don't want to lose more cats." He paused for a moment, then added, "We'll keep watch on it for a while. Pass the word around not to hunt at Snakerocks for the time being. With any luck, it will move on before leaf-bare, when prey gets scarce."

"And hedgehogs might fly," Cloudtail grumbled, stalking past Brambleclaw toward the warriors' den. "Badgers and cats don't mix, and that's the end of it."

CHAPTER 3

*"Squirrelpaw is upset,"* Leafpaw remarked, watching her sister leave the medicine cat's clearing with the twig of mouse bile clenched in her jaws.

"She deserves to be." Cinderpelt glanced up from counting juniper berries. She spoke firmly, though not unsympathetically. "If apprentices think they can go off by themselves, without telling any cat, then where would we be?"

"I know." While Leafpaw prepared the mouse bile, she had listened to her sister raging about how unfair the punishment was. Squirrelpaw's anger churned deep within Leafpaw's belly, as if the air in the camp were water and her sister was sending ripples of cold frustration into the medicine cat's den. Ever since they were tiny kits they had always known what the other was feeling. Leafpaw remembered how her fur had tingled with excitement when Squirrelpaw was made apprentice, and how her sister had been unable to sleep on the night when Leafpaw had been apprenticed as a medicine cat at the Moonstone. Once she had felt an excruciating pain in her paw, and limped around the camp from sunhigh to sunset, until Squirrelpaw returned from a hunting patrol with a thorn driven deep into her pad.

Leafpaw shook her head as if she had a burr clinging to her pelt, trying to push away her sister's emotions and concentrate on her task of sorting yarrow leaves.

"Squirrelpaw will be fine," Cinderpelt reassured her. "It'll all be forgotten tomorrow. Now, did you get any of that mouse bile on your fur? If you did, you'd better go and wash it off."

"No, Cinderpelt, I'm fine." Leafpaw knew her voice was filled with the strain she was feeling, however hard she tried to hide it.

"Cheer up." Cinderpelt limped out of her den to join her apprentice, pressing her muzzle comfortingly against Leafpaw's side. "Do you want to come to the Gathering tonight?"

"May I?" Leafpaw spun to face her mentor. Then she hesitated. "Squirrelpaw won't be allowed to come, will she?"

"After today? Certainly not!" Cinderpelt's blue eyes glowed with understanding. "Leafpaw, you and your sister aren't kits anymore. And you have chosen a very different path from hers, to be a medicine cat. You will always be friends, but you can't do everything together, and the sooner you both accept that, the better."

Leafpaw nodded and bent over the yarrow leaves again. She struggled to calm her feelings of excitement over the Gathering, so that Squirrelpaw would not feel even more upset over being left out. Cinderpelt was right, but all the same she couldn't help wishing that she and Squirrelpaw had been able to attend the Gathering together.

※　※　※

The full moon rode high in the sky as Firestar led the cats from ThunderClan up the slope toward Fourtrees. Padding along beside Cinderpelt, Leafpaw shivered with anticipation. This was the place where the territories of all four Clans joined together. At every full moon, the Clan leaders met here with their warriors under the sacred truce of StarClan to exchange news and make decisions that would affect the whole forest.

Firestar paused at the top of the slope and gazed down into the clearing. Leafpaw, near the back of the group, could only just see the tops of the four great oak trees that gave the clearing its name, but she could hear the sounds of many cats, and the breeze brought to her the mingled scents of ShadowClan, RiverClan, and WindClan.

Before her first Gathering, the only other cats Leafpaw had met were the three medicine cats from the other Clans, when she made her journey to Highstones at the half moon to be formally apprenticed. When she had attended a Gathering for the first time, she and Squirrelpaw had been overwhelmed by all the strangers, and had stayed close to their mentors. But this time Leafpaw felt more confident, and she was looking forward to meeting warriors and apprentices from other Clans.

Crouching in the undergrowth, she watched her father for the signal to move down into the clearing. Brambleclaw was standing just in front of her with Mousefur and Sorreltail. Leafpaw could see from the tautness in the young tabby's muscles that he was eagerly waiting for the Gathering to start, while Sorreltail's whole body quivered with excitement at the prospect of her first Gathering as a warrior. Farther ahead, Graystripe and Sandstorm were exchanging a few words, while Cloudtail shifted impatiently from paw to paw. Briefly Leafpaw felt a pang of sadness that Squirrelpaw was not there as well, but to her relief her sister had not minded too much about being left behind, saying that she was looking forward to a good night's sleep after caring for the elders all day.

At last Firestar raised his tail as the sign for his cats to move forward. Leafpaw sprang over the edge of the hollow and found herself racing down the slope just behind Brambleclaw, weaving her way through the bushes until she came out into the clearing.

The shimmering moonlight revealed a mass of cats, some already seated around the Great Rock in the center, others trotting across the clearing to greet cats they had not seen for a moon, or lying in the shelter of the bushes to gossip and share tongues. Brambleclaw slipped into the throng right away, and Cinderpelt went over to speak to Littlecloud, the ShadowClan medicine cat. Leafpaw hesitated, still a little daunted by the number of warriors in front of her, the unfamiliar scents, and the glowing of so many eyes that all seemed to be trained on her.

Then she caught sight of Graystripe with a group of cats who all had the scent of RiverClan. Leafpaw recognized a warrior with dense blue-gray fur whom they had met at the last Gathering, and remembered her name: Mistyfoot, the

RiverClan deputy. The two younger warriors were strangers to her, but Graystripe greeted them affectionately, pressing his muzzle against theirs.

Leafpaw was just wondering if she would be welcome to go and talk to them when Mistyfoot caught her eye and beckoned to her with her tail. "Hi—it's Leafpaw, isn't it? Cinderpelt's apprentice?"

"That's right." Leafpaw padded over. "How are you?"

"We're all well, and the Clan is thriving," Mistyfoot replied. "Have you met Stormfur and Feathertail?"

"My kits," Graystripe added proudly, though it was several moons since these strong cats had left the nursery.

Leafpaw touched noses with the young warriors, realizing that she should have guessed Stormfur was Graystripe's kin. The two cats had the same muscular bodies and long gray pelt. Feathertail's fur was a lighter silver-gray tabby; her blue eyes glowed with warmth and friendliness as she greeted Leafpaw.

"I know Cinderpelt well," she meowed. "She looked after me once when I was ill. You must be proud to be her apprentice."

Leafpaw nodded. "Very proud. But she knows so much, sometimes I wonder if I'll ever learn it all!"

Feathertail purred sympathetically. "I felt the same about becoming a warrior. I'm sure you'll be fine."

"You say the Clan's thriving, Mistyfoot," Graystripe meowed quietly, "but you're looking worried. Is there a problem?"

Now that he mentioned it, Leafpaw could see a glimmer of

uneasiness in the RiverClan deputy's eyes. Mistyfoot hesitated for a couple of heartbeats and then shrugged. "It's probably nothing but . . . Well, you'll hear about it soon enough when the Gathering starts."

As she spoke she glanced toward the Great Rock. Leafpaw saw that two cats were already waiting on the summit. Silhouetted against the shining circle of the full moon was Tallstar, leader of WindClan, easily recognizable by his long tail. Beside him stood Leopardstar, the RiverClan leader, staring around impatiently at the cats below. As Leafpaw watched, she saw Firestar leap up to join them.

"Where is ShadowClan's leader?" Leopardstar called out. "Blackstar, what are you waiting for?"

"Just coming." A heavy white tom with jet black paws shouldered his way through the cats not far from Leafpaw. He crouched at the base of the rock and sprang up to land lightly beside the RiverClan leader.

As soon as his paws touched the rock Leopardstar threw back her head and let out a yowl. At once the noise in the clearing died down and every cat turned to face the Great Rock. Feathertail settled down beside Leafpaw with a friendly glance, and Leafpaw found herself warming to the gentle young warrior.

"Cats of all Clans, welcome." Tallstar, the eldest of all the Clan leaders, moved to the front of the Great Rock, raising his voice to address the assembled cats. Glancing at his fellow leaders, he asked, "Who will speak first?"

"I will." Firestar stepped forward, his flame-colored pelt

turned silver in the moonlight.

Leafpaw listened as her father passed on the news about the badger at Snakerocks. It caused little stir; the creature was unlikely to move from there onto another Clan's territory as long as the forest was full of prey.

"And we have a new warrior," Firestar went on. "The ThunderClan apprentice Sorrelpaw has taken the warrior name of Sorreltail."

A murmur of appreciation rippled around the clearing; Sorreltail was popular and well-known among the other Clans, having been to several more Gatherings than the average apprentice. Leafpaw caught a glimpse of her sitting up very straight and proud beside Sandstorm.

Firestar stepped back and Blackstar took his place. He had taken over the leadership of ShadowClan after the death of Tigerstar. Under his leadership ShadowClan was trusted more than before, though it was still believed that cold winds blew over the hearts of the ShadowClan cats and darkened their thoughts.

"ShadowClan is strong and prey is plentiful," Blackstar announced. "The heat of greenleaf has dried up part of the marshes on our territory, but we still have plenty of water to drink."

His glance raked defiantly around the clearing, and Leafpaw reflected that even if ShadowClan had less than a single raindrop left in their territory, Blackstar was unlikely to admit as much to the Gathering.

Tallstar flicked his tail at Leopardstar, inviting her to

speak, but she drew back, leaving the next place to him. The WindClan leader hesitated for a moment, and Leafpaw saw that his eyes were clouded with worry.

"Blackstar spoke truly of the heat of greenleaf," he began. "It is many days since the forest saw rain, and the moorland streams on WindClan's territory have been scorched away completely this last quarter moon. We have no water at all."

"But the river borders your territory," a cat called out from the shadows beneath the Great Rock; craning her neck to see, Leafpaw recognized Russetfur, the ShadowClan deputy.

"The river runs through a deep, sheer-sided gorge for the whole length of our border," Tallstar replied. "It's too dangerous to go down there. Warriors have tried, and Onewhisker fell, though thank StarClan he was not hurt. Our kits and elders cannot manage the climb. They are suffering badly, and I fear that some of the younger kits might die."

"Can't your kits and elders chew grass for the moisture?" another cat suggested.

Tallstar shook his head. "The grass is parched. I tell you, there is no water anywhere on our territory." Turning with clear reluctance to the RiverClan leader, he meowed, "Leopardstar, in the name of StarClan I must ask that you let us come into your territory to drink from the river there."

Leopardstar came to stand beside the WindClan leader, her dappled golden fur rippling in the moonlight. "The water in the river is low," she warned. "We have not escaped the effects of this drought in my Clan."

"But there is far more than you need," Tallstar responded,

desperation creeping into his tone.

Leopardstar nodded. "That is true." Coming to the very edge of the rock, she looked down into the clearing and asked, "What do my warriors think? Mistyfoot?"

The RiverClan deputy rose to her paws, but before she could speak one of her Clan mates cried out, "We can't trust them! Let WindClan set one paw over our border, and they'll be taking our prey as well as our water."

Leafpaw could see the speaker, a smoky black tom, sitting a few foxlengths away, but she did not recognize him.

"That's Blackclaw," Feathertail murmured into her ear. "He's loyal to the Clan, but . . ." She trailed off, obviously unwilling to say anything bad about her Clan mate.

Mistyfoot turned and fixed Blackclaw with a clear blue stare. "You forget the times when RiverClan has needed help from other Clans," she meowed. "If they had not helped us then, we would not be here today." To Leopardstar she added, "I say we should allow this. We have water to spare."

The clearing fell silent as the cats waited for Leopardstar to make her decision. "Very well, Tallstar," she meowed at last. "Your Clan may enter our territory to drink from the river just below the Twoleg bridge. But you will come no farther, and you do not have leave to take prey."

Tallstar bowed his head, and Leafpaw heard the relief in his voice as he replied, "Leopardstar, RiverClan has our thanks, from the oldest elder to the youngest kit. You have saved our Clan."

"The drought will not last forever, and you will have water

in your territory soon. We will discuss this again at the next Gathering," Leopardstar meowed.

"I'm sure they will," Graystripe muttered darkly. "If I know Leopardstar, she'll make WindClan pay for that water somehow."

"Let us hope that StarClan have sent rain by then," Tallstar meowed, stepping back to let Leopardstar address the Gathering.

Leafpaw's interest quickened as she wondered if they were about to hear what had been troubling Mistyfoot earlier, but at first the RiverClan leader's news was unremarkable: a litter of kits had been born, and Twolegs had left rubbish by the river, attracting rats that had been killed by Blackclaw and Stormfur. Graystripe looked ready to burst with pride when his son was praised, while Stormfur scuffed the ground with his paws, his ears flat with embarrassment.

At last Leopardstar meowed, "Some of you have met our apprentices Hawkpaw and Mothpaw. They are now warriors, and will be known as Hawkfrost and Mothwing."

The cats around Leafpaw craned their necks to see the warriors the RiverClan leader had named; Leafpaw turned to look too, but she could not distinguish them among the throng. The traditional welcoming murmur for all new warriors broke out at the announcement, but to Leafpaw's surprise it was mingled with a few disconcerting growls, which she realized were coming from RiverClan cats.

Leopardstar glared down from the rock and stilled the noise with a flick of her tail. "Do I hear protests?" she spat out angrily. "Very well, I will tell you everything, to stop rumors flying once and for all.

"Six moons ago, at the beginning of newleaf, a rogue cat came to RiverClan, with her two surviving kits. Her name was Sasha, and the birth of her kits had weakened her so much that she needed help with hunting and caring for them. For a time she thought of joining the Clan, and we would have welcomed her as a warrior, but in the end she decided the warrior code was not the way of life for her. She left us, but her kits chose to stay."

A flood of protest surged up from the cats around the rock. One voice rose clear above the yowling. "Rogue cats? Taken into a Clan? Has RiverClan gone mad?"

Graystripe shot a questioning glance at Mistyfoot, who shrugged.

"They are good warriors," she murmured defensively.

Leopardstar made no attempt to quiet the clamor, only staring stonily down until it died away. "They are strong young cats and they have learned their warrior skills well," she meowed when she could make herself heard. "They have sworn to defend their Clan at the cost of their lives, just as all of you have sworn." With a glance at Blackstar, she added, "Were not some of ShadowClan's warriors rogues once?" Before he could reply, her gaze swiveled to Firestar. "And if a kittypet can become Clan leader, why should rogues not be welcome as warriors?"

"She has a point there," Graystripe admitted.

Firestar dipped his head toward Leopardstar. "True," he

mewed. "I will be glad to see these cats fulfill their promise as loyal members of their Clan."

Leopardstar nodded in reply; his words had clearly appeased her.

"Is that what was worrying you, Mistyfoot?" Graystripe asked. "It's no big deal, if they've settled down well."

"I know." Mistyfoot sighed. "And I know I'm the last cat to criticize any warrior for being born outside the Clan, but . . ."

"You do know that Mistyfoot's mother was your old leader, Bluestar?" Feathertail whispered to Leafpaw.

Leafpaw nodded.

"But Leopardstar hasn't told you everything," Mistyfoot went on. The blue-gray warrior broke off as Leopardstar began to speak again.

"Mothwing has chosen a special place within our Clan," she explained. "Mudfur, our medicine cat, is growing old, and the time has come for him to take an apprentice."

This time her voice was drowned completely by the howls of protest. The three other leaders on top of the Great Rock drew together for an anxious conference. Tallstar was clearly unwilling to speak out after Leopardstar had agreed to give him access to the river, and in the end it was Blackstar who replied. "I'm ready to admit that a rogue can learn enough of our code to become a warrior," he rasped. "But a medicine cat? What do rogues know of StarClan? Will StarClan even accept her?"

"*That's* what's bothering me," Mistyfoot muttered to Graystripe.

Leafpaw felt a tingle spread through her fur. She remembered her own conviction, back when she had been little more than a kit, that it was right for her to heal and comfort her Clan mates, and to interpret the signs of StarClan for them. *Had Mothwing felt the same?* Leafpaw wondered. *Could* she have felt the same, if she was not Clan-born? Even Yellowfang, the medicine cat before Cinderpelt, had been forest-born, though ThunderClan had not been the Clan of her birth.

Voices all around the clearing echoed Blackstar's questions. At the base of the rock an old brown tom heaved himself to his paws and waited for quiet; it was Mudfur, the RiverClan medicine cat.

As the noise died down, he raised his voice. "Mothwing is a talented young cat," he meowed. "But because she was born a rogue, I am waiting for a sign from StarClan that she is the right medicine cat for RiverClan. Once I have received that sign, I will take her to Mothermouth at the half-moon time. If I act without the blessing of StarClan, then you can all complain—but not until then." He flopped back down again, his whiskers twitching irritably.

The crowd had parted so that Leafpaw could make out the young cat crouched beside him. She was startlingly beautiful, with glowing amber eyes in a triangular face, and a long golden pelt with rippling tabby stripes.

"Is that Mothwing?" she whispered to Feathertail.

"That's right." Feathertail gave Leafpaw's ear a quick lick. "When the leaders have finished I'll take you to meet her, if you like. She's quite friendly, once you get to know her."

Leafpaw nodded eagerly. She was sure that Mudfur would soon receive the sign that Mothwing could be accepted. There were no other medicine cat apprentices in the forest, and she looked forward to making friends with another one—someone she could talk to about her training and all the mysteries of StarClan that were slowly being revealed to her.

The protests had died down after Mudfur's speech, and as Leopardstar had no more to say Tallstar brought the meeting to an end.

Feathertail leaped to her paws. "Come on, before we all have to leave."

As Leafpaw followed the RiverClan warrior across the clearing, she felt sympathy already for Mothwing. Judging by the response of the other cats tonight, it was easy to imagine the hard path that lay ahead of her before she would be fully accepted by her Clan.

As the Gathering drew to a close and the cats began to separate into their own Clans, Brambleclaw looked around for his sister, Tawnypelt. He had not seen her, and wondered if she had not been chosen to come this time.

He saw Firestar halt in front of a young tabby tom who was sitting near Mudfur, the RiverClan medicine cat.

"Congratulations, Hawkfrost," Firestar meowed. "I'm sure you'll make a fine warrior."

*So that's Hawkfrost*, Brambleclaw thought with interest, pricking up his ears. *The rogue-born RiverClan cat.*

"Thank you, Firestar," the new warrior replied. "I'll do my

best to serve my Clan."

"I'm sure you will." Firestar touched Hawkfrost on the shoulder with the tip of his tail in a gesture of encouragement. "Pay no attention to all the fuss. It'll all be forgotten in a moon."

He walked on, and Hawkfrost raised his head to look after him. Brambleclaw couldn't quite suppress a shiver when he glimpsed the tom's eyes, an eerie ice blue that seemed to stare through the ThunderClan leader as if he were made of smoke.

"Great StarClan!" he murmured aloud. "I wouldn't like to meet him in battle."

"Meet who?"

Brambleclaw spun around to see Tawnypelt standing behind him. "There you are!" he exclaimed. "I've been looking everywhere for you." Answering her question, he added, "Hawkfrost. He looks dangerous."

Tawnypelt shrugged. "So are you dangerous. I'm dangerous. It's what warriors are for. This whole full-moon thing could be broken by the slash of a claw—and has been before."

Brambleclaw nodded. "True. So how are you, Tawnypelt? How's life in ShadowClan?"

"Pretty good." Tawnypelt hesitated, looking uncharacteristically uncertain. "Look, there's something I wanted to ask you about." Brambleclaw sat down and pricked his ears expectantly. "The other night I had this weird dream. . . ."

"What?" He couldn't bite back the exclamation, and Tawnypelt's green eyes flew wide with alarm. "No, go on," he meowed, forcing himself to be calm. "Tell me about the dream."

"I was in a clearing in the forest," Tawnypelt explained, "but I didn't recognize exactly where it was. There was a cat sitting on a rock—a black cat; I think it was Nightstar. You know, ShadowClan's leader before our father? I . . . I guess if StarClan were going to send a cat to ShadowClan, it wouldn't be Tigerstar."

"What did he say to you?" Brambleclaw asked hoarsely, already knowing what his sister's answer would be.

"He told me that there was some great trouble coming to the forest, and a new prophecy had to be fulfilled. I had been chosen to meet with three other cats at the new moon, and listen to what midnight would tell us."

Brambleclaw stared at her, his fur crawling with ice.

"What's the matter?" Tawnypelt asked. "Why are you looking like that?"

"Because I had exactly the same dream, except that the cat who spoke to me was Bluestar."

Tawnypelt blinked and her brother saw a shiver pass through her tortoiseshell fur. At last she meowed, "Have you told any other cat about your dream?"

Brambleclaw shook his head. "I didn't know what to make of it. To be honest, I thought it was due to something I ate. I mean, why would StarClan send a vision like that to me, instead of to Firestar or Cinderpelt?"

"I thought the same," his sister agreed. "And I expected the other three cats to be from ShadowClan, so when no other cat mentioned it . . ."

"I know, me too. I thought they would be from Thunder-Clan. But it looks as if we were wrong."

Brambleclaw glanced around the clearing. The Gathering was thinning out as cats began to leave, and in spite of the protests over Hawkfrost and Mothwing the general mood was good-humored. No other cats looked as if they had received doom-laden dreams. What possible trouble could be coming—and if it did, what could he and Tawnypelt do about it?

"What do you think we should do now?" Tawnypelt echoed his thoughts.

"If the dream was true, then two other cats should have had it," Brambleclaw replied. "It makes sense that there would be one from each of the other two Clans. We should try to find out who."

"Oh, yes." Tawnypelt sounded scornful. "Are you going to walk into WindClan or RiverClan territory and ask every cat if they had a weird dream? I'm not. They would think we were mad, if they didn't claw our ears off first."

"What do you suggest, then?"

"We're all supposed to meet at the new moon," Tawnypelt mewed thoughtfully. "Nightstar didn't say where, but it must be here at Fourtrees. There isn't anywhere else where cats from four different Clans can get together."

"So you think we should come here at the new moon?"

"Unless you can think of a better idea."

Brambleclaw shook his head. "I only hope the other cats do the same. If . . . if the dream is real, of course."

He broke off as he heard a cat calling his name, and turned to see Firestar standing a short distance away, with the other ThunderClan cats gathered around him. "It's time to go," Firestar said.

"Coming!" Turning back to Tawnypelt he meowed urgently, "At the new moon, then. Say nothing to any cat. And trust StarClan the others will come."

Tawnypelt nodded and slipped into the bushes, following her Clan mates. Brambleclaw hurried over to join Firestar, hoping that his shock and fear did not show on his face. He had tried to forget his dream, but if Tawnypelt had dreamed it as well, he had no choice but to take it seriously. Trouble was coming, and he did not know what to do about it, nor understand how midnight could tell him anything.

*Oh, StarClan,* he mewed silently. *I hope you know what you're doing!*

# CHAPTER 4

*Brambleclaw emerged from the warriors' den* and glanced around the clearing. Another quarter moon had passed, and still there was no rain. Over all the forest, the air was hot and heavy. The streams near the camp had dried up, so the Clan had to travel to the stream that flowed past Fourtrees when they needed water. Luckily it ran deep through the rocky soil, and flowed even in the driest greenleaf.

Ever since the Gathering Brambleclaw's sleep had been disturbed, and when he woke each morning he struggled with the foreboding that something terrible had happened to the camp during the night. But everything seemed as peaceful as it had been the day before. This morning, Whitepaw and Shrewpaw were practicing their fighting moves outside the apprentices' den. Mousefur emerged from the gorse tunnel with a squirrel clamped in her jaws, followed by her apprentice, Spiderpaw, and Rainwhisker, who also carried fresh-kill. Firestar and Graystripe were talking together at the base of the Highrock, with Squirrelpaw and Dustpelt listening close by.

Firestar beckoned Brambleclaw over with his tail. "Are you up for an extra patrol?" he asked. "I want to check the border with ShadowClan, in case they get the idea of coming across here to find water."

"But Blackstar said that his Clan has all the water they need," Brambleclaw reminded him.

Firestar's ears twitched. "True. But we don't necessarily believe what Clan leaders say at a Gathering. Besides, I've never trusted Blackstar. If he thinks we have richer prey in our territory, he'll send warriors in to help themselves, for sure."

Graystripe growled agreement. "ShadowClan have been quiet for too many moons. If you ask me, it's about time they started making trouble."

"I just thought—" Brambleclaw stopped, embarrassed to be seen objecting to his leader's order, and amazed that he could see a possibility Firestar didn't seem to have considered.

"Go on," Firestar prompted.

Brambleclaw took a deep breath. He couldn't get out of this now, in spite of the green glare that Squirrelpaw was giving him for daring to disagree with her father. "I just think that if there is trouble, it's more likely to come from WindClan," he ventured. "If their territory is as dry as Tallstar said, then they're bound to be short of prey."

"WindClan!" Squirrelpaw burst out. "Brambleclaw, are you completely mouse-brained? RiverClan gave WindClan permission to drink at the river, so if they steal prey from anywhere they'll steal it from RiverClan."

"And that strip of RiverClan territory is really narrow between the river and our border," Brambleclaw retorted. "If

WindClan do hunt, the prey could easily cross into our territory."

"You think you're so clever!" Squirrelpaw sprang to her paws, her fur bristling. "Firestar ordered you to check the ShadowClan border, so you should do what you're told."

"Of course, you've never disobeyed a warrior, have you?" Dustpelt put in dryly.

Squirrelpaw ignored her mentor. "ShadowClan have always caused trouble," she persisted. "But we're friends with WindClan now."

Brambleclaw found himself getting angrier and angrier. Of course he didn't want to question Firestar's authority. Firestar was the hero who had saved the forest from the terrible ambitions of Tigerstar and the rogue cats who followed him. There would never be another cat like him. Yet Brambleclaw really believed that ThunderClan should take a possible threat from WindClan seriously. He would have liked to discuss it properly with Firestar, but that was impossible when Squirrelpaw insisted on arguing with everything he said.

"You're the one who thinks she knows it all," he spat, taking a step toward her. "Will you just listen for one moment?"

He ducked to avoid her paw as she lashed at him, claws unsheathed, and his last scrap of self-control deserted him. Falling into a crouch, he got ready to spring at her, his tail twitching back and forth. If Squirrelpaw wanted a fight, she could have one!

But before either of the young cats could attack, Firestar

pushed in between them. "That's enough!" he snarled.

Brambleclaw froze in dismay. Straightening up, he gave his chest an anxious lick and murmured, "Sorry, Firestar."

Squirrelpaw stayed silent, giving him a mutinous glare, until Dustpelt prompted her. "Well?"

"Sorry," Squirrelpaw muttered, and instantly spoiled her apology by adding, "But he's still a mouse-brain."

"Actually, I think he's got a point, don't you?" Dustpelt meowed to Firestar. "I agree that ShadowClan have always been trouble and always will be, but if WindClan happen to spot a juicy vole or a squirrel on our side of the border, don't you think they might be tempted?"

"You could be right," Firestar conceded. "In that case, Brambleclaw, you'd better take a patrol up the RiverClan border as far as Fourtrees. Dustpelt, you and Squirrelpaw can go as well." His eyes narrowed as he glanced from his daughter to Brambleclaw and back again. "And you *will* get along with each other, or I'll want to know why."

"Yes, Firestar," Brambleclaw replied, relieved that he had gotten off so lightly for nearly flattening Squirrelpaw.

"That's two patrols, then," Graystripe mewed cheerfully. "I'll find some more cats to go with me up the ShadowClan side." He jumped to his paws and vanished into the warriors' den.

Firestar nodded to Dustpelt, giving him authority over the patrol, and padded away to his den on the other side of the Highrock.

"Right, let's go," meowed Dustpelt. He set off toward the

gorse tunnel, only to glance back at Squirrelpaw, who had not moved. "What's the matter now?"

"It's not fair," Squirrelpaw muttered. "I don't want to patrol with *him*."

Brambleclaw rolled his eyes, but had the sense not to start their quarrel again.

"Then you shouldn't have said what you did," Dustpelt told his apprentice. Pacing back, he stood over her and gazed sternly down at her. "Squirrelpaw, sooner or later you must learn there are times to speak, and times to be silent."

Squirrelpaw heaved a noisy sigh. "But it seems like it's *always* time to be silent."

"There, you've got the idea." Dustpelt flicked her ear with his tail, and Brambleclaw caught a glimpse of the affection there was between mentor and apprentice. "Come on, both of you. We'll renew the scent markings, and with any luck we'll come across a mouse or two while we're out."

Squirrelpaw recovered her good temper when she caught a plump vole at Sunningrocks. Brambleclaw had to admit that she was an efficient hunter, patiently stalking her prey and pouncing on it to dispatch it with one blow of her paw.

"Dustpelt, I'm *starving*," she announced. "May I eat it?"

Her mentor hesitated for a heartbeat and then nodded. "The Clan has been fed," he replied. "And this isn't a hunting patrol."

Squirrelpaw shot a glance at Brambleclaw as she crouched over the fresh-kill and took an eager bite. "Mmm . . .

delicious," she mumbled. Then she stopped and nudged the remains of the vole toward Brambleclaw. "Want some?"

Brambleclaw was on the brink of telling her that he could catch his own prey until he realized that Squirrelpaw was trying to make friends again. "Thanks," he meowed, taking a bite.

Dustpelt leaped down from the top of the rock. "When you've quite finished stuffing yourselves . . ." he began. "Squirrelpaw, what can you scent?"

"Apart from vole, you mean?" Squirrelpaw mewed cheekily. Springing to her paws, she tasted the air. The breeze was blowing from RiverClan territory, and she soon replied, "RiverClan cats—strong and fresh."

"Good." Dustpelt looked pleased. "A patrol just went by. Nothing to do with us."

*And no sign of WindClan*, Brambleclaw commented to himself as they moved off again. Not that this meant his suspicions were wrong—he did not expect to see any of their cats this far downstream, the whole length of ThunderClan territory away from their own border.

As they drew closer to Fourtrees and passed the Twoleg bridge, all three cats paused to scan the slope. The breeze had dropped and the air was still and heavy with the scent of cats.

"WindClan and RiverClan," Brambleclaw mewed quietly to Dustpelt.

The older warrior nodded. "But they're allowed to go down to the river," he reminded him. "There's no sign that they've crossed our border."

"So there!" Squirrelpaw couldn't resist adding.

Brambleclaw shrugged, telling himself that he would rather be proved wrong. He didn't *want* trouble with WindClan.

Dustpelt was just moving off again toward Fourtrees when Brambleclaw caught another scent—WindClan again, but much stronger and fresher than before. Not daring to call out, he signaled frantically to Dustpelt with his tail, angling his ears in the direction where he thought the scent was coming from. Dustpelt crouched down in the long grass and signaled to his companions to do the same.

*Please, StarClan,* Brambleclaw begged, *don't let Squirrelpaw make a smart remark!*

But the apprentice remained silent, flattening herself to the ground and staring at the clumps of bracken that Brambleclaw had indicated. For a while, the only sound was the slap and murmur of the river nearby. Then there was a dry, rustling sound, and a mottled brown cat peered out of the bracken before creeping into the open a couple of tail-lengths on the ThunderClan side of the border. Brambleclaw recognized Mudclaw, the WindClan deputy. He was followed by Onewhisker and a smallish dark gray cat Brambleclaw had never seen before—an apprentice, he guessed—carrying a vole in his jaws.

Glancing back, Mudclaw murmured, "Head for the border. I can smell ThunderClan."

"I'm not surprised," Dustpelt growled, rising up out of the grass.

Mudclaw recoiled and drew his lips back in a snarl. At

once Brambleclaw leaped up to stand beside his Clan mate, and Squirrelpaw dashed up to her mentor's other side.

"What are you doing on our territory?" Dustpelt demanded. "As if I need to ask."

"We're not stealing prey," Mudclaw retorted.

"Then what's that?" Squirrelpaw asked, flicking her tail toward the vole that the apprentice was carrying.

"It's not a ThunderClan vole," Onewhisker explained. An old friend of Firestar's, he looked thoroughly embarrassed to be caught like this on ThunderClan territory. "It ran across the border from RiverClan."

"Even if that's true, you're stealing it from RiverClan," Brambleclaw pointed out. "You're allowed to drink from the river, not to take prey."

The gray-black apprentice dropped the vole and launched himself across the grass at Brambleclaw. "Mind your own business!" he spat.

He barreled into Brambleclaw and knocked him over; Brambleclaw let out a surprised yowl as the apprentice's teeth closed in the loose skin on his neck. Twisting his body, he managed to score his claws down the other cat's shoulder, and felt strong hind paws scrabbling at his belly. With a screech of fury he tore his neck free and dived for his opponent's throat.

As his teeth found their mark, Brambleclaw caught a glimpse of Onewhisker aiming a blow with his paw. He braced himself to fight both cats at once, before he realized that the WindClan warrior had batted the apprentice away and was standing over him, rage smoldering in his eyes.

"That's enough, Crowpaw!" he snarled. "Attacking a ThunderClan warrior when we're trespassing on their territory? What next?"

Crowpaw shot him a furious look through narrowed eyes. "He called us thieves!"

"And he was right, wasn't he?" Onewhisker turned to Dustpelt, who was standing a few fox-lengths away. As Brambleclaw scrambled to his feet he saw that the Thunder-Clan warrior had thrust himself in front of Squirrelpaw, preventing her from joining in the fight.

"I'm sorry, Dustpelt," Onewhisker went on. "It is a RiverClan vole, and I know we shouldn't have taken it, but there's hardly any prey in our own territory. Our elders and kits are hungry, and—" He stopped as if he thought he had already said too much. "What will you do now?"

"The vole's between you and RiverClan," Dustpelt meowed coldly. "I see no need to tell Firestar about this—unless it happens again. Just get out of our territory, and stay out."

Mudclaw nudged Crowpaw to his paws. The WindClan deputy still looked furious at being found out, and Brambleclaw noticed that he did not add his apology to Onewhisker's. Without a word he headed for the border, with Onewhisker close behind him. Crowpaw hesitated; then with a defiant glance he snatched up the vole and streaked after his Clan mates.

"I suppose we'll never hear the last of *that*!" Squirrelpaw spat at Brambleclaw. Her eyes glittered with annoyance. "Happy now you've been proved right?"

"I didn't say a word!" Brambleclaw protested.

Squirrelpaw didn't reply, but stalked off with her tail in the air. Brambleclaw looked after her with a sigh. He would much rather the incident had never happened. His fur prickled with the sense of impending disaster. Clans were becoming so thirsty and desperate that even decent cats like Onewhisker were prepared to trespass, steal, and lie. Heat lay over the forest with the weight of a huge, choking pelt, and it seemed as if every living thing was waiting for a storm to break. Could this be the trouble that StarClan had foretold?

The next few days and nights, as the moon waned to the merest scratch in the sky, seemed never-ending to Brambleclaw. When he thought of what might happen at Fourtrees when he went to meet Tawnypelt, he felt every hair in his pelt rise up with dread. Would the other Clan cats come? And what exactly would be revealed at midnight? Perhaps StarClan themselves would come down and speak with them.

At last the night came when there was almost no moon at all, but the stars of Silverpelt glittered so brightly that Brambleclaw had no difficulty in finding his way through the gorse tunnel and up the ravine. Leaves rustled as he brushed through the undergrowth from one patch of shade to the next, trying to tread as lightly as if he were creeping up on a mouse. Other ThunderClan warriors might be out late, and Brambleclaw did not want to be seen, nor to explain where he was going. He had not told any cat about his dream, and he knew that Firestar would not approve of his going to meet with cats of other Clans at Fourtrees when he was not protected by the full-moon truce.

The air was cool now, but there was a dusty scent in the air, rising from the parched earth. Plants were drooping or lay withering on the ground. The whole forest cried out for rain like a starving kit, and if it did not come soon, it would not be only WindClan who were short of water.

When Brambleclaw reached Fourtrees the clearing was empty. The sides of the Great Rock glimmered with starshine, and the leaves of the four oak trees rustled gently overhead. Brambleclaw shivered. He was so used to seeing the hollow full of cats that it seemed more daunting than before: so much bigger, with so many unexplained shadows. He could almost imagine that he had stepped into the mystical world of StarClan.

He padded across the clearing and sat at the base of the Great Rock. His ears were pricked to catch the smallest sound, and every nerve from ears to tail-tip was stretched with anticipation. Who would the other cats be? As moments slipped by, his excitement was replaced by anxiety. Not even Tawnypelt had arrived. Perhaps she had changed her mind, or perhaps this was the wrong meeting place after all.

At last he saw movement in the bushes about halfway up the side of the hollow. Brambleclaw tensed. The breeze was blowing away from him, so he could not pick up the scent; from the direction it was coming it could have been either a RiverClan or WindClan cat.

He followed the movement with his eyes as far as a clump of bracken at the bottom of the slope. The fronds waved wildly, and a cat stepped into the clearing.

Brambleclaw stared, frozen for a heartbeat, then sprang to his paws, his neck fur bristling in fury.

"Squirrelpaw!"

# CHAPTER 5

*Brambleclaw stalked stiff-legged across the* clearing until he stood face
to face with the apprentice. "Just what do you think you're
doing here?" he hissed.

"Hi, Brambleclaw." Squirrelpaw tried to sound calm, but
her sparkling eyes betrayed her excitement. "I couldn't sleep,
and I saw you leaving, so I've been following you." She gave a
little purr of delight. "I was good, wasn't I? You never knew I
was there, all the way through the forest."

That was true, though Brambleclaw would have died
rather than tell her he was impressed. Instead, he let out a
low growl. For two mousetails he felt like springing at the
ginger she-cat to claw the smug expression off her face. "Why
can't you mind your own business?"

The she-cat narrowed her eyes. "It's any cat's business
when a Clan warrior sneaks out of camp at night."

"I wasn't *sneaking*," Brambleclaw protested guiltily.

"Oh, no?" Squirrelpaw sounded scornful. "You leave camp,
come straight up here to Fourtrees, and sit waiting for ages,
looking like you expect every warrior in the forest to jump out
at you. Don't tell me you're just enjoying the beautiful night."

"I don't have to tell you anything." Brambleclaw heard his voice grow desperate; all he wanted was to get rid of this annoying apprentice before any cats from other Clans arrived. She hadn't mentioned the dream, which meant she couldn't have had it as well, so she had no right to be here and find out the next part of the prophecy—if that was what was really going to happen. "This has got nothing to do with you, Squirrelpaw. Why don't you just go home?"

"No." Squirrelpaw sat down and curled her tail around her front paws, glaring at Brambleclaw with wide green eyes. "I'm not leaving until I find out what's going on."

Brambleclaw let out a snarl of sheer frustration, only to jump when a voice growled behind him, "What's *she* doing here?"

It was Tawnypelt, slipping out from behind the Great Rock. She padded across the clearing and narrowed her eyes at Squirrelpaw. "I thought we weren't going to tell any other cats?"

Brambleclaw felt his fur prickle. "I *didn't* tell her. She saw me leaving and followed me."

"And it's a good thing I did." Squirrelpaw stood up and met Tawnypelt's gaze, her ears flat against her head. "You creep out at night and come up here to meet a ShadowClan warrior! What's Firestar going to think about that when I tell him?"

Brambleclaw's belly lurched uncomfortably. Perhaps he ought to have told Firestar about the dream right from the start, but it was too late now.

"Listen," he meowed urgently. "Tawnypelt isn't just a ShadowClan warrior; she's my sister. You know that as well as any cat. We're not plotting anything."

"Then why all the secrecy?" Squirrelpaw demanded.

Brambleclaw was searching for a reply when Tawnypelt interrupted him, flicking her tail toward the slope. "Look."

Brambleclaw caught a glimpse of something gray moving among the bushes, and a heartbeat later Feathertail and Stormfur stepped into the clearing. They glanced around warily, but as soon as Feathertail spotted the other cats she raced across the clearing toward them.

"I was right!" she exclaimed, skidding to a halt in front of Brambleclaw and the two she-cats. Her eyes widened, beginning to look puzzled and a little daunted. "Did you have the dream as well? Is it the four of us?"

"Tawnypelt and I have had it," Brambleclaw replied, at the same moment Squirrelpaw asked, "What dream?"

"The dream from StarClan, telling us that there's trouble ahead." Feathertail sounded more uncertain still, and her gaze flicked tensely from cat to cat.

"Did you both have the dream?" Brambleclaw asked, glancing at Stormfur as the RiverClan warrior caught up with his sister.

Stormfur shook his head. "No, only Feathertail."

"It scared me so much," Feathertail confessed. "I couldn't eat or sleep for thinking about it. Stormfur knew something was wrong, and he pestered me so much that I told him what I'd dreamed. We decided that I should come to Fourtrees tonight, at the new moon, and Stormfur wouldn't let me come by myself." She gave her brother's ear a friendly lick. "He . . . he didn't want me to be in danger. But I'm not, am I?

I mean, we all know each other."

"Don't be so quick to trust every cat," Stormfur growled. "I don't like meeting cats from other Clans in secret like this. It's not what the warrior code tells us."

"But we have each had a message from StarClan, telling us to come," Tawnypelt pointed out. "Bluestar visited Brambleclaw, and Nightstar came to me."

"And I saw Oakheart," Feathertail meowed. "He said great trouble was coming to the forest, and I would have to meet with three other cats at the new moon to hear what midnight tells us."

"I was told that, too," Tawnypelt confirmed. With a twitch of her ears at Stormfur she added, "I don't much like it either, but we should wait and see what StarClan want."

"At midnight, I suppose," Stormfur meowed, glancing up at the stars. "It must be nearly that now."

Brambleclaw's heart sank as he noticed Squirrelpaw's eyes getting wider and wider. "You mean that StarClan told all of you to meet here?" the young she-cat burst out. "And they say there's trouble coming? What kind of trouble?"

"We don't know," Feathertail replied. "At least, Oakheart didn't tell me. . . ." She trailed off, looking flustered, but Brambleclaw and Tawnypelt shook their heads to show that their dream-cats hadn't shared this with them either.

Stormfur's eyes narrowed. "Your Clan mate hasn't had the dream," he mewed to Brambleclaw. "What's she doing here?"

"You didn't have it either." Squirrelpaw wasn't afraid to

stand up to the RiverClan warrior. "I've as much right to be here as you."

"Except I didn't invite you," Brambleclaw growled.

"Chase her off, then," Tawnypelt suggested. "I'll help."

Squirrelpaw took a step toward the ShadowClan warrior, her fur fluffed out and her tail bristling. "Just lay one paw on me . . ."

Brambleclaw sighed. "If we chase her off now she'll go straight to Firestar," he meowed. "She's heard pretty much everything, so she might as well stay."

Squirrelpaw gave a disdainful sniff and sat down again. She drew her tongue down her paw and calmly began to wash her face.

"Honestly, Brambleclaw," Tawnypelt growled. "You should have been more careful. Letting an apprentice track you!"

"What's going on?" A new voice came from behind them, high-pitched and aggressive. "This can't be right—Deadfoot said there were only supposed to be four of us."

Brambleclaw jumped and looked around. His eyes narrowed into a furious glare as he recognized the cat with smoky gray-black fur, lean limbs, and small, neat head. "You!" he spat.

Standing a couple of fox-lengths away was the WindClan apprentice Crowpaw, who had trespassed on ThunderClan territory and stolen a vole.

"Yes, me," he retorted, his fur bristling as if at any moment he might spring and finish off the fight.

Tawnypelt pricked her ears. "This is a WindClan cat, right?" She looked Crowpaw up and down dismissively.

"Undersized specimen, isn't he?"

"He's an apprentice," Brambleclaw explained, as Crowpaw drew his lips back in a snarl. "His name's Crowpaw."

He glanced at Squirrelpaw, willing her to keep silent about the incident with the vole. He wanted WindClan brought to justice over the prey stealing, but properly, at a Gathering, not by provoking a fight here. After all, what they were doing here was already a long way outside the warrior code. Squirrelpaw twitched the tip of her tail, but to Brambleclaw's relief she said nothing.

"You had the dream too?" Feathertail asked; Brambleclaw saw the anxiety beginning to fade from her blue eyes, as if she were drawing courage from a growing certainty that the dreams were true.

Crowpaw gave her a curt nod. "I spoke with our old deputy, Deadfoot," he meowed. "He told me to meet three other cats at the new moon."

"Then that's one cat from each Clan," replied Feathertail. "We're all here."

"Now we just have to wait for midnight," Brambleclaw added.

"Do you know what this is about?" Crowpaw turned his back on Brambleclaw and appealed directly to Feathertail.

"If it were *me*," Squirrelpaw meowed before Feathertail could reply, "I'd be a bit less quick to believe in these dreams. If there was really trouble on its way, do you think StarClan would come to you first, before the Clan leaders or medicine cats?"

"Then how do you explain it?" Brambleclaw asked, all the more defensive because he had felt exactly the same doubts that Squirrelpaw was voicing now. "Why else would we all have had the same dream?"

"Maybe you've all been stuffing yourselves with too much fresh-kill?" Squirrelpaw suggested.

Crowpaw whipped around with an angry hiss. "Who asked you, anyway?" he demanded.

"I can say what I like," Squirrelpaw shot back at him. "I don't need your permission. You're not even a warrior."

"Nor are you," the gray-black cat snapped. "What are you doing here, anyway? You didn't have the dream. No cat wants you here."

Brambleclaw opened his jaws to defend Squirrelpaw. Even though he had been annoyed with her for following him, it was no business of Crowpaw's to tell her what to do. Then he realized that Squirrelpaw wouldn't thank him; with her ready tongue she was quite capable of defending herself.

"I don't see them falling over themselves to welcome you, either," she growled.

Crowpaw spat, his ears flattened and his eyes glaring fury.

"There's no need to get angry," Feathertail began.

The small black cat ignored her. Lashing his tail from side to side, he sprang at Squirrelpaw. An instant later Brambleclaw leaped too, barreling into him and rolling him over before his claws could score down her flank.

"Back off," he hissed, pinning Crowpaw down with a paw on his neck. He could hardly believe that the WindClan apprentice would start a fight now, when they were waiting for a message from StarClan, and linked in the prophecy through their dreams. If StarClan had really chosen them for a mysterious destiny, they would surely not fulfill it by shedding one another's blood.

The light of battle died from Crowpaw's eyes, though he still looked furious. Brambleclaw let him get up; he turned his back and started to groom his ruffled fur.

"Thanks for nothing!" Brambleclaw was hardly surprised to see that Squirrelpaw was glaring at him with just as much hostility as Crowpaw. "I can fight my own battles."

Brambleclaw let out a hiss of exasperation. "You can't start fighting here. There are more important things to think about. And if these dreams are true, then StarClan wants the Clans to work together."

He glanced around the clearing, half hoping that a cat from StarClan would appear to tell them what they were supposed to be doing, before a fight broke out that he couldn't stop. But Silverpelt shone on a clearing empty of any cats but themselves. He could smell nothing but the ordinary night scents of growing plants and distant prey, and hear nothing but the sigh of wind through the branches of the oaks.

"It must be after midnight now," Tawnypelt meowed. "I don't think StarClan are coming."

Feathertail turned to look all around the clearing, her blue eyes once more wide with anxiety. "But they have to come! Why did we all have the same dream, if it wasn't true?"

"Then why is nothing happening?" Tawnypelt challenged her. "Here we are, meeting at the new moon, just as StarClan told us. We can't do any more."

"We were fools to come." Crowpaw gave them all another unfriendly stare. "The dreams meant nothing. There's no prophecy, no danger—and even if there were, the warrior code should be enough to protect the forest." He began to stalk across the clearing to the slope on the WindClan side, and his last words were flung over his shoulder. "I'm going back to camp."

"Good riddance!" Squirrelpaw yowled after him.

He ignored her, and a moment later had disappeared into the bushes.

"Tawnypelt's right. Nothing is going to happen," Stormfur meowed. "We might as well go too. Come on, Feathertail."

"Just a minute," mewed Brambleclaw. "Maybe we got it wrong—maybe StarClan was angry because of the fighting. We can't just pretend that nothing has happened, that none of us had those dreams. We ought to decide what we're going to do next."

"What can we do?" Tawnypelt asked. She flicked her tail toward Squirrelpaw. "Maybe she's right. Why would StarClan choose us and not our leaders?"

"I don't know, but I think they *have* chosen us," Feathertail meowed gently. "But somehow we haven't understood properly. Maybe they'll send us all another dream to explain."

"Maybe." Her brother didn't sound convinced.

"Let's all try to come to the next Gathering," Brambleclaw suggested. "There might be another sign by then."

"Crowpaw won't know to meet us there," Feathertail murmured, glancing at the spot in the bushes where the

WindClan apprentice had vanished.

"No loss," Stormfur remarked, but at his sister's anxious look he added, "We can keep an eye open for him when he comes to the river to drink. If we see him we'll pass the message on."

"All right, that's decided," meowed Tawnypelt. "We meet at the Gathering."

"And what do we tell our Clans?" Stormfur asked. "It's against the warrior code to hide things from them."

"StarClan never said we had to keep the dream secret," Tawnypelt put in.

"I know, but . . ." Feathertail hesitated and then went on, "I just feel it's wrong to talk about it."

Brambleclaw knew Stormfur and Tawnypelt were right; he was already feeling guilty that he had said nothing about his dream to Firestar and Cinderpelt. At the same time he shared Feathertail's instinct to keep silent.

"I'm not sure," he meowed. "Suppose our leaders forbade us to meet again? We could end up having to choose between obeying them or obeying StarClan." Aware of uneasy glances from the others, he went on earnestly; "We don't know *enough* to tell them. Suppose we wait until the next Gathering, at least. We might have other signs by then that will explain it all to us."

Feathertail agreed at once, obviously relieved, and after a pause Stormfur gave a small, reluctant nod.

"But only until the next Gathering," Tawnypelt meowed. "If we haven't found out any more by then, I'll have to tell Blackstar." She gave a huge stretch, her back arched and her forepaws extended. "Right, I'm off."

Brambleclaw touched noses with her in farewell, breathing in her familiar scent. "It must mean something that we were both chosen—brother and sister," he murmured.

"Maybe." Tawnypelt's green eyes were unconvinced. "The other cats aren't kin, though." Her tongue rasped once over Brambleclaw's ear in a rare gesture of affection. "StarClan willing, I'll see you at the Gathering."

Brambleclaw watched her bound across the clearing, before turning to Squirrelpaw. "Come on," he meowed. "I've things I want to say to you."

Squirrelpaw shrugged and padded away from him, toward ThunderClan territory.

Saying good night to Feathertail and Stormfur, Brambleclaw headed up the slope after her. When he emerged from the hollow a hot, clammy breeze was blowing into his face, ruffling his fur and turning back the leaves on the trees. Clouds had begun to mass above his head, cutting off the light of Silverpelt. The forest was silent and the air felt heavier than ever. Brambleclaw guessed that the storm was on its way at last.

As he began trotting down toward the stream, Squirrelpaw paused to wait for him. Her fur was relaxed on her spine now, and her green eyes shone.

"That was *exciting!*" she exclaimed. "Brambleclaw, you have to let me come with you to the next meeting, *please!* I never thought I'd be part of a prophecy from StarClan."

"You're not part of it," Brambleclaw meowed sternly. "StarClan didn't send *you* the dream."

"But I know about it, don't I? If StarClan didn't want me involved, they would have kept me away from Fourtrees somehow." Squirrelpaw faced him, forcing him to halt, and gazed at him with pleading eyes. "I could help. I'd do everything you told me."

Brambleclaw couldn't keep back a puff of laughter. "And hedgehogs might fly."

"No, I will, I promise." Her green eyes narrowed. "And I wouldn't tell any cat. You can trust me on that, at least."

For a few heartbeats Brambleclaw returned her gaze. He knew that if she told Firestar what had happened he would be in deep trouble. Her silence must be worth something.

"Okay," he agreed at last. "I'll let you know if anything else happens, but *only* if you keep your mouth shut."

Squirrelpaw's tail went straight up and her eyes blazed with delight. "Thank you, Brambleclaw!"

Brambleclaw sighed. Somehow he could sense that he would be in even deeper trouble because of the bargain he had just made. He followed Squirrelpaw into the shadows that lay thickly under the trees, feeling a shiver of fear at the thought of what might be watching them, unseen. But the forest around him was no darker or more threatening than the half-offered prophecy. If the trouble that was coming to the forest was as serious as Bluestar had said, then Brambleclaw was in great danger of making a fatal mistake simply because he did not know enough.

CHAPTER 6

All night Leafpaw's sleep had been disturbed by strange, vivid dreams. At first she thought she was following a scent trail toward Fourtrees, running through the forest along the invisible path. Then the dream changed and she felt the fur on her neck and shoulders rise as if she confronted an enemy, with battle only a heartbeat away. The threat of danger faded, but now she grew colder and colder, until she jerked awake to find the clump of ferns where she slept heavy with raindrops, and rain drumming softly on the forest all around her.

Scrambling to her paws, she dashed across the small, fern-enclosed clearing and took shelter just inside Cinderpelt's den. The medicine cat was sleeping soundly in her mossy nest beside the back wall and did not move when Leafpaw came in, shaking water from her pelt.

The young apprentice blinked and yawned as she gazed out into the clearing. Above her head she could just make out the black outlines of trees against a sky that was growing gray with the first light of dawn. Part of her rejoiced that the long, dry spell was coming to an end with this downpour that the forest needed so badly. The rest of her could not help feeling troubled about what her dreams might mean. Was StarClan sending her a sign? Or had she somehow picked up thoughts from Squirrelpaw? This would not be the first time she had known what her sister was doing without being told.

Leafpaw let out a long sigh. Little as she liked the idea, she was almost convinced that Squirrelpaw must have slipped out of camp to hunt by night, sending Leafpaw the images of running through the forest. There was no way she had been on an official patrol. What sort of trouble would Squirrelpaw be in if Firestar found out?

As Leafpaw crouched there, she realized that the rain was easing off and the clouds were turning pale yellow and thinning out. With a last glance at the sleeping Cinderpelt she slipped outside again, ignoring the water that soaked her fur as she pushed through the fern tunnel into the main clearing. Perhaps if she could find Squirrelpaw quickly, she could help her hide whatever she had been up to.

But when she reached the clearing there was no sign of her sister. The other three apprentices had emerged from their den and were lapping eagerly at a shallow puddle that had pooled on the sun-scorched earth. Ferncloud's three kits crept out of the nursery, their eyes huge as they examined this strange new water that had fallen from the sky. Ferncloud looked on with pride in her eyes as they dabbed at it, squealing with excitement as shining drops spun away from their paws.

Leafpaw watched them for a moment, then whirled around when she saw movement at the mouth of the gorse tunnel. *An early hunting patrol,* she wondered, *caught out by the rain? Or could it be Squirrelpaw, returning after her illicit outing?*

Then she realized that the newcomer did not have ThunderClan scent. She drew breath to yowl a warning to the Clan before she recognized the sleek black pelt: it was Ravenpaw, who had once been a ThunderClan apprentice but now lived as a loner in a Twoleg barn on the edge of WindClan territory. Leafpaw had met him once before, on her journey to Highstones with Cinderpelt. Living so close to Twolegs, Ravenpaw hunted mainly by night and was perfectly comfortable with traveling through the forest in pitch dark. He might be just the cat to tell Leafpaw if there had been a ThunderClan apprentice hunting in the forest before dawn.

The visitor crossed the clearing slowly, skirting the deepest puddles and delicately picking up his paws to shake off the water. "Hi—it's Leafpaw, isn't it?" Ravenpaw meowed, pricking his ears toward her. "That was some storm! I'd have been soaked through if I hadn't managed to shelter in a hollow tree. Still, the forest needs the rain."

Leafpaw returned his greeting politely. She was trying to find the right words to ask him if he had seen Squirrelpaw on his way to the camp, when a cheerful yowl interrupted her. "Hey, Ravenpaw!"

Whitepaw and Shrewpaw were bounding across the clearing toward them. Ferncloud's kits abandoned their raindrop games and scuttled after them.

The biggest of the three kits skidded to a halt in front

of Ravenpaw and took an enormous sniff. "New cat," she growled. "New scent."

The loner dipped his head in greeting, the tip of his tail flicking back and forth in amusement.

"Hollykit, this is Ravenpaw," Shrewpaw told her. "He lives on a Twoleg farm, and feasts on more mice than you three have seen in your life."

Hollykit's amber eyes grew huge. "*Every* day?"

"That's right," Whitepaw put in solemnly. "Every day."

"*I* want to go there," the little gray kit mewed. "Can we? Now?"

"When you're bigger, Birchkit," Ferncloud promised, coming up to join them. "Welcome, Ravenpaw. It's good to— Hollykit! Larchkit! Stop that at once!"

The two brown tabby kits had pounced on Ravenpaw's twitching tail, and were batting at it with outstretched paws. Ravenpaw winced. "Don't do that, little kits," he scolded gently. "It's my tail, not a mouse."

"Ravenpaw, I'm sorry," meowed Ferncloud. "They haven't learned how to behave properly yet."

"Don't worry, Ferncloud," Ravenpaw replied, though he drew his tail closely against his side, out of harm's way. "Kits will be kits."

"And these particular kits have been out for long enough." Ferncloud swished her tail around to gather the three kits together and herded them back toward the nursery. "Say good-bye to Ravenpaw now."

The kits mewed good-bye and scampered off.

"Can we do anything for you, Ravenpaw?" Whitepaw asked politely. "Would you like some fresh-kill?"

"No, I ate before I left home, thank you," the black cat replied. "I've come to see Firestar. Is he around?"

"I think he's in his den," Shrewpaw told him. "Shall I take you there?"

"No, I will," meowed Leafpaw. She was getting increasingly anxious to ask the loner if he had seen Squirrelpaw on his journey through the forest. Just then Thornclaw, Shrewpaw's mentor, emerged from the warriors' den. Leafpaw twitched her ears toward him. "Er . . . is your mentor looking for you?" she asked Shrewpaw.

As she spoke, Thornclaw called to Shrewpaw, and the apprentice dashed off with a quick word of farewell. Whitepaw also meowed her good-byes, and went over to join Brackenfur at the fresh-kill pile.

Suddenly the thorny branches that formed the gorse tunnel trembled, and relief flooded over Leafpaw as she watched Squirrelpaw emerge, dragging a rabbit behind her through the mud. Leafpaw had taken a couple of paces toward her before she remembered the Clan's visitor, and turned awkwardly back to him.

"That's your sister, isn't it?" Ravenpaw meowed. "Go and talk to her if you want. I can find my own way to Firestar's den."

Released, Leafpaw bounded toward her sister, who was heading for the fern tunnel. Catching sight of her, Squirrelpaw stopped to wait, dropping the rabbit at her paws; its fur

was plastered with mud from being dragged across the clearing, and rain had flattened Squirrelpaw's own pelt against her
flanks, but her eyes gleamed with triumph. "Not bad, is it?"
she announced, nodding toward her prey. "It's for you and
Cinderpelt."

"Where have you *been*?" Leafpaw hissed. "I've been worried
sick about you."

"Why?" Squirrelpaw's green eyes looked injured. "Where
did you think I had gone? I . . . I only slipped out to hunt
when the rain started to ease off. And you might at least say
thank-you!"

Snatching up the rabbit, she plunged into the ferns that
led to the medicine cats' clearing without waiting for
Leafpaw to respond. Leafpaw followed more slowly, not sure
whether to be relieved or furious. She had the uneasy feeling
that Squirrelpaw was lying to her, for the first time ever. If
she had really picked up her sister's thoughts in her dream,
then Squirrelpaw had done a lot more than just slip out of
camp for a quick chase after a rabbit.

When she emerged into the clearing, she saw that
Squirrelpaw had already dumped the rabbit at the mouth of
Cinderpelt's den. Her sister gave it an admiring sniff and
meowed, "You might at least say I did well to catch it." She
still sounded indignant, but she didn't meet Leafpaw's gaze
when she spoke.

"You did," Leafpaw admitted. "It's huge! Especially as you
had such a disturbed night," she added more sharply.

Squirrelpaw froze; only her green eyes moved, flicking up

to rest on her sister's face. "Who says I did?"

"I know you did. You were awake nearly all night. What was the matter? It was more than a short hunt, I know that."

Squirrelpaw dropped her eyes to the ground. "Oh, I ate a frog late in the evening," she muttered. "It must have disagreed with me, that's all."

Leafpaw unsheathed her claws and dug them into the rain-softened earth. Inwardly she was fighting to stay calm. She *knew* that Squirrelpaw was lying to her, and part of her wanted to start wailing like a kit: *You're my sister! You should trust me!*

"Oh, a frog," she mewed. "You should have come to me for some herbs to chew."

"Yes, well . . ." Squirrelpaw scraped the earth with her one white paw. Leafpaw could see her discomfort in her flattened ears and the guilty look she shot at her, but didn't feel in the least bit sorry. Why was Squirrelpaw lying?

"I'm fine now," Squirrelpaw insisted. "It wasn't anything to make a fuss about."

She glanced around in relief as Cinderpelt appeared from the mouth of her den. Her smoky gray fur was ruffled, and she carried a leaf-wrapped packet in her jaws. "Fresh-kill, I see," she meowed, setting the packet down. "Squirrelpaw, that's a splendid rabbit! Thank you."

Squirrelpaw gave her shoulder a quick lick, her eyes glowing at the medicine cat's praise. But she still avoided her sister's gaze.

Cinderpelt picked up the packet again and padded unevenly across the clearing to set it down in front of Leafpaw.

Many seasons ago, when she was Firestar's apprentice, she had injured her hind leg in an accident on the Thunderpath. She had been unable to finish her warrior training, but while recovering in the care of Yellowfang, the ThunderClan medicine cat, she had found a new path to follow in the service of her Clan.

"Leafpaw, take that to Dappletail, please," Cinderpelt meowed. "It's poppy seed to help her sleep, because her teeth are aching so badly. Mind you tell her to go easy on it."

"Yes, Cinderpelt." Leafpaw picked up the packet and hurried out of the clearing, casting one last glance at her sister as she went. There was no chance to ask Squirrelpaw any more questions, and her sister was still refusing to look at her. Leafpaw felt every hair in her pelt prickle with foreboding as she wondered what could have happened to open up this gulf between them.

"Water! Help! Water everywhere! Swim!" Brambleclaw yowled, then choked as a sharp, salty wave filled his mouth, dragging at his fur and pulling him under. His paws worked frantically as he struggled to keep his head above the surface. He stretched up his neck, straining to find the line of reeds he expected to mark the opposite bank, but all he could see were endless, heaving, blue-green waves. On the horizon, he caught a glimpse of the sun sinking into the waves in a pool of flame, its dying rays tracing a path of blood that stretched toward him. Then his head went under and the cold salt water flooded into his mouth again.

*I'm drowning!* he wailed silently as he fought for his life. *StarClan help me!*

His head broke the surface and a strong current spun him around with his back legs dangling helplessly beneath him. Choking and gasping for air, he found himself gazing up at a sheer wall of smooth sand-colored rock. Had he been swept into the gorge? No, these cliffs were higher still. At their base, the waves sucked at a dark hole, edged by jagged rocks that made it look like a gaping mouth with teeth. Brambleclaw's terror increased as he realized that the swirling water was carrying him straight toward the stony jaws.

"No! No!" he yowled. "Help me!"

He kicked and thrashed in a panic but he was growing weaker and his sodden fur was dragging him down. The waves drove him onward, crashing against the rocks; now the black mouth loomed over him, spitting salty foam, as if it were about to swallow him alive. . . .

Then his eyes flew open, and there were leaves above him, not sheer cliffs, and he was supported by moss-cushioned sand rather than sinking in bottomless water. Brambleclaw lay shuddering with relief as he realized that he was lying in his nest in the warriors' den. The thunder of the waves became the rushing of wind in the branches above his head; water had dripped through the thick canopy of leaves and formed an icy trickle in his neck fur, and he knew the rain must have come at last. His throat was as sore as if he had swallowed a riverful of salty water, and his mouth was parched.

Brambleclaw sat up restlessly. Dustpelt lifted his head and muttered, "What's wrong with you? Can't you keep quiet and let the rest of us sleep?"

"Sorry," Brambleclaw meowed. He began grooming the moss out of his fur, his heart still thudding as if it were going to break out of his chest. He felt as limp and exhausted as if he had really been struggling to save himself in that strange salt water.

Gradually the strengthening of the light in the den told him that the sun had come out. He heaved himself to his paws and poked his head out between the branches, blinking as he looked for a puddle where he could quench his thirst.

A fresh breeze was driving the clouds away. In front of Brambleclaw the clearing was filled with pale yellow light from the rising sun, reflecting from puddles on the ground and water droplets hanging on every branch and frond of fern. The whole forest seemed to be drinking in the life-giving water, the trees lifting their dusty leaves to catch each sparkling drop.

"Thank StarClan!" Mousefur meowed as she pushed her way out of the den beside Brambleclaw. "I'd almost forgotten what rain smells like."

Brambleclaw staggered across the clearing to a puddle near the base of the Highrock, where he lowered his head and lapped, trying to wash the taste of salt from his mouth. He had never imagined that water could taste like that; like the other cats, he would sometimes lick salt from the surface of rocks, or taste it in the blood of prey, but the memory of drinking that salt-laden water made every hair on his pelt prickle.

A final gust of rain ruffled the pools of water and rinsed the sticky feel of salt from Brambleclaw's fur. Raising his head to enjoy the sharp, cold shower, he spotted Firestar emerging from his den under the Highrock and turning to speak to the cat who followed him out. Brambleclaw was surprised to see that the second cat was Ravenpaw.

"Twolegs are always doing strange things," Firestar was saying as they came into earshot. "I'm grateful that you came all this way to tell us, but I really don't think it's got anything to do with us."

Ravenpaw looked uneasy. "I know Twolegs often act without reason, but I've never seen anything like this. There are far more of them on the Thunderpath than before, walking along the edge with shiny, bright-colored pelts. And they have new kinds of monsters—huge ones!"

"Yes, Ravenpaw, so you said." Firestar sounded faintly impatient with his old friend. "But we haven't seen any of them in our territory. I'll tell you what. . . ." He paused to press his muzzle affectionately against Ravenpaw's side. "I'll tell the patrols to keep their eyes open for anything unusual."

Ravenpaw twitched the fur on his shoulders. "I suppose that's all you can do."

"And you could drop in on WindClan on your way home," Firestar suggested. "They're closer than we are to that part of the Thunderpath, so Tallstar ought to know if something strange is going on."

"Yes, Firestar, I'll do that."

"Wait a moment, I've got a better idea," meowed Firestar. "Why don't I come with you part of the way? I could take a patrol up to Fourtrees at the same time. Stay there, and I'll fetch Graystripe and Sandstorm." He bounded off into the warriors' den without waiting for Ravenpaw to reply.

When the Clan leader had gone, Ravenpaw caught sight of Brambleclaw and gave him a friendly nod. "Hi, how are you?" he meowed. "How's the prey running?"

"Fine. Everything's fine." Brambleclaw was aware that his voice still sounded shaky, and he wasn't surprised when Ravenpaw peered at him more closely.

"You look like you've been chased all night by a horde of badgers," the loner meowed. "Is anything the matter?"

"Nothing really . . ." Brambleclaw scuffled his paws on the ground. "I had a dream, that's all."

Ravenpaw's eyes were sympathetic. "Do you want to tell me about it?"

"It was nonsense really," Brambleclaw murmured. His ears filled again with the sound of the saltwater waves crashing and bellowing against the cliffs, and he suddenly found himself spilling everything to Ravenpaw: the vast expanse of water, the salt taste of it when it filled his mouth, the gaping black jaws in the cliff that had threatened to swallow him, and, most alarmingly of all, the sun sinking in a pool of bloodred fire. "That place can't be real," he finished. "I don't know why it's gotten to me like this. It's not like I don't have anything else to think about," he added grimly.

To his surprise, Ravenpaw did not leap in to agree that Brambleclaw had had a meaningless dream about a place that existed only in his troubled imagination. Instead, the black cat was silent for a long time, his eyes clouded with thought.

"Salt water, cliffs," he murmured. Then, "The place is real," he meowed. "I've heard of it before, though I've never seen it for myself."

"Real? Wh-what do you mean?" Brambleclaw stared at him, his fur standing on end.

"Rogue cats come to the Twoleg farm sometimes, when they have traveled far and are in need of shelter for the night and a spare mouse or two," Ravenpaw explained. "Cats who live toward the place where the sun sets. They have told Barley and me about a place where there is more water than you could possibly imagine, like a river that has only one bank, and it's too salty to drink. Every night it swallows the sun in a flash of fire, bleeding into the waves without a sound."

Brambleclaw shivered; the loner's words brought his dream back far too vividly for comfort. "Yes, I saw the place where the sun drowns. And the dark cave with teeth?"

"I can't tell you about that," Ravenpaw admitted. "But this dream must have been sent to you for a reason. Be patient, and perhaps StarClan will show you more."

"StarClan?" Brambleclaw felt his belly flip over.

"How could you dream of a place you have never seen unless StarClan willed it?" Ravenpaw pointed out.

Brambleclaw had to admit the logic in what the loner said.

"Say it was StarClan who sent me this dream about the sun-drown place," he began. "Do you think they could possibly be telling me to *go* there?"

Ravenpaw's eyes widened in surprise. "Go there? Why?"

"Well, I had another dream first," Brambleclaw explained uncomfortably. "I . . . I thought I met Bluestar in the forest. She told me about a new prophecy, that great trouble is coming to the forest. She said that I'd been chosen. . . ." He said nothing about the cats from the other Clans. Even though Ravenpaw lived outside the warrior code, he would not approve of meeting with the others in secret, as Brambleclaw had done. "Why me?" he finished in confusion. "Why not Firestar? He would know what to do."

The loner gazed at him solemnly for a long moment. "There was a prophecy once about Firestar, too," he meowed at last. "StarClan promised that fire would save the Clan, though they didn't say exactly how. Firestar never understood it, never knew the prophecy was about him, until Bluestar told him just before she died."

Brambleclaw met his gaze and could find nothing to say. He had heard about the fire prophecy—every Clan cat had, as part of the stories told about their leader—but it had never occurred to him that Firestar might once have felt as con-fused as he felt now.

"There was a time when Firestar was a young warrior just like you," Ravenpaw went on as if he could read Brambleclaw's thoughts. "He often wondered if he was making the right decisions. Oh, yes, he's a hero now, he saved the forest, but to begin with, his task looked as impossible as yours—whatever it might be. His prophecy has been fulfilled," he added. "Maybe it's your time now. Remember that StarClan don't like to make things obvious. They send us prophecies, but they never tell us exactly what we should do. They expect us to show courage and loyalty to achieve what has to be done, just as Firestar did."

Brambleclaw was puzzled by the reverence with which Ravenpaw, a loner who chose not to dwell in a Clan, spoke of StarClan. Disconcertingly, the black cat murmured, "Just because I live outside the forest doesn't mean that I reject the warrior code. It is a noble path for cats to walk, and I would defend it as willingly as any warrior."

He gave Brambleclaw a friendly nod as Firestar returned with Graystripe and Sandstorm. Brambleclaw murmured farewell and watched the four cats pad across the clearing and vanish into the gorse tunnel.

If the dreams were true—both of them—then an enormous task lay in front of him. He had no idea how he could find the salt water, except that he would need to follow the setting sun. And he did not know how far away it was: farther than any forest cat had ever gone before, that was for sure.

Ravenpaw's words echoed in his ears. *Maybe it's your time now.*

Had the other three cats dreamed of the sun-drown place too? *What if he's right?* Brambleclaw asked himself. *What should I do next?*

# CHAPTER 7

*Brambleclaw emerged warily from the undergrowth* at the edge of the trees above the riverbank, tasting the air for the scent of cats. The traces of ThunderClan were all stale, though fresher RiverClan scents drifted across from the other side of the river. Hoping that no cat from either Clan would see him, Brambleclaw slipped swiftly down the bank to the water's edge.

Brown water churned along past his paws. More rain had fallen during the day, though the clouds were thinning now to let pale sunshine through, so that the forest steamed. The river was swollen, half submerging the stepping-stones, and Brambleclaw had to brace himself before he dared leap out onto the first of them.

He was on his way to visit Feathertail and Stormfur. All day he had been thinking about the second dream, becoming more and more convinced that they had to travel to the sun-drown place before they could learn what StarClan had to tell them. The dream had been too real to ignore—he could still taste salt in his mouth, and he flinched as droplets splashed against his nose from the stepping-stone, expecting the same sharp tang. And they ought to leave at once; his fur prickled with a strange sense of urgency, warning him that there was no time to wait until the next Gathering. If the other chosen cats had also had the dream, they shouldn't be hard to persuade.

He still had not told Squirrelpaw about the second dream. Although he felt guilty that he was not keeping his promise, he was well aware that if she knew about the journey he was planning she would want to come too. And what would Firestar think if Brambleclaw dragged his daughter off into the unknown?

Water lapped cold around his paws as Brambleclaw landed on the first stone and crouched, ready for his leap to the next. Before he pushed off, he scanned the far bank again. Although there was friendship now between ThunderClan and RiverClan, he was not sure of his welcome if he trespassed uninvited on their territory. He would prefer to find Feathertail and Stormfur before any other cats knew he was there.

He managed to reach the next stone, and the one after that, shivering as cold water splashed up onto his fur. The next stepping-stone had vanished completely, with only a ripple of water flowing over it to tell him where it was. Keeping his gaze fixed on the spot, he leaped, but as he landed his paws slipped off the edge, and he found himself splashing into the river. He let out a yowl of alarm as his head went under.

Terror surged over him as he was plunged into bottomless,

blue-green waves like those of his dream. Clawing his way upward, he surfaced to see reeds instead of sand-colored cliffs, and gray-brown water running in ripples, not waves. The current was carrying him close to the opposite bank, and Brambleclaw struck out, kicking strongly across the flow of water. To his relief, his paws scraped on pebbles; a heartbeat later he managed to stand and flounder into the shallows. Panting, he hauled himself onto the bank and shook himself vigorously.

Suddenly fresh RiverClan scent wafted into his nostrils; he dived into a clump of bracken and peered out between the fronds. A moment later he murmured thanks to StarClan as Feathertail and Stormfur—the two cats he wanted to see— appeared farther along the riverbank.

Brambleclaw plunged out of the bracken and stood shivering in front of them. "Hi," he mewed.

"Great StarClan!" Stormfur looked him up and down. "Have you been for a swim?"

"I fell off the stepping-stones. Feathertail, can I have a word with you?"

"Of course. Are you sure you're all right?"

"Yes, I'm fine. Feathertail, have you had another dream?"

The gray she-cat looked puzzled. "No. Why, have you?"

"Yes." Settling into the grass so they could talk more comfortably, Brambleclaw told them quickly about the sun-drown place and the cave with teeth, feeling his fur bristle with fear again. "I spoke to Ravenpaw this morning—you know, the loner who lives near Highstones? He says the sun-drown place is real. And he told me that StarClan's prophecies are always vague. We need the faith and courage of warriors to under-stand them, and to trust that what StarClan wants us to do is right."

"Which is what?" Stormfur queried.

"I . . . I think we should go to the sun-drown place," Brambleclaw replied, his belly churning with tension. "*That's* where StarClan will tell us what we need to know."

Feathertail had listened in silence, her blue gaze fixed on his face. When he stopped speaking, she nodded slowly. "I think you're right."

"What?" Stormfur sprang to his paws. "Are you mad? You don't even know where this place is."

Feathertail flicked him with her tail. "No, but StarClan will guide us."

Brambleclaw waited tensely. If Stormfur refused to agree, he might tell Leopardstar what was going on, and the Clan could stop Feathertail from leaving with him.

The gray warrior paced along the bank and back again, his tail fluffed up in agitation. "Faith and courage—we'd certainly need those if we went to this place," he muttered. "I'm still not convinced that you're right, mind you," he added wryly to Brambleclaw. "But if you're not, maybe StarClan will send another sign to turn us back."

Feathertail's blue eyes glowed. "Does that mean you'll come with us?"

"Try to stop me," her brother meowed grimly. He swung around to face Brambleclaw. "I know I've not had any dreams, but an extra warrior could be useful."

"You're right." Brambleclaw was so relieved to have won their agreement that he did not try to argue. "Thanks, both of you."

"So when do we leave?" Stormfur mewed.

"I thought the day before half-moon," Brambleclaw suggested. "That should give us enough time to talk to the others."

Rising to his paws, he padded down to the water's edge. The sun was going down, red behind bars of dark cloud. A breeze ruffled his drying fur and he shivered again, less from cold than from the thought of the path they had to travel.

"I know Tawnypelt will come if I ask her," he meowed, "but what about Crowpaw? He'd rather eat fox dung than go on a journey with us. But if all the cats StarClan have chosen don't go together, we might fail the prophecy."

"Crowpaw will understand," Feathertail tried to reassure him, though Brambleclaw wished he had her confidence.

"We'll help you persuade him," Stormfur offered. "He comes to the river to drink every day about sunset. It's too late now, so why don't we meet there tomorrow and talk to him together?"

"Okay." Brambleclaw blinked his gratitude. Somehow, the prophecy seemed to weigh less heavily when he was sharing it with friends. "Provided he comes, after this rain. WindClan should have water of their own now, remember."

"If he doesn't come," mewed Feathertail, sounding determined, "we'll just have to think of something else."

⚜ ⚜ ⚜

More rain fell during the night. WindClan's moorland streams would be flowing again without a doubt, making Brambleclaw more anxious than ever that the WindClan apprentice would not come into RiverClan territory to drink. He was restless all day; Cloudtail, on hunting patrol with him and Dustpelt, kept asking if he had ants in his fur.

When the fresh-kill pile had been restocked, Brambleclaw managed to slip out of camp again on his own. He especially wanted to avoid Squirrelpaw, who was bound to ask him where he was going.

The sun was sinking by the time he reached the border with RiverClan, in sight of the Twoleg bridge. It wasn't long before he saw the two RiverClan warriors climbing the river-bank and scooting across the bridge with their heads low. Stormfur beckoned with his tail, and Brambleclaw raced across the border to meet him and Feathertail at the near end of the bridge.

"Better hide," Stormfur meowed. "We don't know how many WindClan cats will come, and you're not supposed to be here."

Brambleclaw nodded. The three cats crept into the shelter of a thornbush near the place where the WindClan cats came to drink. Just below their hiding place the river raced noisily past, its brown water flecked with foam as it poured out of the gorge.

They did not have long to wait before Brambleclaw caught a strong WindClan scent and a group of cats appeared from the direction of Fourtrees. The Clan leader, Tallstar, came first, followed by Onewhisker and a ginger warrior Brambleclaw didn't recognize. Other cats came after them and Brambleclaw's heart began to race uncomfortably when he spotted Crowpaw among them with his mentor, Mudclaw.

The WindClan cats padded down the slope to the riverbank and crouched at the water's edge to drink. Frustrated, Brambleclaw saw that Crowpaw stayed in the middle of the group, too far away to call to him without other cats hearing.

"I'll have to go and fetch him," Feathertail murmured. She slipped out from underneath the bush and headed for the river.

Brambleclaw watched her greet the WindClan cats, stopping to speak briefly with Morningflower, one of the WindClan elders. Their exchange was polite, though not friendly; Brambleclaw wondered how long the Clans' uneasy alliance over the water would last if WindClan went on coming to drink now that the drought was over.

Soon Feathertail went to crouch beside Crowpaw at the water's edge. Brambleclaw dug his claws into the ground as he watched her straighten up again, shake water from her whiskers, and set off back to the thornbush. Crowpaw was not following her; had the WindClan apprentice decided he wanted no more to do with the mission, or had Feathertail been unable to tell him about the meeting?

"What's the matter?" he hissed as Feathertail crawled back into the shelter of the branches. "Did you talk to him?"

"It's okay." Feathertail pushed her muzzle into his side. "He's coming. He just doesn't want WindClan to see."

While she was speaking, Crowpaw backed away from the river and began to pad up the bank toward the bush. His Clan mates were still drinking. A couple of foxlengths away he glanced around casually and then dived for the bush before any cat could notice him go.

As the leaves rustled into place around him he glared at Brambleclaw with hostility in his green eyes. "I thought I could smell ThunderClan," he growled. "What do you want now?"

Brambleclaw exchanged an apprehensive glance with Feathertail. This wasn't a good start. "I've had another dream," he began, swallowing nervously.

"What sort of dream?" Crowpaw's voice was cold. "I haven't had one. Why would StarClan send you a dream and not me?"

Stormfur raised his hackles and Brambleclaw bit back a sharp response. "I don't know," he admitted.

A grunt was Crowpaw's only reply, but he listened in silence as Brambleclaw described what he had seen. "Ravenpaw, the loner who lives on the far side of your territory, visited the camp yesterday," he finished. "He told me that the sun-drown place is real. I . . . I think StarClan are telling us to go there. And we should go soon, all of us, in case the rest of the prophecy comes true and the Clans are in too much trouble to be saved."

Crowpaw's eyes stretched wide. "I can't believe I'm hearing

this," he meowed. "You're asking us to leave our Clans and go trekking off into the unknown—StarClan knows how far!—just because you've had a dream that none of us have had? Who died and made you leader?"

Brambleclaw found it hard to meet his eyes; Crowpaw was only echoing his own doubts. "I'm not trying to be leader," he stammered. "I'm just telling you what I think StarClan want."

"I'm willing to go," Feathertail added. "Even though I haven't had another dream."

"Then you're more mouse-brained than he is," Crowpaw retorted. "Well, I won't go. I'll be made a warrior soon. I've worked hard for it, and I'm not leaving the Clan so close to the end of my training."

"But Crowpaw—" Brambleclaw started to protest.

"No!" The apprentice showed his teeth in a snarl. "I'm not coming. What would my Clan think?"

"Maybe they'll honor you," Stormfur meowed. The gray warrior's eyes were serious. "Think, Crowpaw! If trouble is really coming, worse than anything we've seen before, what will the Clans think of the cats who help them? They'll understand how much faith we had to place in StarClan, that they were leading us on a genuine mission, and they'll know how much courage it took to do this."

"But you weren't chosen!" Crowpaw pointed out. "It doesn't matter to you one way or the other."

"Maybe not, but I'm coming anyway," Stormfur told him.

"And the reason StarClan aren't giving us clear instructions is because they want us to show faith and courage,"

Brambleclaw added. "Those are the qualities that a true warrior needs."

"Please, Crowpaw!" Feathertail's eyes shone. "The mission might fail without you. Remember that you *were* chosen—the only apprentice singled out by StarClan. They must believe that you can do this."

Crowpaw hesitated, looking at her. The red light of sunset had faded, leaving them in twilight, and Brambleclaw could hear and scent the WindClan cats as they passed the bush on their way back to their own territory. Crowpaw would have to leave with them before they noticed he was missing; there was no more time to plead or reason with him.

"All right," Crowpaw meowed at last. "I'll come." His eyes narrowed as he gazed at Brambleclaw. "Just don't start telling me what to do. Dreams or no dreams, I'm not going to take orders from you!"

Brambleclaw picked his way along the stone-lined tunnel under the Thunderpath, skirting the puddles that had formed there since the rain. Darkness lay all around, along with the reek of ShadowClan.

He had come here straight from the encounter with Crowpaw. The RiverClan warriors had offered to come with him, but Brambleclaw thought it was too risky. Alone, he would be less of a threat if ShadowClan warriors found him on their territory. Emerging on the other side of the Thunderpath, he tasted the air for fresh scents of ShadowClan warriors, but detected nothing except the damp odors of the marshy ground.

His belly skimming the earth, he darted across an open space and into the shelter of some bushes.

There were few tall trees in ShadowClan territory. Most of the ground was choked with brambles and nettles, separated by shallow pools of water. Brambleclaw's paws sank into the peaty earth at every step, and he shivered as his belly fur grew soaked.

"How do ShadowClan stand it?" he muttered. "It's so wet, I'm surprised they haven't all got webbed paws!"

He had a pretty good idea of where he might find Tawnypelt. She had once told him about a huge chestnut tree beside the stream that led down into ThunderClan territory. Her eyes had glowed as she described this favorite spot for sunning herself and catching squirrels, making Brambleclaw wonder if she was secretly missing the trees of ThunderClan. With any luck, she might be there now.

Brambleclaw located the stream and began to follow it, sometimes gritting his teeth and splashing through the shallows in the hope of hiding his scent from ShadowClan warriors. He saw a patrol crossing the stream a short way ahead, and crouched down behind a clump of sedge until they had vanished into the undergrowth and their scent faded away.

Not long after that he came to the chestnut tree. Its roots twisted around him, stretching down into the stream. Brambleclaw thought he could detect his sister's scent, but under the thick canopy of leaves it was too dark to see her.

"Tawnypelt!" he called softly. "Are you there?"

The answer came as a weight that crashed down on him,

bowling him over. He let out a startled yowl that broke off as his muzzle was pressed into the damp earth. A paw landed on his neck, pinning him with barely sheathed claws, and a voice growled close to his ear, "What are you doing here, you stupid furball?"

Brambleclaw let out a gasp of relief. The claws retracted and the weight lifted off him, letting him scramble to his paws. Tawnypelt was perched on a tree root, looking down at him.

"If you're found here, you'll be crowfood," she hissed. "What's gotten into you?"

"Something's happened. I've had another dream." Brambleclaw quickly told her about it.

Tawnypelt settled herself on the root to listen. "So Ravenpaw reckons it's a real place," she mused when he had finished. "And you think StarClan wants us to go there. They don't ask much, do they?"

Brambleclaw felt his ears droop. "You mean you won't come?"

His sister's tail twitched irritably. "Did I say that? Of course I'm coming. But no cat says I have to like it. And what about Stormfur? Why does he have to get involved? StarClan haven't chosen him."

Brambleclaw sighed. "I know. But try stopping him. Besides, he's a good warrior, and we might be glad of his support. We don't know what we're going to meet out there. And another thing," he added. "He and Feathertail do everything together. I think it comes of having their father in another Clan."

"I can understand that." Tawnypelt's tone was dry, and her brother realized how much sympathy she might have for the two RiverClan warriors. Her father was dead and both her brother and her mother, Goldenflower, remained in ThunderClan. Tawnypelt might well feel like a stranger in the Clan she had chosen. But Brambleclaw recognized the pride that would not let her voice her loneliness, and her determination to be a loyal ShadowClan warrior. Regret surged through him, not for the first time, as he thought what a loss she was to ThunderClan.

"You will serve your Clan well by coming on this journey," he reminded her.

"That's true." A trace of eagerness crept into Tawnypelt's voice, and grew stronger as she went on. "StarClan must have chosen us because they think we're the right cats. We must have something to offer that no other cats can give." She sprang down from the root and landed with a soft thud at Brambleclaw's side. "ShadowClan has many strong warriors to keep up the patrols. They can do without me for a while. When do we leave?"

Brambleclaw let out an affectionate purr. "Not right now! I told the others the night before the half-moon. We'll meet at Fourtrees."

Tawnypelt's tail lashed with enthusiasm. "I'll be ready. And now," she added, "I'd better show you to the border. Even one of StarClan's chosen can get his fur ripped off for trespassing."

CHAPTER 8

*"Snakerocks is the best place in* the forest to find chervil," Cinderpelt explained over her shoulder as she limped along the fern-shaded path. "But we can't go there just now, thanks to that wretched badger."

"It's still there, then?" Leafpaw asked. She and the medicine cat were on an herb-gathering expedition. The sun shone brilliantly from a sky that was clear again, but the rain had revived the forest plants, and Leafpaw was enjoying the delicious coolness on her paws as she followed her mentor along the narrow track.

"So the dawn patrol said," Cinderpelt replied. "Keep your eyes open for—Ah!"

She swerved into the ferns and up a sandy slope, where several clumps of a strongly scented herb were growing; the flowers were gone but Leafpaw recognized the large, spreading leaves, and as she drew closer she smelled the sweetish scent of chervil.

"Tell me what we use it for," Cinderpelt prompted, beginning to gnaw one of the stems at its base.

Leafpaw narrowed her eyes and tried to remember. "The

juice of the leaves for infected wounds," she mewed. "And if you chew the root it's good for bellyache."

"Well done," Cinderpelt purred. "Now you can dig up a few roots—not too many, though, or there'll be no more in seasons to come."

She went on biting the stems while Leafpaw obediently began to scrape at the ground to uncover the roots. The chervil scent was all around them, making her feel light-headed, but after a few moments she began to scent something else—something that reminded her of the acrid tang of the Thunderpath, though it was not quite the same.

She glanced up and spotted a thin thread of smoke rising from a clump of dead bracken a little way down the slope. "Cinderpelt, look," she mewed uneasily, pointing with her tail.

The medicine cat looked around and froze, her neck fur bristling and her blue eyes blazing. "Great StarClan, no!" She gasped. Awkwardly, because of her injured leg, she began scrambling down toward the burning bracken.

Leafpaw leaped after her and passed the medicine cat in a couple of bounds. As she drew closer to the clump of bracken, a searing light flashed, dazzling her eyes. Blinking, she made out something shiny and clear sticking out of the ground, some spiky scrap of Twoleg rubbish. The sun was falling straight onto it and the bracken behind was slowly blackening and sending the wisp of smoke into the sky.

"Fire!" Cinderpelt yowled, coming up behind her. "Quick!"

Suddenly the bracken burst into flame. Leafpaw sprang back from the wave of heat. Turning to flee, she saw that

Cinderpelt stood still, gazing into the scarlet and orange blaze that leaped hungrily at the brittle stalks.

*Was she frozen in panic?* Leafpaw wondered. Sandstorm had told her about the terrible fire that once swept through the ThunderClan camp. Cinderpelt had survived, but several cats had not, and fire must be especially frightening to the medicine cat when her injured leg made it hard for her to run away.

Then Leafpaw saw that Cinderpelt's eyes were not wide with fear, but something else. Her gaze was fixed and remote, and Leafpaw realized with a shiver from her ears to her tail tip that her mentor was receiving a message from StarClan.

As quickly as it had blazed up, the fire began to die, and Leafpaw let out a sigh of relief. The flames sank into bright embers and began to wink out, the fronds of bracken disintegrating into flecks of ash. Cinderpelt took a step backward. She was even more unsteady than usual; Leafpaw darted forward to press up against her side, supporting her and helping her to sit down.

"Did you see it?" Cinderpelt whispered.

"See what, Cinderpelt?"

"In the flames . . . a leaping tiger. I saw it clearly, its huge head, the leaping paws, stripes as black as night along its body. . . ." The medicine cat's voice was hoarse. "An omen from StarClan, fire and tiger together. It must mean something, but what?"

Leafpaw shook her head. "I don't know," she confessed, feeling scared and helpless.

Cinderpelt got shakily to her paws, shrugging off Leafpaw's

attempt to help her up. "We must go straight back to camp," she mewed. "Firestar should hear about this at once."

The ThunderClan leader was alone in his den under the Highrock when Cinderpelt and Leafpaw returned. Cinderpelt paused outside the curtain of lichen that covered the entrance and called out, "Firestar? I need to talk to you."

"Come in," Firestar's voice replied.

Leafpaw followed her mentor into the den to see her father curled up on the bed of moss by the far wall. His head was raised as if Cinderpelt had roused him from sleep, and when the medicine cat and her apprentice entered he rose and stretched, arching his back so that the muscles rippled under his flame-colored pelt.

"What can I do for you?"

Cinderpelt padded across the den toward him, while Leafpaw sat quietly beside the entrance, wrapping her tail around her paws as she tried to push down her sense of approaching danger. She had never seen Cinderpelt receive a message from their warrior ancestors before, and she was unsettled by the fear she had seen in her mentor's eyes on the journey back through the damp green forest.

"StarClan have sent me an omen," the medicine cat began. She described how the Twoleg rubbish had caught the sun's rays and set fire to the bracken. "In the flames I saw a leaping tiger. Fire and tiger together, devouring the bracken. Such power, unleashed, could destroy the forest."

Firestar was crouched in front of her, with his paws tucked in and his green gaze fixed on her face so intently that

Leafpaw almost expected her mentor's gray fur to start smoking like the bracken burning under the hot sunlight. "What do you think it means?"

"I've been trying to work it out," Cinderpelt meowed. "I'm not sure I'm right, but . . . in the old prophecy, 'fire will save the clan,' 'fire' meant you, Firestar."

The ThunderClan leader gave a start of surprise. "You think it refers to me now? Well . . . perhaps, but what about 'tiger'? Tigerstar is dead."

Leafpaw felt uneasiness stir inside her as her father calmly named the fearsome cat who had shed so much blood in his quest for power.

"He is dead—but his son still lives," Cinderpelt pointed out quietly. She glanced at Leafpaw sitting in the shadows, as if she were uncertain her apprentice should be hearing this. Leafpaw stayed absolutely still, determined to listen to the rest.

"Brambleclaw?" Firestar exclaimed. "Are you saying *he's* going to destroy the forest? Come on, Cinderpelt. He's as loyal as any warrior in the Clan. Look at the way he fought for us in the battle against BloodClan."

Leafpaw felt a sudden urge to say something in Brambleclaw's defense, though it was not her place to speak here. She did not know the young warrior particularly well, but some instinct inside her cried out, *No! He would never harm his Clan, or the forest.*

"Firestar, use your head." Cinderpelt sounded irritable. "I haven't said that Brambleclaw will destroy the forest. But if 'tiger' doesn't mean him, then which cat does it mean? And something else . . . if 'tiger' is Tigerstar's son, then maybe 'fire' is Firestar's daughter."

Leafpaw flinched as if a badger had sunk its teeth into her fur.

"Oh, I don't mean you." Cinderpelt turned to her apprentice with amusement gleaming faintly in her blue eyes. "I'll keep an eye on you, don't worry." Glancing back at Firestar, she added, "No, I think it more likely means Squirrelpaw. She has a flame-colored pelt like you, after all."

Leafpaw's brief sense of relief was swallowed up in fear and dismay as she realized where the medicine cat's logic was leading. Her own sister, the cat who was dearer to her than all others—was she prophesied to do something so terrible that her name would be cursed by all the Clans, just as queens told their kits now that if they were naughty the terrible Tigerstar would come and get them?

"My own daughter . . . she's headstrong, yes, but not dangerous . . ." Firestar's eyes were deeply troubled; Leafpaw saw that he had too much respect for Cinderpelt's wisdom to argue with her interpretation, though it was bitter as mouse bile to hear. "What do you think I should do?" he asked helplessly.

Cinderpelt shook her head. "That's your decision, Firestar. I can only tell you what StarClan have shown me. Fire and tiger together, and danger to the forest. But I'd advise you not to tell the Clan yet, not until I receive another sign. They'll only panic, and that will make things worse." Her head swiveled to fix an icy stare on Leafpaw. "Say nothing about this, on your loyalty to StarClan."

"Not even to Squirrelpaw?" Leafpaw asked nervously.

"Especially not to Squirrelpaw."

"I must tell Graystripe," Firestar mewed. "And Sandstorm—StarClan know what Sandstorm will think about this!"

Cinderpelt nodded. "That is wise, I think."

"And it might be as well to keep the two of them apart." Firestar spoke half to himself. Leafpaw could see how he was torn between doing his best for his Clan, and his deep feelings for his daughter and the warrior who had once been his apprentice. "She's an apprentice, he's a warrior; it shouldn't be hard," Firestar went on. "We'll make sure they have enough to do, and not in each other's company. Maybe StarClan will send another omen to tell us when the danger is past?" he suggested, glancing hopefully at Cinderpelt.

"Maybe." But the medicine cat's tone was not reassuring. She rose and flicked her tail for Leafpaw to follow her. "If they do, you'll be the first to know."

She dipped her head and backed out of the den. Leafpaw moved to follow her, hesitated, then rushed across to her father and buried her muzzle in his pelt, wanting to be comforted as much as to comfort him. Whatever this omen might mean, she was scared by it. She felt Firestar's tongue rasp warmly over her ear. Her eyes met his and she saw her own sorrow and fear reflected there.

Then Cinderpelt called "Leafpaw!" from outside, and the moment was over. Leafpaw bowed her head to her leader and left him alone, to wait for further news from StarClan about the destiny of his cats.

# CHAPTER 9

❧

*Brambleclaw chose a plump starling from* the fresh-kill pile, carrying it a few paces away before he began to gulp it down. Sunhigh was just past, and the clearing was full of cats enjoying the warmth. Brambleclaw caught a glimpse of Leafpaw padding over to the elders' den, a wad of herbs in her jaws. He was surprised to see how unhappy she looked; perhaps she was in trouble with her mentor, though he found it hard to imagine that Cinderpelt would drive any cat to look so worried.

Closer to the nettle patch, Firestar was eating with Graystripe and Sandstorm. As Brambleclaw bit into his prey he saw his leader raise his head and give him a hard stare, as if he might be in trouble. Brambleclaw couldn't remember anything he had done wrong that his leader knew about, but his fur prickled uneasily; surely Firestar hadn't found out about the dreams?

He braced himself for his leader to call him over and tell him what was on his mind, but when he heard a cat speak his name it was Squirrelpaw. She snatched a mouse from the heap of fresh-kill and bounced across to sit by his side.

"Whew!" she exclaimed, dropping the mouse. "I thought

I'd never finish feeding the elders. Longtail has the appetite of a starving fox!" She took a bite from her piece of prey and gulped it down. "So what's happening?" she asked. "Have you had any more messages from StarClan?"

Brambleclaw swallowed his mouthful of starling. "Ssshhh, not so loud," he hissed.

It was the day after his encounter with Crowpaw and his visit to ShadowClan territory, and he had still not decided how much to tell Squirrelpaw about the second dream. If he vanished on the day before the half-moon without confiding in her, he would have broken his part of their bargain, but he did not know what he would say if she demanded to come with them.

"Well, have you?" Squirrelpaw persisted, lowering her voice.

Brambleclaw chewed slowly, playing for time. He had just decided that he would have to tell the nosy she-cat something, if only to stop all her questions, when he realized that Firestar had padded over from the nettle patch and was standing over them. He stiffened, instinctively unsheathing his claws so that they sank into the breast of the starling.

"Squirrelpaw, I want you to go out with Thornclaw," Firestar ordered. "He's going to show Shrewpaw the best hunting places near Fourtrees."

Squirrelpaw took another gulp of mouse and swiped her tongue over her whiskers. "Do I have to? I've been up there with Dustpelt loads of times."

The tip of Firestar's tail twitched back and forth. "Yes, you do. When your leader gives you an order, you obey it."

Squirrelpaw rolled her eyes at Brambleclaw before picking up the last of the mouse and swallowing it.

"*Now*, Squirrelpaw." Firestar's tail twitched again. "Thornclaw's waiting." He nodded toward the tabby warrior, who was padding across the clearing with Shrewpaw.

"You could at least let me finish my mouse in peace," Squirrelpaw argued. "I've been on my paws all morning, chasing after the elders."

"And so you should be!" Firestar's voice was sharp. "That's what being an apprentice is all about. I don't want to hear you complaining."

"I'm *not* complaining!" Squirrelpaw leaped to her paws, her fur bristling. "I only said I wanted a bit of peace and quiet to eat. Why are you always nagging at me? You're not my *mentor,* so stop acting like you are. Or are you just afraid that I'll let you down, and not live up to our great leader's shining example?"

Without waiting for a response, she spun around and flounced off to meet Thornclaw and Shrewpaw near the entrance to the camp. Brambleclaw noticed that the tabby warrior looked surprised when Squirrelpaw spoke to him, though he was too far off to hear what she said, and it crossed his mind that Thornclaw hadn't been expecting her to join the patrol at all. Then the warrior nodded, and all three cats vanished into the gorse tunnel.

Firestar watched Squirrelpaw go with a grim look. He didn't say a word to Brambleclaw, but turned and padded back to Sandstorm and Graystripe.

Brambleclaw heard Sandstorm growl, "You know that's the wrong way to handle her. If you order her about, she'll just get more stubborn."

Firestar replied in a low voice that Brambleclaw couldn't catch; then the cats got up and headed toward Firestar's den.

*What was all that about?* Brambleclaw wondered. *Firestar was annoyed with Squirrelpaw, so he made up an excuse to get her out of the camp.* His blood ran chill. *To get her away from me, maybe?*

If he was right, there could only be one reason. Squirrelpaw must have told her father about the first dream, and the meeting with the other cats at Fourtrees. She might have done it deliberately, or she might have let something slip because she wasn't thinking. Whatever had happened, Brambleclaw knew there would be more trouble to come, but at least it meant he didn't have to tell her about the second dream; she had obviously broken the agreement they had made at Fourtrees.

Trying to put his fears about what Firestar might do next out of his mind, he went back to the fresh-kill pile. If he was going to set off on a long journey in a few days' time, it would be a good idea to eat more and build up his strength. He would also ask Cinderpelt about the traveling herbs that cats ate to give them strength for the journey to Highstones, as long as he could think of a way to do it without arousing the medicine cat's suspicions.

He was just reaching down to pick up a juicy-looking vole when he heard a voice behind him. "Hey—what do you think you're doing?"

It was Mousefur. Brambleclaw looked around to see the brown she-cat glaring at him from a few foxlengths away.

"I've been watching you," she went on. "You've already eaten. You haven't hunted enough today to take any more prey."

Embarrassment flooded over Brambleclaw. "Sorry," he mumbled.

"So I should think," Mousefur snapped.

Cloudtail, who was standing beside her, let out an amused purr. "He's trying to compete with Graystripe," he teased. "Looks like one big eater isn't enough for ThunderClan. Never mind, Brambleclaw. Do you want to hunt with me and Brightheart? We'll catch as many voles as you can eat, and double the fresh-kill pile."

"Er, thanks," Brambleclaw stammered.

"Hang on, I'll just fetch Brightheart." Cloudtail raced over to the warriors' den, and Mousefur, with a last glare at Brambleclaw, followed him.

While Brambleclaw waited for his friends to reappear, he decided to suggest going up to Fourtrees, where they might come across Thornclaw's patrol. He needed to get hold of Squirrelpaw and find out exactly what she had told her father. If Firestar knew that StarClan had chosen four cats, each from a different Clan, would he try to warn the other leaders, and put a stop to their journey before it even started?

But Brambleclaw's patrol saw nothing of Squirrelpaw and the others while they were out, and by the time he returned to camp with Cloudtail and Brightheart, with plenty of prey to add to the pile, night was falling. Most of the cats were already heading for their dens. Brambleclaw kept watch until the evening patrol had left and the moon had appeared above the trees, but he still did not see Squirrelpaw. He slept badly that night, worried about the prophecy and Squirrelpaw's unwanted involvement.

The next morning he pushed his way out of the warriors' den as soon as he woke, determined to find the ginger apprentice and get some answers to his questions. But it seemed as if StarClan itself were against him, making him hiss out loud with frustration. No sooner had he set paw in the clearing than Graystripe called him to join the dawn patrol with Sorreltail and Rainwhisker. By the time they returned, after a circuit of the whole territory, it was almost sunhigh. When Brambleclaw checked the apprentices' den it was empty, and as he could not see Dustpelt in the camp either, he assumed that Squirrelpaw had gone out training with her mentor.

He took a nap in the heat of the day, his worries soothed for a short while by the quiet murmur of bees and the sigh of wind in the branches, and woke to catch sight of Squirrelpaw disappearing into the gorse tunnel, a wad of old bedding clamped in her jaws. Springing to his paws, he was about to follow her when a cat called his name.

Brackenfur was padding toward him with his apprentice, Whitepaw. For some reason the golden brown tom looked uneasy. "Hi, Brambleclaw. I . . . I thought you might like to come and watch a training session," he meowed.

Brambleclaw stared at him in surprise. Warriors hardly ever watched the apprentices training, unless they were mentors themselves. With a swift glance at the tunnel where Squirrelpaw was now out of sight, he replied, "Er . . . thanks, Brackenfur, but some other time, okay?"

He headed quickly toward the camp entrance, but realized after a couple of heartbeats that Brackenfur was keeping pace with him.

"It's just that Firestar thought it might be good practice for you," the older warrior explained. "For when you have an apprentice of your own."

Brambleclaw halted. "Let me get this straight," he meowed. "*Firestar* asked you to tell me to watch you and Whitepaw training?"

Brackenfur's gaze slid past him and he looked acutely embarrassed. "That's right," he mewed.

"But we *never* do that," Brambleclaw protested. "Anyway, it'll be moons before Ferncloud's kits are ready for mentors."

Brackenfur shrugged. "An order's an order, Brambleclaw."

Brambleclaw blinked. "It's an *order*?" He shook his head crossly. It wasn't StarClan that was against him—it was his own leader. And it was hardly surprising, if Squirrelpaw had told Firestar that one of his warriors had been having prophetic dreams without telling the rest of the Clan.

Fuming, he followed Brackenfur and his apprentice out of the camp and along the ravine to the sandy hollow where the training sessions took place. He sat on the edge, watching

Brackenfur put Whitepaw through her fighting moves. A little later, Mousefur arrived with Spiderpaw, and the two apprentices started a mock battle. Brambleclaw watched as Whitepaw darted in to give Spiderpaw a quick nip in the neck; Spiderpaw spun around at once, his long black limbs whirling as he leaped on her and pinned her to the ground. They were both making good progress, Brambleclaw noticed idly, yawning with boredom.

*I could be doing something useful*, he thought miserably. There were only two days to go before he was due to meet the other cats at Fourtrees and set out on their journey. He needed to talk to Squirrelpaw soon.

When Mousefur called a halt and the two apprentices climbed out of the hollow, shaking sand from their fur, Brambleclaw returned to camp even more determined to find Squirrelpaw and get some answers. To his relief, when he emerged from the gorse tunnel he spotted her with Shrewpaw beside the apprentices' den.

Racing across the clearing, he halted in front of her and demanded, "I want to talk to you."

He knew that issuing orders was not the way to handle Squirrelpaw. Ready for her to snarl or spit, he was surprised when she mewed in a hurried, low voice, with an uneasy glance at Shrewpaw, "Okay, but not here. Meet me behind the nursery."

Brambleclaw nodded and padded away to greet Sootfur and Ashfur, who were returning with fresh-kill. He paused at the entrance to the nursery where Ferncloud was watching her kits play, forcing himself to sound normal as he commented on how strong and healthy they were growing. Finally he made his way behind the nursery, a sandy area bounded by nettles where the cats went to make their dirt.

Squirrelpaw was already waiting for him, her dark ginger fur almost hidden in the shadows. "Brambleclaw, I—"

"You've told your father something, haven't you?" Brambleclaw interrupted. "After you promised to keep your mouth shut."

Squirrelpaw straightened up to face him, her neck fur bristling furiously. "I have *not*! I haven't said a word to any cat."

"Then why is Firestar so determined to keep us apart?"

"Oh, you've noticed too, have you?" Squirrelpaw tried to sound calm, but her voice rose to a wail as she went on, "I don't *know*! I promise I didn't tell him anything. But he looks at me like I've done something bad, and I *haven't*."

Suddenly feeling sorry for the confused, unhappy she-cat, Brambleclaw padded up to her to press his muzzle against her side, but she whisked away from him, her teeth bared in the beginnings of a snarl.

"It's nothing I can't handle. Leafpaw's upset, too," she added. "She hasn't said anything, but I can tell."

Brambleclaw sat down and stared across the nettles to the thorn hedge around the camp, without really seeing it. He couldn't make any sense of Firestar's behavior if Squirrelpaw was telling the truth about keeping quiet. Brambleclaw couldn't bring himself to think that she was lying to him, which meant there had to be another reason Firestar was angry with them both. But what on earth could it be?

"Perhaps we should ask him?" he suggested. "If he told us what the matter is, we might be able to put it right."

Squirrelpaw looked doubtful, but before she could reply Brambleclaw heard the sound of more cats pushing their way through the nettles. Springing to his paws, he whipped around to see Firestar himself, with Graystripe just behind.

"So." The ThunderClan leader stepped forward until he stood between his daughter and Brambleclaw. "Shrewpaw said I'd find you here."

"We weren't doing anything wrong!" Squirrelpaw blurted out.

"But I wonder what you think you *are* doing." Firestar gave his daughter a hard stare and then transferred it to Brambleclaw. "Wasting your time, for one thing, when there's work to be done."

"We've worked hard all day, Firestar," Brambleclaw meowed, ducking his head respectfully.

"That's true, Firestar, they have," Graystripe put in.

Firestar shot him a quick glance, but did not respond. "Does that mean you think there's nothing more to do?" he asked Brambleclaw. The younger warrior opened his mouth to protest, but his leader did not give him the chance. "If you're so sure," he went on, "then take a look at the elders. Frostfur got burrs tangled in her pelt today. You can help her get them out."

Anger flared inside Brambleclaw. That was an apprentice task! But he could see from Firestar's cold green gaze that there was no point in arguing. He mumbled, "Yes, Firestar," and padded away toward the main clearing.

Once the nettles had rustled back into place, screening him from the little group of cats, he paused to hear Firestar speaking to Squirrelpaw, still in that same hard, displeased tone. "Squirrelpaw, you must have better things to do than hang about with an inexperienced warrior like Brambleclaw. Stay with your own mentor in the future."

Brambleclaw couldn't hear Squirrelpaw's response, and it wasn't safe to stay there listening any longer. Sadness flooded over him as he made his way to the elders' den. Somehow he had lost his leader's respect, and if Squirrelpaw really hadn't told her father about the dream and the meeting with the other cats at Fourtrees, he couldn't imagine why.

In two nights' time he was supposed to leave on his journey with the cats from the other Clans to find the sun-drown place, and see what midnight told them. How could he possibly go, Brambleclaw wondered despairingly, when Firestar was watching him so closely? A chill ran through him from ears to tail-tip as he realized that to be loyal to the prophecy and to StarClan, he might have to be disloyal to his leader.

CHAPTER 10
❧

*Brambleclaw scarcely slept that night, and* when he did, his dreams were full of Firestar's anger, and images of his leader driving him away from the camp. When he pushed his way out of the warriors' den the next morning, he still felt exhausted—even more so when he reflected that this was his last day in camp before his journey would begin.

A gray dawn light was filtering through the camp, and the wind was chilly. Tasting the air, Brambleclaw thought he could make out the first scent of approaching leaf-fall. Change was on the way, he realized, whatever he and the other chosen cats tried to do.

Throughout the day he did not even bother trying to speak to Squirrelpaw. Though Firestar had not ordered them to stay apart, he obviously didn't like them to be together. There was no point in deliberately looking for trouble. Brambleclaw caught a glimpse of the young apprentice leaving the camp with Dustpelt; she looked oddly subdued, with her tail trailing against the earth and her ears flat.

"You look as if you've lost a rabbit and found a shrew," a brisk voice spoke beside him.

Brambleclaw looked up; it was Mousefur.

"Do you want to come hunting with me and Spiderpaw?" the she-cat meowed.

For once Brambleclaw felt he hardly had the energy for hunting or anything else. With his journey due to start the next day, worries were crowding around him like cats at a Gathering. Was he really meant to lead four other cats out into the unknown, to face dangers they could not even imagine?

Mousefur was still waiting for Brambleclaw to answer. He couldn't help wondering if her suggestion of hunting together was another of Firestar's orders to keep him busy. But the brown she-cat blinked at him in a friendly way, and he realized that he would be better off hunting than hanging about the camp worrying. Perhaps if he brought back plenty of prey he would start to regain Firestar's good opinion.

But the hunt didn't go well. Spiderpaw was too easily distracted, as playful as a kit on its first outing. Once, as he was creeping up on a mouse, a leaf spiraled down past his nose, and he lifted one paw to bat at it. Startled by the clumsy movement, the mouse vanished under a root.

"Honestly!" Mousefur sighed. "Do you expect the prey to come and jump into your mouth?"

"Sorry," Spiderpaw mewed, looking abashed.

He made more of an effort after that. When the patrol came upon a squirrel nibbling an acorn in the middle of a clearing, Spiderpaw began stalking it, moving each long black leg stealthily. He was almost ready to pounce when the wind changed and carried his scent to his prey. The squirrel started, tail flicking up, and bounded toward the edge of the clearing.

"Bad luck!" Brambleclaw called.

Instead of answering, Spiderpaw raced after the squirrel and disappeared into the undergrowth.

"Hey!" Mousefur shouted after him. "You'll never catch a squirrel like that." Spiderpaw did not reappear, and his mentor bared her teeth in a resigned growl. "One day he'll learn." She padded off into the undergrowth to find him.

Left to himself, Brambleclaw stood still, listening for the sound of prey. There was a faint rustling in the leaves under the nearest tree. A mouse appeared, scuffling after seeds. Brambleclaw dropped into a hunting crouch and crept up on it, trying to make his paws float over the ground. Then he sprang, and killed his prey with one swift snap.

He scraped earth over it so that he could collect it later, half wishing that Mousefur had been there to see his success. At least she could have told Firestar that he was still hunting well for his Clan—whatever the leader's complaint was, it couldn't be about that. Listening for more prey, promising himself one last good hunt before he left, he pricked up his ears instead at the sound of something bigger rustling among the bushes a little way off, in the opposite direction from where Spiderpaw and Mousefur had disappeared. Brambleclaw drew the air into his mouth, but could scent nothing except ThunderClan cats. He began to pad forward, only to quicken his pace as the rustling grew louder and was followed by a furious yowl. He ran around the edge of a bramble thicket and stopped dead.

There was a gorse bush in front of him, and Squirrelpaw

was struggling madly among its thick, spiky branches. Her front paws were off the ground and her fur was tangled in the thorns. Brambleclaw couldn't suppress a *mrrow* of laughter. "Having fun?"

Instantly Squirrelpaw's head whipped around and her green eyes flashed fury at him. "That's right, have a good laugh, you stupid furball!" she snapped. "Then maybe you'll have time to get me out of here!"

She sounded so much like the old Squirrelpaw rather than the dejected creature that had left the camp that morning that Brambleclaw felt better at once. Tail waving, he strolled toward her. "How did you manage to get so stuck?"

"I was chasing a vole." Squirrelpaw sounded exasperated. "Dappletail said she fancied one, so I thought I'd better oblige, seeing that Firestar seems to want me to feed the elders, like, forever. It ran under here, and I thought there was room for me to run after it."

"There isn't," Brambleclaw pointed out helpfully.

"I know that now, mouse-brain! Do something!"

"Keep still, then." Approaching the bush, Brambleclaw saw where the worst tangles were, and began to tease out her fur, carefully using his teeth and claws. Some of the thorns pierced his nose, making his eyes water, but he kept on without complaining.

"Hang on," Squirrelpaw muttered after a while. "I think I'm loose."

Brambleclaw jumped out of the way as the apprentice plunged forward, forepaws scrabbling the earth as she dragged her hindquarters clear of the branches. A moment later she was free, shaking herself irritably while she stared at the tufts of ginger fur she had left behind.

"Thanks, Brambleclaw," she meowed.

"Are you hurt at all?" he asked. "Maybe you ought to let Cinderpelt have a look at—"

"Squirrelpaw!"

Brambleclaw froze and his heart sank. He slowly turned around to see Firestar stalking toward them.

The Clan leader had an expression like ice in his eyes as he looked from Brambleclaw to his daughter and back again. "Is this how you obey orders?" he growled.

The unfairness of Firestar's attitude took Brambleclaw's breath away. For a couple of heartbeats he couldn't find words to answer, and when he did he knew he sounded guilty. "I'm not disobeying orders, Firestar."

"Oh? I'm sorry." Firestar's voice was as dry as a sun-scorched rock. "I thought you were supposed to be on a hunting patrol, but I must have heard wrong."

"I *am* on a hunting patrol," Brambleclaw mewed desperately.

Firestar made a great show of looking around. "I don't see Mousefur or Spiderpaw."

"Spiderpaw went off after a squirrel." Brambleclaw pointed with his tail. "Mousefur went after him."

"Why are you being so horrible?" Squirrelpaw interrupted, glaring at her father. "Brambleclaw isn't doing anything wrong."

"Brambleclaw isn't doing what he was told," Firestar growled. "That isn't the warrior code as I was taught it."

Squirrelpaw sprang forward to stand nose-to-nose with her father and lifted her voice in a yowl of pure fury. "I was stuck in the bush! Brambleclaw helped me! It's not his fault!"

"Be quiet," Firestar rasped. Brambleclaw was struck by how much alike father and daughter looked: green eyes flashing, ginger pelts bristling angrily. "This has nothing to do with you."

"It looks like it has," Squirrelpaw argued. "You growl at Brambleclaw every time he so much as glances at me—"

"*Silence!*" Firestar hissed.

Brambleclaw stared in alarm. Just at that moment, Graystripe thrust his way into the clearing, a vole clamped in his jaws.

"Firestar?" he meowed, dropping his prey. "What's going on?"

Firestar lashed his tail, then straightened up with an impatient shake of his head. Brambleclaw forced himself to relax the fur on his neck.

"Oh, right." Graystripe's amber eyes glowed with understanding as he looked at the other cats in the clearing, and Brambleclaw realized that whatever was making Firestar act like this, his deputy knew all about it. "Come on, Firestar," he went on, padding up to the Clan leader and giving him a nudge. "These two aren't doing any harm."

"And not much good, either," Firestar retorted. He faced the two younger cats. "My decisions, and the orders I give, are for the good of the whole Clan," he reminded them. "If you can't understand that, then maybe you aren't fit to be warriors."

"What?" Squirrelpaw's jaws opened on a howl of outrage, but a furious hiss from her father silenced her.

Brambleclaw was too bewildered even to try protesting. Something—some knowledge Firestar and Graystripe shared—had turned Firestar against him. If Squirrelpaw hadn't told her father about the dream, then it had to be something else. But he had no idea what it could be, or what he could do about it.

"You," Firestar went on crisply, flicking his tail at Squirrelpaw, "take that vole of Graystripe's to the elders, and then carry on hunting for them. You"—with a flick at Brambleclaw—"find Mousefur and see if you can possibly bring back some fresh-kill before dark. Do it now."

Without waiting to see if his orders were obeyed, he whipped around and stalked off through the bushes.

Graystripe paused before following him. "He's got a lot on his mind," he murmured apologetically. "Don't take it too much to heart. Everything will work out okay; you'll see."

A yowl of "Graystripe!" came from the direction where Firestar had disappeared. Graystripe twitched his ears, nodded farewell to the two younger cats, and hurried after his leader.

Squirrelpaw stared after them. Now that Firestar had gone and she no longer had to go on defying him, her tail drooped, and the gaze she turned on Brambleclaw was full of distress.

"I can't do anything right," she meowed. "You heard what he said. He thinks I'm not fit to be a warrior. He'll never give me my warrior name."

Brambleclaw did not know what to say. His bewilderment was melting into a slow, furious anger. He *knew* he hadn't done anything wrong. Whatever was making Firestar behave like this, it wasn't his fault. It wasn't Squirrelpaw's, either. She could be annoying, but she was a loyal and hardworking apprentice. Any leader worth a couple of mousetails could see what a great warrior she would make.

He glared down at the ground, and when Squirrelpaw spoke his name he scarcely heard her. He felt his mind clearing, like a gray sky when the wind tore the clouds away and the sun shone through. The day before, after the confrontation behind the nursery, he had felt torn between the demands of the prophecy and loyalty to Firestar. Now he looked ahead to see day after day of struggling to please his leader with no chance of success, because he did not know why Firestar was angry with him in the first place. There was only one solution. He must leave on the journey with only the word of StarClan to guide him, and not come back until he had discovered answers that would prove to Firestar how loyal he had been all along. Or else he would not come back at all.

"Go on," Brambleclaw meowed roughly, nodding toward the dropped vole. "Take that back, or he'll have another go at you."

"What about you?" Squirrelpaw, usually so bright and confident, sounded nervous.

"I . . ." He had been about to lie to her, and tell her that he was going to look for Mousefur. Then he realized how deeply betrayed she would feel when he didn't come back. After all, they were in this together, at least as far as Firestar's hostility was concerned. "I'm leaving," he told her.

"Leaving?" Squirrelpaw echoed in dismay. "Leaving ThunderClan?"

"Not leaving for good," Brambleclaw put in quickly. "Squirrelpaw, listen. . . ."

She sat in front of him, and her wide green eyes never left his face as he told her about the second dream, of drowning in endless salty water and being swept toward the cave with teeth.

"Ravenpaw says it's a real place," he explained. "I think StarClan are telling me to go there, and the other cats agree. We're starting at sunrise tomorrow."

The hurt in Squirrelpaw's eyes was clear. "You told them and not me?" she wailed. "Brambleclaw, you *promised!*"

"I know." Brambleclaw felt guilt gnawing at him. "I was going to, and then all this trouble with Firestar started— StarClan know why, and if they do, they're telling me even less about it than they've told me about the prophecy."

"And you're really going all that way? But you don't even know how far it is."

"None of us do," Brambleclaw admitted. "But Ravenpaw has spoken to cats who have seen the place, so it must be possible to get there. I'm not coming back to the camp," he added. "I'll spend the night somewhere in the forest, and meet the others at Fourtrees in the morning. Please, Squirrelpaw, don't give us away. Don't tell any cat where we've gone."

As he spoke, Squirrelpaw's eyes brightened until they were gleaming with excitement. Brambleclaw knew what she was going to say a heartbeat before she said it.

"I won't breathe a word to any cat," she promised. "I can't, because I'm coming with you."

"Oh, no, you're not!" Brambleclaw retorted. "You're not one of the chosen cats. You're not even a warrior yet."

"Crowpaw isn't a warrior," Squirrelpaw flashed back at him. "And I'd bet a moon of dawn patrols Stormfur is coming. He'd never let Feathertail go without him. So why do I have to be left out?" She hesitated, and then added, "I didn't tell any cat about the first dream, Brambleclaw. I never said a word. Not even to Leafpaw."

Brambleclaw knew that was true. If Squirrelpaw had dropped even a hint, it would have been all around the camp by now.

"I didn't promise you could come," he reminded her. "I promised to tell you, and I've done that."

"But you *can't* leave me behind," Squirrelpaw cried. "If I don't know what happens next, my fur will fall out from wondering!"

"It's just too dangerous, Squirrelpaw; can't you see that? The prophecy is a heavy enough weight for me to bear, without having to look after you as well."

"Look after me!" Squirrelpaw's eyes blazed indignantly. "I

can look after myself, thank you. I'm coming, whether you like it or not. If you won't let me come with you, I'll follow you. Think about what happened today. I don't want to go back to camp and be told off for nothing, over and over again, any more than you do!"

Brambleclaw stared at her, indecisive. He did not want the responsibility of taking a young apprentice into danger . . . but she would be in much more danger if she tried to follow him alone through unknown territory. And if she returned to the camp, once Firestar realized that Brambleclaw had gone missing, he would badger Squirrelpaw until she told him what she knew, and maybe even send an expedition to bring him back. For a couple of heartbeats Brambleclaw understood what it meant to be a leader, his fur weighed down with doubts and questions heavier than a whole riverful of floodwater.

He heaved a sigh that seemed to go down to the tips of his paws. "All right, Squirrelpaw," he meowed. "You can come."

CHAPTER 11

*"Where are we going to sleep?"* Squirrelpaw asked.

As soon as Brambleclaw agreed to take her with him on the journey, her hurt and anger had vanished like dawn mist under a hot sun. He did not think she had stopped talking for a moment since they left the clearing where Firestar had found them.

*"Quiet!"* he hissed. "If any cat is looking for us, they'll be able to hear you right across the forest."

"But where?" Squirrelpaw persisted, though she did lower her voice.

"Somewhere not too far from Fourtrees," Brambleclaw replied. "Then we'll be ready to meet the others at sunrise."

Darkness had fallen as he led the way through the undergrowth. Clouds had massed to cover the sky, so that no gleam of star or moon broke through. A cold breeze whispered in the grass, and once again Brambleclaw tasted the scents of approaching leaf-fall.

With possible pursuit in mind, he had considered finding shelter near Snakerocks, which the Clan had been ordered to avoid, but the risk of encountering the night-hunting badger was too great. Instead he decided to make for the Thunder-path, hoping that the acrid smells of Twoleg monsters would mask his own scent and Squirrelpaw's.

"I know a good tree by the Thunderpath," Squirrelpaw suggested. "You can get right inside. We could hide there."

"And have spiders and beetles crawling through our fur all night?" Brambleclaw mewed discouragingly. "No, thanks."

Squirrelpaw sniffed. "Why do you always know better?"

"Maybe because I'm a warrior?"

Distracted by a rustling in the undergrowth, the appren-tice made no reply. Barely pausing to track her prey, she dived into a clump of bracken and came back a couple of heartbeats later with a mouse dangling from her jaws.

"Well done," meowed Brambleclaw.

The sight of the fresh-kill made him realize how hungry he was. Not long after, he managed to catch a mouse for himself, and the two cats paused to eat in quick, wary gulps, their ears pricked to catch the faintest traces of a ThunderClan patrol. But Brambleclaw could hear nothing except the ordinary night sounds of the forest and the nearby roar of monsters on the Thunderpath. Their stench was so strong here that it masked most others, as Brambleclaw had hoped, though he shrank from the thought of spending the night with that in his nostrils.

While they ate, a thin, cold rain began to fall, growing steadily heavier until Brambleclaw's fur was soaked and he was colder than he could remember feeling in moons.

"We need shelter," Squirrelpaw mewed, shivering. She

looked small and vulnerable, with her fur plastered darkly to her body. "What about finding that tree?"

Brambleclaw was about to agree when they emerged from the undergrowth at the top of a grassy bank, and he found himself looking down at the Thunderpath. A Twoleg monster roared past, its glaring eyes cutting shafts of yellow brightness through the night. Before it swept by, the light showed Brambleclaw a looming dark shape, the biggest monster he had ever seen, squatting on the verge of the Thunderpath. The reek of it flooded his senses.

"What's *that?*" exclaimed Squirrelpaw, brushing close beside him.

"I don't know," Brambleclaw admitted. "I've never seen anything like it before. Stay here while I take a look."

Cautiously he padded forward until he stood a couple of foxlengths away from the monster. Was it dead, he wondered, and was that why its Twolegs had abandoned it here? Or was it crouching, watching, waiting to spring as he would spring on a helpless mouse?

"Look, we could get underneath it," Squirrelpaw pointed out, trotting up to join him; of course she had not obeyed his order to wait at the top of the bank. "We could shelter from the rain."

There was just enough light for Brambleclaw to make out a darker gap between the monster's belly and the ground. His fur bristled at the thought of crawling into the narrow space, but he didn't want to seem a coward in front of Squirrelpaw, and her suggestion was a good one. The overwhelming scent would certainly hide them from any pursuers.

"Okay," he meowed. "But let me—" He broke off as Squirrelpaw bounded forward, flattened herself to the ground, and wriggled underneath the monster.

"—go first," Brambleclaw finished resignedly, following her.

A faint dawn light seeping under the monster's belly roused Brambleclaw the next morning. Squirrelpaw was curled beside him. For a heartbeat he couldn't remember why she was sleeping in his den instead of her own. Then the acrid reek of the monster, and a continuous roar from the Thunderpath close by, reminded him where he was and why. This was the morning when the journey would really begin! But instead of excitement, he felt only uncertainty dragging at his paws, along with the dismal thought that he had as good as exiled himself from his Clan by disappearing without his leader's permission.

Brambleclaw crept out from beneath the monster and lifted his head to taste the air. The grass was still wet from the previous night's rain, and the bushes at the top of the bank were heavy with drops of water. Mist curled through the trees in the gray dawn. There was no sound or scent of other cats.

Turning back to the monster, he called to Squirrelpaw, "Wake up! It's time we were on our way to Fourtrees."

He was beginning to think he would have to slide back under the monster's belly to rouse the apprentice when she crawled out, blinking. "I'm starving," she complained.

"We'll have time to catch prey on the way," Brambleclaw told her. "But we *must* get moving. The others will be waiting."

"Okay." Squirrelpaw raced up the bank and headed toward Fourtrees, following the line of the Thunderpath. Brambleclaw caught up to her, and for a time the two cats loped along side by side. The mist cleared and a golden light gathered on the horizon where the sun would rise. Birds began to sing in the branches overhead.

Once she was properly awake, Squirrelpaw seemed to forget about stopping to hunt. She hurried on, paying no attention to anything around her. Brambleclaw was torn between wanting to get to Fourtrees as soon as possible, and staying alert for possible trouble. When he heard rustling in the bushes behind them he halted, ears flicking up and jaws parted to detect the scent of their pursuer.

"Squirrelpaw!" he hissed. "Get out of sight!"

But Squirrelpaw whirled around a heartbeat before he spoke, and stood staring in the direction of the sound, her green eyes wide. At the same moment, Brambleclaw picked up the strong, familiar scent of a ThunderClan cat. Then the branches of a nearby bush quivered and parted to reveal Leafpaw.

The two sisters stood rigid for a moment, their gazes locked together. Then Leafpaw padded forward and set down the packet of herbs she was carrying at Squirrelpaw's feet.

"I brought you some traveling herbs," she murmured. "You're going to need them."

Brambleclaw stared from her to Squirrelpaw. "I thought you said you hadn't told any cat!" His voice was loud with outrage. "How does she know? You've been lying to me!"

"I have not!" Squirrelpaw spat.

"No, she hasn't," Leafpaw's gentler voice added. "But she didn't need to tell me anything. I just knew, that's all."

Brambleclaw shook himself. "You mean, you know everything?" he asked. "About the dreams, and the journey to the sun-drown place?"

Leafpaw turned her serious gaze on him, and he saw unhappiness and bewilderment in the depths of her eyes. "No," she mewed. "Only that Squirrelpaw is going away." She hesitated, closing her eyes briefly. "And there will be great danger."

A pang of pity for her stabbed through Brambleclaw, sharp as a thorn, but he could not afford to give in to it. He had to know what Leafpaw had done with her knowledge.

"Who else knows?" he demanded roughly. "Have you told your father?"

"No!" The flash of anger in Leafpaw's eyes suddenly made her look very much like her sister. "I wouldn't tell on Squirrelpaw, not even to Firestar."

"She wouldn't, Brambleclaw," Squirrelpaw added.

Brambleclaw nodded slowly.

"I almost wish I had," Leafpaw went on, bitterness in her voice. "Perhaps I could have stopped it all, and kept you here. Squirrelpaw, do you really have to go?"

"I must! This is the most exciting thing that has ever happened to me. Don't you see? It's a command from *StarClan*, so it's not like we're going against the warrior code."

She began pouring out to Leafpaw the whole story of Brambleclaw's dreams, and the meeting with the cats from other Clans. Leafpaw listened, her eyes widening in dismay. Brambleclaw fidgeted from paw to paw, acutely aware of the passing of time as the daylight strengthened.

"But *you* don't need to go!" Leafpaw wailed when Squirrelpaw had finished. "You haven't been chosen."

"Well, I'm not going back. I can't do anything right, as far as Firestar is concerned. Do you know he even told me I might not be fit to be a warrior? I'll show him whether I'm fit or not!"

Brambleclaw glanced at Leafpaw. She knew as well as he did how useless it was to argue with Squirrelpaw when she had made up her mind. There was something else, too, in Leafpaw's amber eyes: a hint of trouble, as if she knew more than she was telling.

"But you might not come back." Leafpaw's voice shook, and Brambleclaw was reminded even more forcibly that as well as a medicine cat, Leafpaw was Squirrelpaw's sister. "What will I do without you?"

"I'll be okay, Leafpaw." Brambleclaw was amazed at the gentleness of Squirrelpaw's voice, and the way that she pressed her muzzle comfortingly against her sister's side. "I've *got* to go. You do see that, don't you?"

Leafpaw nodded.

"And you won't tell anyone where we've gone?" Squirrelpaw pressed.

"I don't know where you're going—and neither do you," Leafpaw pointed out. "But no, I won't say anything. Just remember that Firestar does love you. He has things on his mind that you know nothing about." She drew in a shaky breath. "Now take the herbs and go."

Squirrelpaw dabbed at the packet of herbs, dividing them between herself and Brambleclaw. As they gulped down the bitter-tasting leaves, Leafpaw looked on, her eyes huge and somber.

"Even if you don't have a medicine cat with you, you can still find herbs as you go along. Don't forget marigold for wounds," she meowed rapidly. "And tansy for coughs—oh, and juniper berries for bellyache. And borage leaves are best for fever, if you can find any." She sounded as if she were trying to pass on the whole of her training in the few moments she had left.

"We won't forget," Squirrelpaw promised. She finished the last mouthful of herbs and swiped her tongue around her mouth. "Come on, Brambleclaw."

"Good-bye, Leafpaw," Brambleclaw mewed. "You—and the rest of the Clan—take care. If trouble is really coming to the forest, we . . . we might not be back in time to help you fight it."

"That is in the paws of StarClan," Leafpaw agreed sadly. "I will do my best to be ready, I promise."

"And don't worry about Squirrelpaw," Brambleclaw added. "I'll look after her."

"And I'll look after him." Squirrelpaw flashed him a

challenging look before padding up to her sister and touching noses with her. "We *will* come back," she murmured.

Leafpaw dipped her head, sadness clouding her eyes. As Brambleclaw headed once again for Fourtrees, he glanced back to see her watching them, a motionless light brown figure against the ferns. As he raised his tail in a gesture of farewell she turned swiftly, and the undergrowth swallowed her up.

# CHAPTER 12

*Leafpaw caught a vole on her* way back to the camp, and slipped down the ravine with it clamped in her jaws, hoping that any cat who saw her would think that she had been out on an early hunting expedition. Her mind was still whirling with her sister's departure, and how the prophecies of StarClan seemed to be gathering around Squirrelpaw and Brambleclaw like mist clinging to the branches of a gorse bush.

As she emerged into the clearing she heard Mousefur's voice raised loudly. "That Brambleclaw is a lazy lump! It's well past sunrise, and he isn't up yet. I want him for a hunting patrol."

"I'll wake him." Brightheart, who was sitting with Mousefur near the nettle patch, got up and went into the warriors' den.

Leafpaw felt a cold knot in her belly at the thought of what would happen when the rest of ThunderClan discovered that Brambleclaw and Squirrelpaw had vanished. At that moment, Dustpelt appeared from the nursery and padded over to the apprentices' den, where Whitepaw and Shrewpaw were sunning themselves.

"Hi," the brown warrior greeted them. "Have you seen

Squirrelpaw? She's not ill, is she? She's usually raring to go by now—before I've even had time for a piece of fresh-kill."

Whitepaw and Shrewpaw exchanged a glance. "We haven't seen her," Whitepaw mewed. "She didn't sleep in the den last night."

Leafpaw saw Dustpelt roll his eyes. "What is she up to now?"

Brightheart pushed her way out of the warriors' den and bounded across to Mousefur. Leafpaw trotted across to the fresh-kill pile with her vole so that she could hear what they were saying.

"Brambleclaw's not there," Brightheart reported.

"What?" Mousefur's tail twitched in surprise. "Where is he, then?"

Brightheart shrugged. "He must have gone hunting on his own. Never mind, Mousefur. Cloudtail and I will come with you."

"Fine." Mousefur shrugged, and as soon as Cloudtail emerged from the den, blinking sleep out of his eyes, she roused Spiderpaw and all four cats left the camp.

Meanwhile, Dustpelt was heading for the fresh-kill pile, irritably calling on StarClan to tell him how he was supposed to mentor an apprentice if she was never where she was meant to be.

"If you see your sister," he growled to Leafpaw, "tell her I'm in the nursery. And she'd better have a good excuse for going off on her own again." He snatched up a starling and headed back to Ferncloud.

Leafpaw watched him go before heading for the fern tunnel that led to the medicine cat's den. She was relieved that Dustpelt had not stopped to question her about Squirrelpaw, but she knew that as time went on and the two cats did not return, there would certainly be questions—lots of them. And she had no idea at all how to answer.

By midday, gossip was beginning to fly around the camp. On her way through the main clearing to fetch fresh-kill for Cinderpelt, Leafpaw overheard Firestar ordering the patrols to keep an eye open for the two missing cats.

"So Brambleclaw is padding after Squirrelpaw, is he?" Cloudtail remarked, his eyes gleaming with amusement. "Well, she's a very attractive young cat; I'll say that for her."

"I can't think what they're up to." Firestar sounded more annoyed than worried. "I'll have something to say to both of them when they come back."

Leafpaw crouched down, pretending to be choosing the best piece of prey, while the warriors dispersed, leaving her father and mother alone together.

"You know," Sandstorm meowed to Firestar, "Graystripe told me what happened last night, when you found them hunting alone. It sounds as if Squirrelpaw and Brambleclaw haven't been back since. From what Graystripe said about the way you spoke to them, I'm not surprised they want to get away for a while."

"Surely I didn't upset them that much?" Firestar sounded anxious. "Not enough to leave the camp?"

Sandstorm gave him a direct look from wide green eyes just like Squirrelpaw's. "I've told you over and over again that you don't get anywhere with Squirrelpaw by criticizing her and ordering her around. She'll do the opposite just to be difficult."

"I know." Firestar let out a heavy sigh. "It's just this prophecy . . . fire and tiger together, and trouble for the forest. I thought after we dealt with BloodClan the Clans would be at peace."

"We've had many moons of peace." Sandstorm padded up to Firestar and pressed her muzzle against his cheek. "All thanks to you. If there is more trouble to come, it's not your fault. I've been thinking about that omen," she went on, sitting down with a quick glance around to make sure none of the warriors were in earshot.

Leafpaw gave a guilty start, wondering if she should creep out of the shadows on the far side of the pile of fresh-kill, but if her mother knew she was there, she paid no attention to her; after all, Leafpaw already knew about the StarClan message.

"It mentions fire and tiger, and trouble," Sandstorm continued, "but it doesn't say that fire and tiger will *cause* the trouble, does it?"

Leafpaw saw a shiver run right through Firestar's body, rippling his flame-colored fur.

"You're right!" he murmured. "The prophecy might mean they'll *save* us from the trouble."

"It might."

Firestar straightened up, suddenly looking very young. "Then it's even more important to get them back!" he burst out. "I'll lead a patrol myself."

"I'll come with you," mewed Sandstorm. Raising her voice, she added, "Leafpaw, you've had time to sniff every piece of fresh-kill on that pile. Cinderpelt will be waiting—and remember that you've promised not to say anything to any cat about this message from StarClan."

"Yes, Sandstorm." Leafpaw grabbed a vole and headed back to the medicine cat's den. She wondered if she ought to confess what her sister had told her about the journey—but she had promised Squirrelpaw to keep silent, too. The weight of the two secret prophecies weighed on her fur like raindrops. She did not know how she would manage to keep both her promises, and stay faithful to her vows as a medicine cat to act only for the good of the Clan, all at the same time.

For the rest of that day, Cinderpelt kept Leafpaw busy going over their stocks of herbs, sorting out what needed to be replenished before leaf-fall set in for good. The sun was going down and the air growing cold with the scent of damp leaves when they heard the noise of a cat brushing through the fern tunnel.

"It's Firestar," Cinderpelt meowed, glancing out of the mouth of the den. "You carry on with that, and I'll see what he wants."

Leafpaw was thankful to stay hidden in the hollow rock and count juniper berries. She caught a glimpse of her father in the clearing outside, the sun turning his pelt to brilliant flame, and shrank farther back so that he would not see her.

"There's no sign of them anywhere." Firestar sounded weary. "I tried to follow their scent, but the rain last night must have washed it away. They could be anywhere. Cinderpelt, what do you think I should do?"

"I don't see what else you can do, except stop worrying." Cinderpelt's voice was brisk but sympathetic. "I remember a couple of apprentices who were always sneaking off for one reason or another. No harm ever came to them."

"Me and Graystripe? That was different. Squirrelpaw—"

"Squirrelpaw has a strong young warrior with her. Brambleclaw will look after her."

There was a short silence. Leafpaw risked another glance out of the opening in the rock to see her father sitting with his head bowed. He looked utterly defeated, and Leafpaw's heart twisted in pity. She wanted to go and comfort him, but there was no comfort she could give without breaking her word.

"It's my fault," Firestar went on in a low, shaken voice. "I should never have said what I did. If they don't come back, I'll never forgive myself."

"Of course they'll come back. The forest is safe at the moment. Wherever they are, they will be well fed and sheltered."

"Maybe." Firestar didn't sound convinced. Without saying any more, he got up and disappeared into the fern tunnel.

When he had gone, Cinderpelt came back into the cave.

"Leafpaw," she meowed, "do *you* know where your sister is now?"

Leafpaw chased with her paw after a juniper berry that had rolled across the floor, not wanting to meet her mentor's gaze. When she thought about Squirrelpaw, she had a sensation of warmth and safety, and the presence of other cats. She guessed they were at Ravenpaw's barn, but she couldn't be sure. She answered truthfully, "No, Cinderpelt, I don't know where she is."

"Hmm . . ." Leafpaw was aware of Cinderpelt's gaze, and she looked up into her mentor's blue eyes to see no anger there, only deep pools of wisdom and understanding. "If you did know, you would tell me, wouldn't you? A medicine cat's loyalties are not the same as other cats', but in the end we are all loyal to StarClan and the four Clans in the forest."

Leafpaw nodded, and to her relief her mentor turned away and started to examine their stocks of marigold leaves.

*I didn't lie to her,* Leafpaw told herself miserably. But it didn't help. StarClan prophecy or not, she knew the warrior code as well as any Clan cat. One of the worst things an apprentice could do was lie to her mentor, and even though the words she had spoken had been the exact truth, Leafpaw felt desperately guilty.

*Oh, Squirrelpaw,* she protested. *Why did you have to go?*

# CHAPTER 13

*"This isn't the quickest way to* Fourtrees," Squirrelpaw protested when Brambleclaw paused on the edge of a bramble thicket. She flicked her tail. "We should be going that way."

"Fine." Brambleclaw sighed. Squirrelpaw had been unusually quiet after saying good-bye to her sister, but unfortunately the silence hadn't lasted. "Go that way, if you feel like a swim. This way the stream is narrower, and there's a rock we can use to jump across."

"Oh—okay." Squirrelpaw seemed disconcerted for a moment, but then she shrugged and raced through the trees at Brambleclaw's side; they crossed the stream in a couple of bounds and headed up the last slope that led to Fourtrees. Brambleclaw realized that the whole disk of the sun had risen above the horizon by the time they reached the edge of the hollow.

He paused, sweeping his tail to hold back Squirrelpaw so that she wouldn't go dashing into the clearing before they knew what they would find there. Drinking in the air, he could taste the mingled scents of the three other Clans, and when he looked down the slope he saw Tawnypelt, Feathertail, and

Stormfur sitting at the base of the Great Rock, while Crowpaw paced restlessly up and down in front of them.

"At last!" Tawnypelt sprang to her paws as Brambleclaw and Squirrelpaw burst out of the bushes at the foot of the slope. "We thought you weren't coming."

"What's *she* doing here?" Crowpaw demanded, glaring at Squirrelpaw.

Squirrelpaw returned the glare, her neck fur bristling angrily. "I can speak for myself, thanks. I'm coming with you."

"What?" Tawnypelt padded up to her brother's side. "Brambleclaw, have you lost your mind? You can't bring an apprentice. This is going to be dangerous."

Before Brambleclaw could reply, Squirrelpaw hissed, "*He's* an apprentice!" and flicked her tail at Crowpaw.

"I was chosen by StarClan," Crowpaw pointed out immediately. "You weren't." Seeming to think that settled it, he sat down and started to wash his ears.

"He's not chosen either," Squirrelpaw protested, transferring the glare to Stormfur. "Don't tell me he's here just to say good-bye to his sister!"

The two RiverClan cats said nothing, just exchanged a worried glance.

"She's coming, and that's that." Brambleclaw's patience was rapidly running out. At this rate the mission would fall apart in bickering and bad temper before it had even started. "Now let's get going."

"Don't order me around!" Crowpaw snapped.

"No, he's right," Tawnypelt sighed. "If we can't stop

Squirrelpaw coming—"

"You can't," Squirrelpaw put in.

"—then we might as well get moving and make the best of it."

To Brambleclaw's relief, even Crowpaw seemed to see the sense in that. He got to his paws, turning his back on Squirrelpaw as if she didn't exist. "Pity you can't leave your Clan without dragging along a burr in your pelt," he jeered at Brambleclaw.

The two RiverClan cats rose too, and padded up to join the group. "Don't worry," Feathertail murmured, touching Squirrelpaw's shoulder briefly with her muzzle. "We're all feeling a bit nervous. It'll be better once we're on our way."

Squirrelpaw's eyes flashed as if she were about to make a sharp reply, but meeting Feathertail's gentle gaze she clearly thought better of it, and dipped her head, her neck fur beginning to lie flat again.

As if obeying an unspoken command, all six cats padded through the bushes to the top of the slope, emerging at the edge of WindClan territory. When Brambleclaw looked out on the moorland slopes, the tough, springy grass ruffled by the wind like the fur of a huge animal, his heart pounded until he thought it would burst right out of his chest. This was the moment he had been waiting for, ever since Bluestar had spoken to him in his dream. The time of the new prophecy was here. The journey had begun!

But as he took his first steps across the moor, he was pierced by a sharp pang of regret for everything he was leaving behind—the familiar forest, his place in the Clan, his friends. From now on, everything would be different.

*Can we really live by the warrior code outside the forest?* Bramble-claw wondered. Glancing back to the dark line of the trees, he added silently, *Will any of us ever see our Clans again?*

Brambleclaw crouched in the shelter of a hedge and looked down at the clustered buildings of a Twoleg farm. Behind him, the other cats shifted restlessly.

"What are we waiting for?" Crowpaw demanded.

"That's the barn where Ravenpaw and Barley live," Brambleclaw replied, indicating it with his tail.

"Yes, I know," meowed the WindClan apprentice. "Mud-claw took me there when I made my apprentice journey to Highstones. We're not stopping there now, are we?"

"I think perhaps we should." Brambleclaw was careful not to sound as if he were giving the touchy apprentice an order. "Ravenpaw knows about the sun-drown place. He might be able to tell us something useful."

"And his barn is crawling with mice." Tawnypelt swiped her tongue around her whiskers.

"We could do worse than spend the night there," Bramble-claw agreed. "A couple of good meals will help to build up our strength."

"But we could easily make Highstones before dark if we keep going," Crowpaw pointed out.

Brambleclaw suspected uncharitably that the WindClan apprentice was arguing just for the sake of it. "I still think it might be best if we stay here for tonight," he meowed. "This way we'll get to Highstones early next morning, with most of the day to get a good start in unknown territory."

"Would you rather sleep on bare stone with no prey," Stormfur murmured, "or warm and comfortable with a full stomach? I vote for Barley's barn."

"Me too!" Squirrelpaw mewed.

"You don't get a vote," Crowpaw retorted.

Squirrelpaw refused to be crushed. Green eyes gleaming with anticipation, she sprang to her paws. "Let's go!"

"No, wait." Feathertail pushed in front of the eager apprentice a heartbeat before Brambleclaw. "There are rats around here. We have to be careful."

"Dogs, too," Tawnypelt added.

"Oh—okay."

Brambleclaw remembered that Squirrelpaw hadn't yet made the journey that all the apprentices took to Highstones before they could be made into warriors. In fact, this must be the first time she had left ThunderClan territory beyond Fourtrees. Privately, he admitted that she had done well so far, crossing WindClan territory without fuss and being sensible about avoiding WindClan patrols so that Crowpaw's departure could remain secret. Perhaps she would cope better than he first feared with the longer path that lay ahead of them.

Brambleclaw emerged from the hedge and led the way past the farm buildings toward the barn. He froze briefly when he heard the barking of a dog, but it sounded distant, and the scent that came to him was faint.

"Get on, if we're going," Crowpaw muttered at his shoulder.

The barn was some way away from the main Twoleg nest. There were holes in the roof, and the door sagged on its supports. Brambleclaw approached warily and sniffed at a gap at the bottom of the door. The scent of mouse flooded his senses; his mouth started to water and he had to concentrate hard to distinguish the cat scent that was almost drowned out.

A familiar voice spoke from just inside. "I smell Thunder-Clan. Come in, and welcome."

It was Ravenpaw. Brambleclaw slid through the gap to see the sleek black loner standing just in front of him. Barley, the black-and-white cat who shared the barn with him, was crouched a pace or two behind, his eyes widening uneasily as Brambleclaw's companions slipped in as well. Brambleclaw realized that Barley had probably not seen so many cats since he came to the forest to help the Clans fight against Blood-Clan, four seasons ago.

"I took your advice, Ravenpaw," Brambleclaw meowed. "I think StarClan sent me the dream because they want me to travel to the sun-drown place. These are the cats StarClan has chosen to go as well."

"Or some of us are," Crowpaw muttered disagreeably.

Brambleclaw ignored him, and introduced the rest of the cats to Ravenpaw and Barley. The older loner merely dipped his head in greeting and slid away into the shadowy depths of the barn.

"Don't mind Barley," Ravenpaw meowed. "It's not often we have so many visitors all at once. So this is Squirrelpaw," he went on, touching noses to greet the young apprentice.

"Firestar's daughter! I've seen you before, when you were a kit in the nursery with Sandstorm, but you won't remember that. I said then that you would look just like your father, and now I see I was right."

Squirrelpaw scuffled her paws in embarrassment; Brambleclaw guessed she was for once lost for words to meet this cat who had played such a large part in the history of her Clan.

"What does Firestar think about the journey?" Ravenpaw asked Brambleclaw. "I'm surprised he let Squirrelpaw go so far when she isn't a warrior yet."

Brambleclaw and Squirrelpaw exchanged an uneasy glance. "It wasn't quite like that," Brambleclaw admitted. "We left without telling him."

Ravenpaw's eyes widened with shock, and for a heartbeat Brambleclaw wondered if he would send them away again.

But Ravenpaw only shook his head. "I'm sorry to hear that you couldn't tell him what's going on," he meowed. "Perhaps you'll tell me more when you've eaten. Are you all hungry?"

"Starving!" Squirrelpaw exclaimed.

A *mrrow* of laughter escaped Ravenpaw. "Feel free to hunt," he invited them. "There are plenty of mice."

A short time later, Brambleclaw was curled up comfortably in the straw, his stomach stuffed full of mice that had almost lined up to leap into his mouth. If Ravenpaw and Barley ate like this every day, it was no wonder they looked so strong and healthy.

His companions were sprawled around him, equally full and growing sleepy as the sun went down, sending shafts of red light through the holes in the barn roof. All around they could hear scuffling noises and faint squeaking in the straw, as if their hunt had made no difference at all to the number of prey.

"If you don't mind, we'll sleep here tonight and leave first thing in the morning," Brambleclaw meowed.

Ravenpaw nodded. "I'll come with you as far as Highstones." Before Brambleclaw could protest that there was no need, he went on, "There are even more Twolegs than before around the Thunderpath. I've been keeping an eye on them, so I know the safest ways to go."

Brambleclaw thanked him, only to feel Crowpaw shift closer to him and mutter into his ear, "Can we trust him?"

Ravenpaw's ear twitched; he had obviously heard the remark. Brambleclaw thought he was going to sink through the floor with embarrassment, and Squirrelpaw lifted her head to aim a furious hiss at Crowpaw.

"Don't be angry with him," Ravenpaw meowed. "That's good thinking, Crowpaw. Thinking like a warrior, in fact. Where you're going, you must trust nothing and no cat without very good reason."

Crowpaw ducked his head, looking pleased at the loner's praise.

"But you can trust me," Ravenpaw continued. "I may not be able to do much to help with the rest of your journey, but at least I can see that you get to Highstones safely."

Wind struck Brambleclaw squarely in the face, flattening his pelt to his sides and almost carrying him off his paws.

When he unsheathed his claws to steady himself, they scraped against bare rock. He and his companions were standing on the summit of Highstones, gazing out over endless, unknown territories.

They had set out in the first faint light of dawn and reached the stony slopes well before sunhigh, led swiftly by Ravenpaw. He stood beside Brambleclaw now, his ears pricked into the distance.

"You'll avoid that tangle of Thunderpaths," he meowed, pointing with his tail to the thick gray smudge in the landscape. "Just as well. That's the place where WindClan took refuge when Brokenstar drove them out. It's full of rats and carrion."

"I know about that!" Squirrelpaw put in. "Graystripe told me how he and Firestar went to fetch WindClan back."

"There are many smaller Thunderpaths to cross," Ravenpaw went on. "And Twoleg nests to avoid. I've traveled that way now and again—not far, but far enough to know that it's not a place for warriors."

Squirrelpaw shot a nervous glance at Ravenpaw. "Is there no more forest at all?" she asked.

"Not that I saw."

"Don't worry," Brambleclaw meowed reassuringly. "I'll look after you."

To his surprise she whirled on him, the light of fury in her green eyes. "How many times do I have to tell you, I don't *need* looking after!" she spat. "If you're going to behave like Firestar all the way to the sun-drown place, I might as well have stayed at home."

"Oh, don't we wish," Crowpaw murmured, rolling his eyes.

Tawnypelt gave Squirrelpaw a curious glance. "Are you going to let an apprentice talk to you like that?" she asked her brother.

Brambleclaw shrugged. "You try stopping her."

His sister's ears twitched. "ThunderClan!"

Feathertail exchanged a glance with Stormfur, and then padded up to Squirrelpaw's side. "I'm nervous, too," she admitted. "I get shivers all along my spine when I think of being so close to all those Twolegs. But StarClan will bring us through."

Squirrelpaw nodded, though her eyes were still troubled.

"If you've all quite finished," Crowpaw mewed loudly, "it's time we were moving."

"Okay." Brambleclaw turned to Ravenpaw. "Thank you for everything," he meowed. "It makes a difference that you understand why we are doing this."

The loner dipped his head. "Think nothing of it. Good luck, all of you, and may StarClan light your path."

He stood aside, and one by one the six cats began to pick their way down the far slope of the hill. The rising sun cast long blue shadows in front of them as they took the first steps on the longest journey of their lives.

CHAPTER 14

*Brambleclaw heaved a sigh of relief* to come down from Highstones and feel grass under his paws again. They were alone now, a tiny band of cats in a vast, unknown territory. Ravenpaw had pointed out a path across fields divided by sharp, shiny Twoleg fences, and there were many scents of Twolegs and dogs, though none of them were fresh. Wooly faced sheep stared at the traveling cats as they slipped past, their heads low and their ears flat, uncomfortable at being out in the open.

"You'd think they'd never seen a cat before," Stormfur grunted.

"Maybe they haven't," Tawnypelt replied. "There's no reason for cats to come here. I haven't had so much as a sniff of prey since we left the barn."

"Well, I've never seen a sheep before," Squirrelpaw pointed out. She padded a little closer to the nearest one, and Brambleclaw unobtrusively moved up behind her; as far as he knew sheep were not dangerous, but he was taking no chances. Squirrelpaw paused a tail-length away, took a good sniff, and wrinkled her nose. "Yuck! They might look like fluffy clouds on legs, but they smell horrible!"

Tawnypelt yawned. "Can we get *on*, for the love of StarClan?"

"I wonder why StarClan are sending us to the sun-drown place," Feathertail meowed, swerving to avoid a grass-cropping sheep that was too close for comfort. "Why couldn't they have told us what we need to know back in the forest? And why do we have to hear the message at midnight?"

Crowpaw snorted. "Who knows?" He narrowed his eyes and stared at Brambleclaw. "Maybe the ThunderClan warrior can tell us. After all, he's the only one of us who has seen this place—or so he says."

Brambleclaw gritted his teeth. "You know as much as I do," he meowed. "We just have to trust StarClan that it will all come clear in the end."

"Easy enough for you to say," Crowpaw retorted.

"Leave him alone!" To Brambleclaw's amazement, Squirrel-paw darted forward and planted herself in front of the WindClan apprentice. "Brambleclaw didn't ask for the second dream. It's not his fault that StarClan chose him."

"And what do you know about it?" Crowpaw growled. "In WindClan, apprentices know when to keep their mouths shut."

"Oh, so you'll be quiet from now on?" Squirrelpaw mewed cheekily. "Good."

With his top lip drawn back in a snarl, Crowpaw stalked around her and went on.

Brambleclaw padded across to his Clan mate. "Thanks for backing me up there," he murmured.

Squirrelpaw's eyes flashed angrily at him. "I'm not doing it for you!" she snapped. "I'm just not letting that stupid furball think WindClan is so much better than ThunderClan." She dashed off with an annoyed hiss, past Feathertail and Storm-fur, who had stopped to watch.

"Don't get too far ahead!" Brambleclaw called after her, but she ignored him.

As he set off in pursuit, Brambleclaw was uncomfortably aware that none of the other cats had tried to defend him, not even Tawnypelt. They must all be full of doubts about his vision of the sun-drown place, and why they had to go there, just like Feathertail. A sense of responsibility was settling more heavily on Brambleclaw with every step he took, and he knew that if any of his companions were injured or even killed on the journey, it would be his fault. Perhaps StarClan had gotten it wrong this time. Perhaps in the end, not even the faith and courage of warriors would be enough to bring them through safely.

Not long after sunhigh, they came to their first Thunder-path. It was narrower than the one they were used to, and curved so that they could not see monsters approaching until the last moment. On the opposite side, a tall hedge stretched as far as they could see in both directions.

Crowpaw approached cautiously and sniffed the hard black edge of the Thunderpath. "Ugh!" he exclaimed, wrinkling his nose. "It's foul stuff. Why do Twolegs spread it all over the place?"

"Their monsters travel on it," Stormfur told him.

"I know that!" Crowpaw snapped. "Their monsters stink, too."

Stormfur shrugged. "That's Twolegs for you."

"Are we going to sit here until sunset discussing the habits of Twolegs?" Tawnypelt interrupted. "Or are we going to cross this Thunderpath?"

Brambleclaw crouched on the grass verge, ears pricked to catch the sound of approaching monsters. "When I say 'now,' run," he told Squirrelpaw, who was crouching beside him. "You'll be fine."

Squirrelpaw didn't look at him. She had been in a bad mood ever since her earlier quarrel with Crowpaw. "I'm not scared, you know," she hissed.

"Then you should be," Tawnypelt grunted from her other side. "Didn't you listen to what we told you when we crossed the Thunderpath near Highstones? Get this straight: they're dangerous even for experienced warriors. Cats have died on them."

Squirrelpaw glanced up at her and nodded, her green eyes huge.

"Good," mewed the ShadowClan warrior. "So listen to Brambleclaw, and when he tells you to go, run like you've never run before."

"Before we cross"—Brambleclaw raised his voice so all the cats could hear him—"I think we should decide what we are going to do on the other side. We can't see beyond that hedge, and I can't pick up any scents for the reek of the Thunderpath."

Stormfur raised his head and opened his jaws to taste the air. "Nor can I," he agreed. "I suggest we cross, go straight through the hedge, and meet up again on the other side. If there is anything dangerous through there, the six of us together should be able to deal with it."

Brambleclaw was impressed by Stormfur's sensible thinking. "Okay," he meowed, and the rest of the cats, even Crowpaw, murmured their assent.

"Brambleclaw, you give the word," Stormfur mewed.

Once more Brambleclaw strained to listen. A low growling in the distance quickly grew into a roar, and a monster leaped around the bend, its unnatural, shiny pelt gleaming as it swept past. It buffeted the cats with a hot, gritty wind and left them choking in the reek it left behind.

Almost at once another monster passed, going in the other direction. Then quiet fell again, heavy like a blanket of snow; when Brambleclaw pricked his ears he could hear nothing but the distant barking of a dog.

"Now!" he yowled.

He sprang forward, aware of Squirrelpaw keeping pace with him on one side and Feathertail on the other. His paws pattered on the hard surface of the Thunderpath; then he reached the narrow strip of grass on the other side and was thrusting through the hedge, spiky branches snagging in his fur.

Pushing hard, he burst through into the open. For a moment he could not make sense of what he saw, and almost froze in panic. He caught a glimpse of leaping flame, and the acrid tang of smoke filled his throat. There was a high-pitched shout and a Twoleg kit came running toward him, not much taller than a fox, with thick, unsteady legs. The barking of the dog was suddenly much louder.

"Squirrelpaw, stay with me!" He gasped, but when he turned to look for her the ginger apprentice had disappeared.

He heard Stormfur yowling, "Stay together! Over here!"

Brambleclaw glanced around, but he could not see any of his companions, and his paws were carrying him into the depths of a holly bush, the closest refuge he could see. His belly brushing the earth, he crawled into shelter, and felt himself pressing up against fur. He heard a frightened whimper; in the dim light he made out a flecked gray pelt and recognized Feathertail.

"It's only me," he murmured.

"Brambleclaw!" Feathertail's voice was shaking. "For a moment I thought it was that dog."

"Have you seen the others?" Brambleclaw asked her. "Did you see where Squirrelpaw went?"

Feathertail shook her head, her blue eyes wide with fear.

"Don't worry, I'm sure they're fine," he mewed, giving her ear a comforting lick. "I'll see what's happening out there."

He crept forward a couple of tail-lengths until he could peer out. The fire, he realized thankfully, was only a heap of burning branches, confined to a small area not far from where he had broken in; a fully-grown Twoleg was feeding more branches to it. The Twoleg kit had joined him. Brambleclaw could still hear the dog barking, but he could not see it, and the smoke prevented him from scenting it. More important, he could not see any of his missing companions.

Wriggling back to Feathertail, he whispered, "Come on, follow me. The Twolegs aren't paying any attention."

"What about the dog?"

"I don't know where it is, but it isn't here. Listen, this is what we'll do." Brambleclaw knew that he had to come up with a plan right away, to get Feathertail out of there before panic froze her completely. Their holly bush was growing close to a wooden fence, and a little farther along a small tree stretched its branches into the next garden. "Over there," he meowed, twitching his ears toward it. "Climb the tree; then we can get on top of the fence. We can go anywhere from there."

He wondered briefly what he would do if Feathertail was so spooked that she refused to move, but the gray she-cat nodded determinedly.

"Now?" she asked.

"Yes—I'll be right behind you."

At once Feathertail dived out of their refuge, raced along the bottom of the fence, and took a flying leap into the tree. Brambleclaw, hard on her paws, heard the Twoleg kit shout again. Then he was clawing at the trunk, scrabbling hard until he reached the safety of a branch and the shelter of thick leaves. He caught Feathertail's scent and saw her blue eyes peering worriedly at him.

"Brambleclaw," she mewed, "I think we've found the dog."

She twitched her whiskers to point down into the next garden. Brambleclaw peered out of the leaves and saw the dog—a huge brown brute—leaping up and scraping the fence with blunt claws in its efforts to climb up and attack them. As Brambleclaw peered down it let out a flurry of hysterical barking.

"Fox dung!" Brambleclaw spat at it.

He wondered what their chances would be of escaping along the top of the fence, but it was flimsier than the ones he had scaled at the edge of ThunderClan territory, and the dog was shaking it so much that any cat trying to balance there was likely to be flung off into the garden. Brambleclaw imagined those teeth meeting in his leg or neck and decided they were better off staying put.

"We'll never find the others at this rate," Feathertail whimpered.

Then Brambleclaw heard the door of the Twoleg nest open. A full-grown Twoleg stood there, shouting at the dog. Still barking wildly, the creature kept up its attack on the fence. The Twoleg shouted again and strode into the garden, grabbed the dog by its collar, and dragged it, protesting, into the nest. The door slammed shut; the barking continued for a moment longer and then stopped.

"See?" Brambleclaw meowed to Feathertail. "Even Twolegs have their uses."

Feathertail nodded, her eyes filled with relief. Brambleclaw slipped out of the tree to the top of the fence and, balancing carefully, padded along it until he reached the hedge that bordered the Thunderpath. From here he had a good view of the gardens on either side. Everything seemed quiet.

"I can't see or hear the others," Feathertail mewed as she joined him.

"No, but that could be a good sign," Brambleclaw pointed out. "If the Twolegs had caught them, they would make such a racket we'd be bound to hear."

He wasn't sure that was quite true, but it seemed to reassure Feathertail.

"What do you think we should do?" she asked.

"The danger is inside these gardens," Brambleclaw decided. "We'll be safer on the other side of the hedge, beside the Thunderpath. The monsters won't bother us if we stick to the verge, and once we get to the end of these Twoleg nests there won't be any more problems."

"But what about the others?"

That was the question Brambleclaw couldn't answer. It was impossible to look for their companions with dogs and Twolegs all around. Anxiety stabbed deep in his belly when he thought of Squirrelpaw alone and bewildered in this strange and frightening place.

"They'll probably do the same," he meowed, hoping he sounded convincing. "They might even be waiting for us. If not, I'll come back and have a look after dark, when the Twolegs will be in their nests."

Feathertail nodded tensely and both cats jumped down from the fence, landing lightly on their forepaws on short, bright green grass. They slipped back through the hedge and along the Thunderpath, keeping well away from its smooth black surface. Monsters passed from time to time, but Brambleclaw was so worried about the missing cats that he hardly noticed the guttural roar and the rush of wind that rocked him on his paws.

Eventually they came to the end of the hedge. The Thunderpath curved away to join another one a little way ahead. Between the two was a wedge of open ground, almost covered by a tangle of hawthorn bushes. On the other side of the Thunderpath, fields stretched away into the distance. A cold breeze ruffled the fur on Brambleclaw's flank as he gazed across the fields to where the sun was beginning to sink.

"Thank StarClan!" Feathertail breathed.

Brambleclaw led the way into the bushes. They would be safer there, and some of their friends might already be waiting. Leaving Feathertail to keep a lookout, he plunged deeper, searching and calling out their names in a low voice. There was no reply, and he could not pick up any familiar scents.

When he returned to Feathertail, she was sitting with her tail wrapped around her paws. A dead mouse lay beside her.

"Do you want to share?" she mewed. "I caught it, but I don't really feel like eating right now."

The sight of prey reminded Brambleclaw how hungry he was. He had eaten well that morning in Ravenpaw's barn, but they had traveled a long way since then.

"Are you sure? I can catch one for myself."

"No, go on." She shoved the mouse toward him with one paw.

"Thanks." Brambleclaw crouched beside her and took a bite, the warm flavors flooding his mouth. "Try not to worry," he mewed as Feathertail bent her head to take a halfhearted mouthful. "I'm sure we'll meet up with the others soon."

Feathertail stopped eating to give him an anxious look. "I hope so. It feels weird being without Stormfur. We've always been closer than most littermates. I suppose it comes from having a father in a different Clan."

Brambleclaw nodded, remembering how close he had felt to Tawnypelt when they were kits, as they struggled to make sense of their bloodstained heritage from their father, Tigerstar.

"Of course, you'll understand that." Feathertail invited him with a twitch of her ears to take more of the mouse.

"Yes," Brambleclaw replied. He shrugged. "But I don't miss my father as much as you must miss Graystripe. I wish I could honor his memory, but I can't."

"That must be very hard." Feathertail pressed her muzzle against his shoulder. "At least we see Graystripe at Gatherings. And we were so proud when he was made Clan deputy."

"He's proud of you, too," mewed Brambleclaw, glad to leave the subject of his father behind.

He took his remaining share of the mouse, and while Feathertail forced herself to finish hers he began to plan what they should do next. Venturing out of the bushes he could see the sun setting in rays of fire, blazing out the path that they must take. But there was no hope of continuing until they had found the others.

"They're not here," Feathertail murmured, padding up to join him so that her breath was soft against his ear.

"No, I'll have to go back. You stay here in case—"

A furious yowling interrupted him: the voices of angry, frightened cats, coming from the last garden in the row. Springing to his paws, he met Feathertail's startled glance.

"There they are!" He gasped. "And they're in trouble!"

# CHAPTER 15

*Leafpaw opened her eyes to see* fronds of fern above her head, outlined against a paling sky. At once she remembered that this was the day of the half-moon, when all the medicine cats and their apprentices made the journey to Highstones to meet with StarClan at the mysterious Moonstone. A shiver of excitement ran through her; she had traveled there only once before, when StarClan had received her as a medicine cat apprentice, and the experience would stay with her for the rest of her life.

Leaping up from her comfortable mossy nest, she stretched and yawned, blinking away the last traces of sleep. She could hear Cinderpelt moving around inside her den, and a few moments later the medicine cat poked her head out and scented the air.

"No smell of rain," she meowed. "We should have a good journey."

Without any more delay she led the way out of camp. Leafpaw cast a regretful look at the pile of fresh-kill as they passed it; no cat who wanted to share tongues with StarClan was allowed to eat beforehand.

Ashfur, who was on guard beside the entrance to the gorse tunnel, dipped his head as Leafpaw and her mentor went by. Leafpaw felt faintly embarrassed. She was conscious that she was still only an apprentice, and was not yet used to the honor with which warriors treated all medicine cats.

Shadows still lay in the ravine and under the trees as Cinderpelt limped toward Fourtrees, where she and Leafpaw would cross into WindClan territory. Faint rustlings in the undergrowth told them where prey was stirring, but the tiny creatures were safe from hunting for now. From time to time a bird uttered an alarm call as the two cats passed by, no more than shadows themselves in the gray light.

"Practice your scenting skills," Cinderpelt instructed Leafpaw after a while. "If you can find any useful herbs, we'll collect them on the way back."

Leafpaw obeyed, concentrating as hard as she could, until they reached the stream. She and Cinderpelt crouched to lap at the water, then padded along the bank until they reached the place where a rock midstream made it easier to cross. Leafpaw kept an eye on her mentor, worried that her injured leg would give her trouble, but Cinderpelt managed the jump with the ease of long practice.

As they climbed the slope that led to Fourtrees, Leafpaw began to pick up the scent of other cats. "ShadowClan," she murmured. "That must be Littlecloud."

Cinderpelt nodded. "He usually waits for me."

Leafpaw knew that Cinderpelt had saved Littlecloud's life when sickness raged through ShadowClan; because of that,

Littlecloud had chosen to follow the path of a medicine cat, and ever since there had been a bond of friendship between him and Cinderpelt, beyond even the common loyalty shared by all medicine cats.

When they reached the top of the hollow, Leafpaw spotted the ShadowClan medicine cat sitting at the base of the Great Rock. The small but dignified tabby figure was alone, as he had no apprentice. He leaped to his paws as soon as he saw them, calling out a greeting. At the same moment the bushes farther around the hollow rustled, and Mudfur from RiverClan stepped into the clearing with his apprentice, Mothwing.

Leafpaw was pleased to see the RiverClan apprentice. She bounded down the slope to join her as Cinderpelt and the other two medicine cats met in the center of the clearing and began to exchange their news.

"Mothwing!" she meowed. "It's good to see you."

The sun had risen fully above the trees, and Mothwing's golden fur glowed amber. Leafpaw thought again how beautiful she was, but she was disconcerted when her friendly greeting was not returned.

Instead, Mothwing nodded coolly. "Greetings. I wondered if Cinderpelt would bring her apprentice."

Something about the way she spoke made Leafpaw feel small, as if Mothwing were trying to put her in her place. Of course, Mothwing was already a warrior, so perhaps she expected respect and not friendship from an apprentice. Disappointment stabbed Leafpaw like a thorn; she dipped her head and fell back a pace to follow the other cats as they made their way up the side of the hollow and across the border into WindClan territory.

Her spirits rose again as they began to cross the moorland; the bright, early leaf-fall sunlight, the breeze ruffling the grass that felt springy under her paws, the scents of gorse and heather were all so different from the lush, shady forest of ThunderClan. Seeing that Mothwing was padding behind her mentor without joining in the talk of the medicine cats, Leafpaw went over to join her.

"I didn't think you would be here," she mewed. "I thought that Mudfur would have taken you to Mothermouth already."

Mothwing swung around to look her full in the face, her amber eyes smoldering as if Leafpaw had said something to offend her. Leafpaw flinched. "I'm sorry . . ." she began.

Suddenly Mothwing relaxed and the hostile light died out of her eyes. "No, I'm sorry," she meowed. "It's not your fault. You heard what Mudfur said at the last Gathering, about waiting for a sign from StarClan that I would be the right medicine cat for the Clan?"

Leafpaw nodded.

"The sign didn't come." Mothwing paused and began to tug at the tough moorland grass with the claws of one forepaw. "There was nothing! I thought that meant StarClan had rejected me—and the other cats were quick enough to start talking about it! Just because my mother was a rogue, and I'm not Clan-born." The fierce light shone briefly in her eyes again, and then faded.

"Oh, no—I'm so sorry!" Leafpaw exclaimed, eyes wide with sympathy.

"Mudfur just told me to be patient." Mothwing's lips twisted wryly. "He may be good at that, but I'm not. I tried, but still the sign didn't come. I was ready to leave the Clan, but Hawkfrost—you remember my brother, Hawkfrost?— told me not to listen. He said I didn't have to prove my loyalty to jealous cats, only to StarClan, and he was sure they would send the sign eventually."

"And he was right," mewed Leafpaw, "or you wouldn't be here now."

"Yes, he was right." Relief sparkled in Mothwing's eyes. "It was only two dawns ago. Mudfur came out of his den and found a moth's wing at the entrance. He showed it to Leopardstar and all the other Clan cats. He said you couldn't have a clearer sign than that."

"And did Leopardstar—" Leafpaw was interrupted by a distant yowling and looked up. The three medicine cats had paused at the top of a distant rise and were looking back toward the two of them.

"Are you coming with us or not?" Mudfur's voice came faintly on the wind.

Leafpaw exchanged a startled glance with Mothwing and let out a *mrrow* of laughter. The sign had been sent from StarClan, so Mothwing could have nothing to worry about. The Moonstone awaited them both, ready to let them into the mysteries of their warrior ancestors. At that moment,

Leafpaw couldn't imagine anything better than being an apprentice medicine cat. "Come on," she mewed excitedly to her companion. "We're being left behind!"

At sunhigh, they met up with Barkface, the WindClan medicine cat, beside the source of one of the moorland streams. Leafpaw watched Barkface and Mudfur greet each other with friendly meows, in spite of the tension between their Clans over WindClan's determination to drink at the river until the next Gathering. Usual Clan rivalries did not exist between medicine cats—their loyalty was to StarClan, which stretched across all forest boundaries.

After a while, Leafpaw noticed that Cinderpelt was beginning to limp badly, and guessed that her old injury was bothering her. But the ThunderClan medicine cat would never admit that the pace was too much for her, so Leafpaw decided to slow the cats down herself. "Can't we have a rest?" she begged, flopping down on a patch of soft heather. "I'm really tired!"

Cinderpelt gave her a keen glance, as if she guessed what Leafpaw was thinking, and then meowed agreement.

"Apprentices," Barkface muttered. "No stamina."

"*He* hasn't traveled as far as us," Mothwing whispered as she settled down beside Leafpaw. "And he doesn't have an apprentice, so what does he know?"

"He's not really unkind," Leafpaw murmured back. "I think he just likes to sound grumpy." She lay on one side and began to give herself a thorough wash, wanting to look her best when she stood before StarClan.

Mothwing started to do the same, and then paused. "Leafpaw, will you test me?" she begged.

"Test you—on what?"

"Herbs." Mothwing's eyes were wide and anxious. "In case Mudfur expects me to know all of them. I don't want to let him down. We use marigold to stop infection, and yarrow leaves to expel poison, but what's best for bellyache? I can never remember."

"Juniper berries, or chervil root," Leafpaw replied, mystified. "But why are you getting so worked up? You can always ask your mentor. He won't expect you to know everything already."

"Not when I meet StarClan!" Mothwing was almost wailing in distress. "I have to show them that I'm fit to be a medicine cat. They might not accept me if I can't remember the things I ought to know."

Leafpaw almost burst out laughing. "It's not like that," she meowed patiently. "StarClan won't ask you questions. They . . . Well, it's difficult to explain, but I'm sure you don't have anything to worry about."

"It's easy enough for you." To Leafpaw's surprise, there was a hint of bitterness in Mothwing's tone. "You were born a forest cat. I have to be better than any other cat, just to be accepted in the Clan."

Her eyes were huge, shining with a mixture of anger and determination. Pity for her squeezed Leafpaw's heart, and she swept her tail around to touch Mothwing's shoulder.

"That might be true of RiverClan," she meowed, "but it isn't true of StarClan. You don't *earn* StarClan's approval—they give it as a gift."

"Well, they might not give it to me," Mothwing muttered.

Leafpaw stared at her friend in amazement. She was so strong and beautiful, she had all of a warrior's skills as well as the chance to learn those of a medicine cat, but she was still afraid that she would never belong in the forest.

Moving closer to her, Leafpaw pressed her muzzle comfortingly into Mothwing's side. "You'll be fine," she murmured. "Look at Firestar. He's not Clan-born, but now he's ThunderClan leader." When Mothwing still looked uncertain, she added, "Trust me. When you stand in front of the Moonstone, you'll understand everything."

The sun was beginning to sink as the medicine cats approached Highstones. The rough moorland grass gave way to a steep slope of bare soil, with here and there a clump of heather. Outcrops of rock poked through it, blotched with yellow lichen.

Barkface, who had taken the lead, paused on a flat rock and gazed upward. Just below the peak a dark hole gaped in the hillside beneath a stone archway.

"There's Mothermouth," Leafpaw explained to Mothwing, and then remembered that her friend would have seen it before, when she made her apprentice journey during her warrior training. "Sorry," she added. "I know this isn't your first time."

Mothwing's eyes widened as she gazed up at the yawning gap. "This is as far as I went," she replied. "I wasn't chosen to go inside."

"It is frightening, I know—but it's wonderful, too," Leafpaw reassured her.

Mothwing drew herself up. "I'm not afraid," she insisted. "I'm a warrior. I'm not afraid of anything."

*Not even rejection by StarClan?* Leafpaw didn't dare put words to her thought, but as she settled down beside her friend to wait for nightfall she couldn't help noticing that Mothwing was trembling.

At last the half-moon floated above the peak and Mudfur rose to his paws. "It's time," he rasped.

Leafpaw felt tension in her belly as she followed her mentor up the slope and underneath the stone archway. Cold, damp air flowed toward them, and it almost seemed as if a river of darkness flowed out too, blacker than the night that surrounded them. Leafpaw took her place at the back of the line of cats, just behind Mothwing.

The tunnel sloped down, winding back and forth until Leafpaw lost all sense of direction. The air seemed thick, as if they were underwater as well as underground. She could see nothing, not even Mothwing padding no more than a rabbit-hop in front of her, though she could hear the RiverClan cat's shallow breathing and smell the fear-scent that came from her.

At last Leafpaw felt a cool ripple in the air around them, and her fur tingled with excitement as she recognized the first sign that they were coming to the heart of the hill. Fresh scents of the world above came faintly to her as she stepped into a large cavern; a glitter of starshine through a hole in the roof showed her soaring walls of stone, and underneath her paws the floor was smooth, well-worn stone. In the center of the cave stood a rock three tail-lengths high. Leafpaw's eyes widened in awe as she gazed at it, though as yet it was dark, a formidable sleeping presence.

Mothwing's fur brushed her lightly. "Where are we?" she whispered. "What's happening?"

"Mothwing, come before the Moonstone," Barkface announced from farther in the cavern. "We must all wait until the time comes to share tongues with StarClan." He and the other medicine cats sat around the stone, about a foxlength from it.

Leafpaw heard a shuddering sigh from her friend, and pressed reassuringly against the RiverClan apprentice's shoulder. "It's okay for us to sit, too," she breathed into Mothwing's ear. As she took her place a tail-length behind Cinderpelt, she felt Mothwing hesitantly sit down beside her.

In the darkness, time stretched out until Leafpaw almost believed that they had been waiting there for seasons. Then, within a heartbeat, brilliant white light flashed into the cave as the moon appeared through the hole in the roof. She heard Mothwing gasp. The Moonstone woke into dazzling life in front of them, glittering in moonlight as if the whole of Silverpelt had swirled down into its crystal surface.

As Leafpaw's eyes became used to the brilliant light she saw Mudfur rise to his paws, turn, and pace slowly across the cavern floor to stand in front of his apprentice. The white light flooded over his fur so that he looked as if he were covered in ice.

"Mothwing," he meowed solemnly, "is it your wish to enter into the mysteries of StarClan as a medicine cat?"

Mothwing hesitated. Leafpaw saw her swallow before she replied, "It is."

"Then come forward."

Mothwing rose and followed her mentor back across the cavern until both cats stood close to the stone. In its light Mothwing looked unearthly, her golden fur pale as ash and a glint of silver in her eyes—almost as if she had already joined the ranks of StarClan. Leafpaw shivered. That could not be a good thought; she pushed it out of her mind, reluctant to believe that it might be an omen.

"Warriors of StarClan," Mudfur continued, "I present to you this apprentice. She has chosen the path of a medicine cat. Grant her your wisdom and insight so that she may understand your ways and heal her Clan in accordance with your will."

He waved his tail and spoke to Mothwing. "Lie down here, and press your nose against the stone."

As if she moved in a dream, Mothwing obeyed. Once she was settled, all the medicine cats moved forward to lie in the same position around the Moonstone, and Cinderpelt gestured to Leafpaw to join them. Her fur crawled with anticipation; she knew what was about to happen.

"It is time to share tongues with StarClan," Barkface murmured.

"Speak with us, warrior ancestors," Littlecloud meowed. "Show us the destiny of our Clans."

Leafpaw closed her eyes and pressed her nose against the surface of the stone. At once the cold gripped her body like the talon of a hawk, or as if she had fallen headlong into dark water. She couldn't see or hear anything, or feel the stone floor of the cavern underneath her; she was floating in a dark night without even the light of Silverpelt.

Then a series of rapid scenes began to flash across her vision. She saw Fourtrees, but the great trees were bare, with only a few ragged leaves still clinging to the branches. One of the trees was shaking back and forth, more violently than in the strongest wind, while the others stood still around it. Almost at once, the picture was replaced with a view of monsters speeding by on the Thunderpath, and a long line of cats trekking through snow, a dark line against the endless white landscape. There were no trees here, and nothing to suggest that it was anywhere in the four territories.

The last scene of all showed her Squirrelpaw, and though Leafpaw knew she was forbidden to speak, she could barely hold back a cry of relief and delight. Her sister was trotting over a broad green field, and Leafpaw had the impression of several other cats with her before the vision was gone, and she was left in darkness once more.

Gradually the cold stone beneath her seeped back into her fur, and the endless space inside the dreams of StarClan dwindled to the ordinary freshness of a night in leaf-fall. Leafpaw opened her eyes, blinking, and drew away from the

Moonstone, before shakily rising to her paws. She felt oddly comforted, as though she were a kit again, protected by her mother while she slept. StarClan had preserved her link with Squirrelpaw, even though they were so far apart.

The other medicine cats were getting to their paws around her, ready to return to the surface. Mothwing stood among them, her eyes blazing with a mixture of triumph and wonder at the things StarClan had shown her. Leafpaw felt a sharp pang of relief as she realized that their warrior ancestors must have accepted Mothwing. Whatever she felt about her Clan mates, the RiverClan cat didn't have to doubt StarClan's approval anymore.

Mudfur touched Mothwing's mouth with his tail-tip, a sign for silence, and led the way out of the cavern. Once again Leafpaw brought up the rear, padding along the twisting underground tunnel, back toward the everyday world.

As soon as they reached the entrance, Mothwing leaped to the top of a jutting spur of rock. She flung back her head and let out a yowl of pure triumph.

Mudfur watched her, shaking his head indulgently. "Not so bad after all, then, was it? Well," he went on as Mothwing sprang down to his side again, "you're a true medicine cat apprentice now. How does it feel?"

"Wonderful!" Mothwing replied. "I saw Hawkfrost leading a patrol, and—" She broke off as Leafpaw widened her eyes at her, trying to signal that medicine cats did not share their dreams until they had some idea of what they meant.

Leafpaw padded over and touched noses with the

RiverClan apprentice. "Congratulations," she murmured. "I told you it would be all right."

"Yes, you did." Mothwing's eyes shone. "Everything will be all right now. RiverClan will hear that StarClan approve of me. They'll have to accept me now!"

She bounded off down the slope, leaving the others to follow more slowly. Leafpaw watched her with her heart full of questions. What had Mothwing seen? And what visions had StarClan sent to Cinderpelt? The ThunderClan medicine cat was looking thoughtful, but her expression gave nothing away.

Suppressing a shiver, Leafpaw remembered her own visions. What was powerful enough to shake one of the great oaks at Fourtrees? And why were cats traveling in the bitter cold of leaf-bare? If StarClan had sent her signs of what the future would bring, how was she supposed to interpret them?

Yet for all her uncertainty, Leafpaw was full of hope. Even though Squirrelpaw was a long way from the forest, StarClan had shown her that she was safe.

*Send her back soon*, Leafpaw prayed as she followed the other cats down the hill. *Wherever this journey leads them, please bring them safely home.*

CHAPTER 16

*Brambleclaw raced back to the hedge* with Feathertail right behind him. All his instincts told him to dash into the garden and rescue the other cats, but the memory of what happened when they had first crossed the Thunderpath warned him to be more careful. Instead, he pushed his way through the branches until he could peer out while still remaining hidden.

What he saw made his belly flip over. Near the Twoleg nest, two huge kittypets had cornered Stormfur and Crowpaw. The WindClan apprentice was crouched close to the ground, his ears flattened and his lips drawn back in a snarl. Stormfur had one paw stretched out in front of him, threatening the kittypets with unsheathed claws. Brambleclaw could see that they wouldn't get away without a fight, and there was nowhere for them to retreat except through the half-open door of the Twoleg nest.

"Great StarClan!" Feathertail gasped in his ear. "Those kittypets are bigger than most warriors!"

Brambleclaw wasn't sure that mattered. Size and a glossy pelt didn't make a warrior. He didn't have any doubts that he and his friends would win the battle, but the two kittypets were defending their territory, and they looked capable of inflicting nasty wounds—wounds the Clan cats could not afford if they were to keep on with their journey.

He tensed his muscles, preparing to leap on the kittypets from behind, but before he could move, a flame-colored streak flashed down from the fence and across the garden.

"Squirrelpaw, no!" Brambleclaw yowled.

The apprentice took no notice; he was not even sure she had heard. Hurling herself into the midst of the bristling cats, she clawed at the nearest kittypet. Both of them swung around, snarling.

At once Brambleclaw called out, "Stormfur, Crowpaw! Over here!"

Crowpaw shot across the grass and crashed into Feather-tail's flank as he charged under the hedge, but Stormfur stayed where he was, screeching at the advancing kittypets with Squirrelpaw beside him. At the same moment Tawnypelt appeared on top of the fence from the next garden and leaped down to join them.

"Back off, fox dung!" Squirrelpaw spat as the two kittypets closed in.

The nearest of them lashed at her with one paw, missing her by a whisker. Then the door to the Twoleg nest was flung open and a female Twoleg appeared, shouting and waving her arms. The kittypets fled around the side of the nest, while the Clan cats dashed for the refuge of the hedge. The Twoleg glared after them for a moment and then retreated into her nest, banging the door behind her.

"Squirrelpaw!" Brambleclaw hissed as the apprentice skidded to a halt. "What were you thinking of out there? Those two could have clawed your fur off."

Squirrelpaw shrugged, quite unrepentant. "No, they couldn't. All kittypets are soft," she meowed. "Anyway, Stormfur and Crowpaw were there."

"Brambleclaw, don't scold her." Stormfur's amber eyes glowed as he gazed at Squirrelpaw. "That was the bravest thing I've ever seen."

Feathertail murmured agreement, and Brambleclaw began to feel uncomfortable. Tawnypelt gave the young cat a nod of approval, too; only Crowpaw looked cross, perhaps aware that Squirrelpaw had come off better than him, perhaps regretting that in the moment of crisis he had obeyed an order from Brambleclaw.

"I never said she wasn't brave," Brambleclaw defended himself hotly. "Just that she needs to think first. We've still got a long way to go, and if any of us is injured it's going to hold us back."

"Well, we're all here now," Tawnypelt pointed out. "Let's get going."

Brambleclaw led the way back to the patch of rough ground where he had waited with Feathertail. By now the sun had gone, but red streaks stained the sky, showing them the path they must follow.

"We could spend the night here," Feathertail suggested. "There's shelter, and prey."

"It's too close to the Twoleg nests," Stormfur argued. "If

we cross the Thunderpath into those fields, we'll be able to find a safer place."

No cat disagreed with that. StarClan sent them an easy crossing of the second Thunderpath, and as twilight gathered they began the trek across the fields. The surface was rough, with boggy patches and heaps of stone, as if once there had been Twoleg nests here that had been allowed to fall into ruin.

It was almost dark when they came to a stretch of broken-down wall. Ferns and grasses had rooted in the cracks, giving some shelter, and moss covered the fallen stones.

"This doesn't look too bad," Stormfur meowed. "We could stop here."

"Oh, yes, please!" Squirrelpaw agreed. "I'm so tired I think my paws will drop off!"

"Well, I think we should go on a bit farther," Crowpaw objected stubbornly. Brambleclaw suspected he was just trying to be difficult. "There's no prey-scent here."

"We've traveled a long way today," Brambleclaw meowed. "If we go any farther we could run into more trouble, or have to spend the night in the open. Let's look around first, though, and make sure there aren't any nasty surprises. No badgers or foxes holed up nearby."

The rest of the cats agreed, all except Crowpaw, who grunted disagreeably. Squirrelpaw went to investigate on the other side of the wall. When she had been gone for a while, Brambleclaw set off after her, bracing himself to find that she had run into trouble again, only to meet her bouncing back around the line of stones.

"This is a great place!" she announced, shaking droplets of water from her whiskers, while Brambleclaw wondered where all her energy came from. "There's a puddle on the other side, with plenty of water."

"Water? Lead me to it," Tawnypelt mewed, trotting in the direction Squirrelpaw indicated. "My mouth's as dry as last season's leaves."

A moment later she came back, and stalked threateningly across to Squirrelpaw with her tail bristling. "That was a dirty trick," she growled.

Squirrelpaw looked bewildered. "Trick? I don't know what you mean."

Tawnypelt spat. "The water tastes disgusting. Full of salt or something."

"No, it doesn't!" Squirrelpaw protested. "I had a good long drink, and it was as fresh as anything."

Tawnypelt turned away and snatched angrily at some juicy stalks of grass. Stormfur shot Squirrelpaw a worried glance. "Wait there," he ordered. A moment later he reappeared with drops gleaming on his whiskers. "No, it's fine," he reported.

"Then why did I get a mouthful of salt?" Tawnypelt mewed.

A shiver ran down Brambleclaw's spine. "What if . . ." he began, his gaze darting from one cat to another. He swallowed. "What if it's a sign from StarClan that we're doing the right thing, trying to find the sun-drown place? My dream was about salt water, remember."

The four chosen cats looked at each other, eyes stretched wide with awe and, Brambleclaw thought, apprehension.

"If you're right," Feathertail murmured, "it would mean that StarClan are watching us, all the time." She glanced around as if she expected to see starry shapes stalking toward them across the darkening field.

Brambleclaw dug his claws into the earth, feeling the need to anchor himself in something real and solid. "Then that's a good thing," he meowed.

"So why haven't we all had a sign?" Crowpaw asked challengingly. "Why just the two of you?"

"Perhaps we'll have one later," Feathertail suggested, brushing her tail against Crowpaw's flank. "Maybe they're spread out to let us know we're staying on the right path."

"Perhaps." Crowpaw shrugged angrily and went off to curl up by himself at one end of the wall.

The rest of the party settled down too. Brambleclaw thought longingly of the mice in Ravenpaw's barn; there was no prey-scent here, and they would have to go to sleep hungry. The next day they would have to spend some time hunting before they went much farther.

The first stars of Silverpelt were beginning to appear above his head. *Warriors of StarClan,* Brambleclaw thought drowsily, *watching us and guiding us on our journey.*

*If only I could speak to you right now,* he thought. *I wish I could ask you if we're really doing the right thing, and why we have to travel so far. I wish I could ask you what trouble you have foreseen for the forest.*

The stars glittered more brightly still, but no answers came.

C H A P T E R   1 7

*Brambleclaw jumped awake when a paw* prodded him in the side.

Squirrelpaw's voice meowed urgently, "Wake up, Bramble-claw! Feathertail and Crowpaw—are gone!"

Brambleclaw sat up, blinking. Tawnypelt was on her paws, and Stormfur was just emerging from the nest he had made for himself under a clump of ferns. But Squirrelpaw was right. There was no sign of Feathertail and Crowpaw.

His head whirling, he staggered to his paws. The sun had already climbed above the horizon in a bright blue sky dotted with puffs of white cloud. A stiff breeze was blowing, rippling the grass in the field, but it brought no scent of the missing cats. For a couple of heartbeats Brambleclaw wondered if they had gone home. They had not received the saltwater sign from StarClan; had that made them feel like giving up, as if they had been judged and found lacking? And if Feathertail and Crowpaw had turned back, could he and Tawnypelt succeed if they went on alone?

Then he realized he was being stupid. Crowpaw might think like that, but Feathertail never would, and wherever the two cats had gone they must be together. And it was unlikely that a predator had taken them; there were no scents of danger here, and in any case the noise would have woken the rest of them.

"See if they've gone for a drink at the pool," he suggested to Squirrelpaw, who was still gazing at him with panic in her green eyes.

"I already have," she mewed. "I'm not mouse-brained."

"No, okay, then . . ." Brambleclaw glanced around wildly, desperate to come up with a plan, and caught sight of two small figures, pale gray and black, approaching across the field. The wind, blowing toward the broken-down wall, had carried their scent away. "There they are!" he exclaimed.

Feathertail and Crowpaw trotted briskly up to the stones. Their mouths were full of fresh-kill, and their eyes gleamed with satisfaction.

"Where have you been?" Brambleclaw demanded. "We were worried about you."

"You shouldn't wander off like that," Stormfur added to his sister.

"What does it look like?" Crowpaw snapped, dropping the two mice he was carrying. "You were all snoring like hedgehogs in winter, so we thought we'd go and hunt."

"There's lots of prey over there." Feathertail gestured with her tail toward a thicket in the next field. "We caught a whole pile, but we'll have to go back and fetch the rest."

"Let these lazy lumps do it themselves," Crowpaw muttered.

"Of course we'll help," meowed Brambleclaw, his mouth

already starting to water at the smell of the fresh-kill. "You've done brilliantly. You stay and eat, and we'll fetch the rest of the prey."

Crowpaw had already crouched down, ready to take a bite from one of the mice. "Don't talk to us as if you're our mentor," he growled.

He was obviously determined to be difficult, so Brambleclaw left him to it. In spite of the younger cat's bad temper, he couldn't help feeling optimistic. They had survived the trouble in the Twoleg gardens, Tawnypelt's sign meant that they were still following the will of StarClan, and now they had a good meal to look forward to. As he led the way toward the thicket he decided that things could be a good deal worse.

"What are *those?*" Brambleclaw asked.

Three days had passed since the trouble in the Twoleg gardens, and the journeying cats had traveled on across farmland, avoiding the Twoleg nests dotted here and there, and meeting nothing more threatening than sheep. Now they were crouched in a ditch that ran along the line of a hedge between two fields. They were peering out at two of the biggest animals Brambleclaw had ever seen, which were running back and forth across the field, snorting and tossing up their heads. The impact of their huge feet made the ground shudder.

"Horses," Crowpaw replied loftily; his eyes gleamed as if he was delighted to know something that Brambleclaw didn't. "They run across our territory sometimes with Twolegs on their backs."

Brambleclaw thought he had never heard anything so mad in his life. "I guess even Twolegs want four legs sometimes," he joked.

Crowpaw shrugged.

"Can we please get going?" Squirrelpaw mewed plaintively. "There's water in this ditch, and my tail is getting wet."

"Fine, go," Brambleclaw muttered. "But I don't fancy getting crushed."

"I don't think horses are dangerous," Stormfur meowed. "We've seen them at the farm on the edge of RiverClan territory. They never pay much attention to us."

"If they did tread on us, they wouldn't mean to," Feathertail added.

Brambleclaw felt that wouldn't be much consolation; a blow from one of those feet, which looked like chunks of weathered stone, could break a cat's spine.

"We just need to run across while they're down at the other end," Tawnypelt pointed out. "I doubt they'd follow us. They must be quite stupid, or they wouldn't let Twolegs on their backs."

"Okay." That sounded like good sense to Brambleclaw. "Straight across this field and through that hedge opposite. And for StarClan's sake, let's stay together this time."

They waited until the horses had cantered off to the other end of the field.

"Now!" mewed Brambleclaw.

He launched himself into the open, wind streaming through his fur, aware of his companions racing beside him. He thought he could hear the pounding of the horses' massive feet, but he did not dare slow down to take a look. Then he was leaping the ditch that bordered the hedge on the far side, and plunging into the shelter of low-growing bushes.

Peering out cautiously, he saw that the others had reached safety with him. "Great!" he meowed. "I think we're starting to get the hang of this."

"It's about time." Crowpaw sniffed.

There were large animals in the next field too, this time standing together in the shade of a couple of trees, swishing their tails and munching grass. These were cows: Brambleclaw had seen them near Ravenpaw's barn on his apprentice journey to Highstones. They had smooth black-and-white pelts and enormous eyes like giant peaty pools.

The cows seemed to take no notice of the group of cats, and so they crossed this field more slowly, keeping an eye on the animals as they brushed through the long, cool grass. It was almost sunhigh, and Brambleclaw would have been happy to settle down for a nap, but he knew that they had to go on. He kept checking the position of the sun in the sky, impatient for it to start going down so that he could be sure they were still traveling in the right direction. Where the sun touched the horizon, that was the sun-drown place. Brambleclaw pushed away his nagging worry that they would have nothing to guide them if clouds came to hide the sun, and he hoped the good weather would hold.

Leaving the cows behind, they came to a field so huge they could not see the other side. Instead of grass, it was covered by thicker stems, yellow and stiff like the straw in Ravenpaw's barn, cut short so they were hard and spiky to walk on. In the distance they could hear the roar of a monster.

"It's over there." Squirrelpaw had leaped onto a low branch of an elder tree that was growing in the hedge. "A huge monster, in the *field!* This far from any Thunderpath!"

"What? It can't be!" Brambleclaw leaped up to the branch beside her. To his amazement, Squirrelpaw was right. A monster far bigger than most of the ones that traveled along the Thunderpath was roaring slowly across the field. Some sort of cloud surrounded it, filling the air with churning yellow dust.

"Satisfied?" Squirrelpaw meowed sarcastically.

"Sorry." Brambleclaw jumped down to rejoin the others. "Squirrelpaw's right. There is a monster in the field."

"Then we'd better get on as quickly as we can, before it sees us," Stormfur meowed.

"They're supposed to stay on the Thunderpath," Feathertail complained. "It's not *fair!*"

Crowpaw dabbed warily at the thick, spiky stems in the field. "This is no good," he spat. "We'll all have scratched pads if we try walking across that. We'll have to go around the edge."

He glared at the other cats as he spoke, as if he were expecting one of them to contradict him, but there was no reply except a murmur of agreement from Feathertail. Crowpaw had good ideas, Brambleclaw decided, if only he'd be less aggressive about sharing them.

The WindClan apprentice led the way and the rest followed, keeping close to the hedge so that they would be able to hide if the monster came after them. There was a narrow grassy space between the hedge and the rough yellow stems, just wide enough for the cats to walk in single file.

"Look at that!" Tawnypelt exclaimed.

She twitched her ears toward a mouse crouched among the spikes, nibbling at seeds that were strewn on the ground. Before any other cat could move, Squirrelpaw pounced, rolled over among the crackling stems, and scrambled to her paws again with the mouse in her jaws.

"Here," she meowed, dropping it in front of Tawnypelt. "You saw it first."

"I can catch my own, thanks," Tawnypelt mewed dryly.

Now that Brambleclaw knew what to look for, he realized there were more mice scuffling among the stems, stuffing themselves on the scattered seeds. It was almost as if StarClan had sent them the chance to hunt and feed well. Once Squirrelpaw had eaten he sent her to keep watch in another tree, to report if the monster changed direction and came toward them.

But the monster kept its distance. Brambleclaw felt more hopeful and stronger from the food when they went on, especially as the sun started to sink and he could check their direction. Before long they were able to leave the strange, spiky field, and the going became easier. The air was heavy with the heat of the day; bees hummed in the grasses and a butterfly flew past. Squirrelpaw dabbed a paw at it, but she looked too drowsy to chase it.

Tawnypelt had taken the lead as they approached the edge of the meadow, with Stormfur and Squirrelpaw just behind her and Crowpaw with Feathertail. Brambleclaw, bringing up the rear, kept a lookout behind for possible danger.

This time there was no hedge, but a Twoleg fence, made of some thin, shiny material. It was a kind of mesh, like interlaced twigs, except that the spaces were regular. They were too small to climb through, but there was a gap at the bottom where a cat could flatten itself against the ground and squeeze underneath.

Brambleclaw scrabbled his way under, feeling the fence stuff scrape against his back. Beside him, Stormfur was doing the same. As Brambleclaw straightened up again, he heard a furious wail from farther down the fence.

"I'm stuck!"

The voice was Squirrelpaw's. Heaving a sigh, Brambleclaw padded along the fence toward her, with Stormfur beside him. Crowpaw and Feathertail were already standing beside the young apprentice, and Tawnypelt came up a moment later.

"Well, what are you all staring at?" Squirrelpaw meowed. "Get me out!"

The ginger apprentice was flat on her belly, halfway beneath the fence. Just where she had tried to slide through, the fence stuff had started to come unraveled, and the ends were tangled in her fur. Every time she wriggled, the sharp ends of fence stuff dug into her skin and made her squeak with pain.

"Keep still," Brambleclaw ordered. He turned and studied the sturdy wooden post. "Then we can see what to do. Maybe if we dig up the fence post the stuff will come loose." The post looked pretty solidly set in the ground, but if they all helped . . .

"It would be quicker to bite through the fence," Stormfur argued. He tugged at the shiny strands with his front teeth, but they did not give way. He straightened up, spitting. "No, it's too tough."

"I could have told you that," Crowpaw meowed. "Far better to bite through her fur and free her that way."

"You leave my fur alone, mouse-brain!" Squirrelpaw snapped.

The WindClan apprentice bared his teeth with the hint of a snarl. "If you'd been more careful, this wouldn't have happened. If we can't get you out, you'll have to stay here."

"No, she won't!" Stormfur rounded on the other cat. "I'll stay with her, if no one else will."

"Fine." Crowpaw shrugged. "You stay here, and the four of us who are actually *chosen* will go on without you."

Stormfur's neck fur bristled and he sank his weight onto his haunches so that his leg muscles bulged under the dark gray fur; the two cats were heartbeats away from a fight. With a stab of panic Brambleclaw realized that two or three sheep had wandered up and were staring at the group of cats, while from farther away came the sharp barking of a dog. They would have to move quickly.

"That's enough," he meowed, thrusting himself between

the two hostile toms. "No cat is being left behind. There must be a way to get Squirrelpaw out of there."

He turned back to the apprentice to see Tawnypelt and Feathertail crouched beside her. Feathertail was chewing up dock leaves. "Honestly!" she exclaimed as she spat out the last of them and shot an exasperated glance at Brambleclaw. "Do you toms never do anything but argue?"

"It's what they do best," Tawnypelt mewed, a gleam of amusement in her eyes. "That's right, spread the dock leaves on her fur. They should make it good and slippery. Breathe in, Squirrelpaw. You've been eating too many mice."

Brambleclaw watched as Feathertail worked the chewed-up dock into Squirrelpaw's pelt, rubbing it with one forepaw into the tangle of fur around the fence stuff.

"Now try again," Tawnypelt directed.

Squirrelpaw scrabbled at the ground with her forepaws and tried to use her hind legs to push herself forward. "It's not working!" She gasped.

"Yes, it is." Feathertail's voice was tense, and she pressed her paw against Squirrelpaw's shoulder, which was slippery with green slime. "Keep going."

"And hurry!" Brambleclaw added.

The dog barked again and the watching sheep scattered. Dog-scent drifted toward them on the breeze, getting stronger. Stormfur and Crowpaw braced themselves to flee.

Squirrelpaw gave one last enormous heave and shot through into the field. A knot of ginger fur slid off the fence stuff; a few strands of it were left behind, but Squirrelpaw was free. She stood up and shook herself. "Thanks," she meowed to Feathertail and Tawnypelt. "That was a brilliant idea!"

She was right; Brambleclaw wished he had been the one to think of it. But at least they could go on now, straight into the path of the setting sun—and quickly, before that dog reached them. He led the way across the next field, confident that StarClan were guiding them.

When he woke the next morning, Brambleclaw was dismayed to see the sky covered by a thick layer of cloud. His confidence in StarClan's guidance faltered. This was what he had been afraid of; perhaps it was just luck that had kept the sky clear until now. How was he supposed to know which way to go if he couldn't see the sun?

Scrambling to his paws, he saw that his companions were still sleeping. The night before they had found no better shelter than a hollow place in a field under a couple of scrawny thorn trees. Brambleclaw found that he was growing more and more nervous without the familiar forest canopy overhead. He had never realized before how much he and his Clan mates relied on the trees: for prey, for shelter, and for concealment. Anxiety over Bluestar's prophecy bit even more sharply, as if badger's teeth were closing in his neck.

Paws itching to be on their way, he climbed the side of the hollow and looked around. The sky was unbroken gray; the air felt damp, as if there were rain to come. In the distance was a belt of trees, and the walls of more Twoleg nests. Brambleclaw hoped that their path would not lead them back among Twolegs.

"Brambleclaw! Brambleclaw!"

Some cat was calling his name excitedly. Brambleclaw turned to see Feathertail racing toward him up the side of the hollow.

"I've had it!" she exclaimed as she drew closer.

"Had what?"

"My saltwater sign!" Feathertail let out a delighted purr. "I dreamed of padding along a stretch of stony ground, with water washing over it. When I bent down to take a drink, the water was all salty, and I woke up tasting it."

"That's great, Feathertail." Brambleclaw's anxiety faded a little. StarClan were still watching over them.

"That means that Crowpaw is the only one of us who hasn't had a sign," Feathertail went on, glancing down into the hollow where Brambleclaw could just see the gray-black curve of Crowpaw's back as he slept in a clump of grass.

"Maybe we shouldn't tell him about your dream, then?" he suggested uneasily.

"We can't do that!" Feathertail looked shocked. "He'd find out sooner or later, and then he'd think we were deliberately deceiving him. No," she added after pausing to think, "let me tell him. I'll wait to catch him in a good mood."

Brambleclaw snorted. "You'll wait a long time, then."

Feathertail let out a faint mew of distress. "Oh, Brambleclaw. Crowpaw's not so bad. It was hard for him, leaving the forest just when he was about to be made a warrior. I think he's lonely—I have Stormfur, and you have Tawnypelt and

Squirrelpaw. We all knew each other before this, but Crow-paw is on his own."

Brambleclaw hadn't thought of that before. It was worth thinking about, though it wouldn't make it any easier to get on with Crowpaw the next time he started arguing the smallest point.

"We're all loyal to our Clans," he meowed. "And to the forest and the warrior code. Crowpaw is no different. He'd be fine if he didn't want to be leader all the time, when he's no more than an apprentice."

Feathertail still looked uneasy. "Even if you're right, it won't make it any easier for him, knowing he's the only one who hasn't had a vision."

Briefly Brambleclaw touched Feathertail's muzzle with his own. "You tell him, then, when you think best." Glancing around, he added, "We'd better wake them all and get moving. If we can work out which way to go."

"That way." Feathertail sounded confident as she waved her tail toward the belt of trees on the far side of the field. "That's where the sun went down last night."

*And after that?* Brambleclaw wondered. If there was no sun, how could they find their way? Would StarClan send them something else to help them find the sun-drown place? As he padded down into the hollow to wake his companions, he sent up a quick prayer to his warrior ancestors.

*Show us the way, please. And guard us all when the trouble comes— whatever it is.*

# CHAPTER 18

✿

*"We're running short of celandine."* Cinderpelt poked her head out of the cleft in the rock. "I've used nearly all of it to soothe Longtail's eyes. Do you think you could go out and get some more?"

Leafpaw looked up from the daisy leaves she was chewing into a paste. "Sure," she meowed, spitting out the last scraps. "This is just about ready. Do you want me to take it along to Speckletail?"

"No, I'd better check on her myself. Her joints have been aching badly since the weather turned so damp." Cinderpelt came out of her den and let out a purr of approval as she nosed the chewed-up leaves. "That's fine. Off you go—and take a warrior with you. The best celandine grows near Fourtrees, along the RiverClan border, and RiverClan aren't happy that WindClan are still coming down to drink at the river."

Leafpaw was surprised. "Still? But there's been so much rain—they must have water of their own by now."

Cinderpelt shrugged. "Try telling that to WindClan."

Leafpaw put the news out of her mind as she brushed through the fern tunnel into the main clearing. That quarrel had nothing to do with ThunderClan, and most of her thoughts were taken up with anxiety about Squirrelpaw and Brambleclaw. The sun had risen four times since she saw them leave. Her private sense of Squirrelpaw told her that her sister was still alive, but she knew nothing about where they were or what they were doing.

She had not eaten that morning, so she padded across to the fresh-kill pile, where Sorreltail was finishing off a vole.

"Hi." The young tortoiseshell warrior flicked her tail in greeting as Leafpaw chose a mouse for herself and settled down to eat.

Leafpaw returned her greeting. "Sorreltail," she asked, "are you busy this morning?"

"No." Sorreltail gulped down the last of her vole and sat up, swiping her tongue appreciatively around her jaws. "Did you want something?"

"Cinderpelt has asked me to go up toward Fourtrees, by the RiverClan border, to collect some celandine. She said I should take a warrior with me."

"Oh, *yes!*" Sorreltail sprang to her paws, excitement gleaming in her amber eyes. "In case WindClan accidentally stray into our territory, yes? Just let them try!"

Leafpaw laughed and quickly ate the rest of her mouse. "Right, I'm ready. Let's go!"

As they approached the end of the gorse tunnel, Firestar appeared, followed by Brackenfur and Rainwhisker. Leafpaw felt a thorn stabbing at her heart when she looked at her father; his head was down and his tail drooping, and even his flame-colored pelt seemed dull.

"Nothing?" Sorreltail asked him quietly; Leafpaw realized that she knew exactly what their leader had been doing.

Firestar shook his head. "Not a trace of them. No scent, no pawmarks, nothing. They've gone."

"They must have left the territory days ago," Brackenfur meowed somberly. "I don't think there's any point in sending out more patrols to look for them."

"You're right, Brackenfur." Firestar let out a heavy sigh. "They're in the paws of StarClan now."

Leafpaw pressed her muzzle against his side, and his tail curled around to brush her ears before he padded off across the clearing. Leafpaw saw Sandstorm meet him at the base of the Highrock, and the two cats went off together toward Firestar's den.

Guilt swept over her as she remembered how much she was hiding—most of all, the certainty that Squirrelpaw was safe, though far from ThunderClan territory—and every hair on her pelt prickled so much that it seemed impossible that no other cat noticed as she followed Sorreltail out of the camp.

As the sun rose higher the morning mists cleared away; the day promised to be hot, although the red-gold leaves on the trees showed that leaf-fall had taken over the forest. Leafpaw and Sorreltail headed toward Fourtrees. The medicine cat apprentice purred with satisfaction as she watched Sorreltail dashing ahead to investigate every bush and hollow that they passed. There was no sign of the shoulder injury that had kept Sorreltail from her warrior ceremony for so long, and no trace of bitterness that she had waited twice as long as other apprentices to receive her warrior name. Though she was older than Leafpaw, she still had all the joyful energy of a kit.

As they drew close to the RiverClan border, Leafpaw heard the soft rush of the river, and caught glimpses of it sparkling through the undergrowth at the edge of the trees. She found huge clumps of celandine where Cinderpelt had suggested, and settled down to bite off as many stems as she could carry.

"I can take some too," Sorreltail offered, glancing back as she padded up to the border. "Yuck—RiverClan scent marks! They make my fur curl."

She stood gazing out over the slope that led down to the river, while Leafpaw got on with her task. It was almost finished when she heard her friend calling to her.

"Come and look at this!"

Bounding to Sorreltail's side, Leafpaw looked down the slope to see a large group of WindClan cats gathered beside the water to drink. She recognized Tallstar and Firestar's friend Onewhisker among them.

"They *are* still drinking at the river!" she exclaimed.

"And look at that." Sorreltail pointed with her tail to where a RiverClan patrol was crossing the Twoleg bridge. "If you ask me, there's going to be trouble."

Mistyfoot was at the head of the patrol; she had brought with her the new warrior Hawkfrost and an older cat Leafpaw did not know, a tom with a black pelt. They padded down the slope and stopped a few foxlengths away from the WindClan cats. Mistyfoot called out something, but she was too far away for Leafpaw to hear what she said.

Sorreltail's tail twitched. "I wish we could get a bit closer!"

"I think crossing the border would be a really bad idea," Leafpaw mewed nervously.

"Oh, I know that. It looks like it could be interesting, that's all." She sounded resigned, as if the thought of helping RiverClan settle their border dispute had appealed to her.

By now, Mistyfoot's fur was bristling furiously, her tail fluffed out to twice its size. Tallstar left his Clan mate and came closer to talk to her. Hawkfrost said something urgently to the RiverClan deputy, but she shook her head and he took a pace back, looking angry.

Eventually Tallstar returned to his Clan mates, who finished drinking and set out for their own territory. They took their time; it looked to Leafpaw as if they were leaving because they had finished, not because Mistyfoot had ordered them off. Several of the WindClan cats hissed at the RiverClan patrol as they passed, and Leafpaw could tell that Mistyfoot had her work cut out holding back her two companions from a fight. They were badly outnumbered— Leafpaw could only guess how frustrated Mistyfoot must feel that she couldn't enforce her territory boundaries, thanks to the agreement at the last Gathering.

When the WindClan cats had vanished in the direction of Fourtrees, Mistyfoot gathered her patrol together to lead them down beside the river. Impulsively, Leafpaw called out to her; the RiverClan deputy turned and spotted her, and after a heartbeat's hesitation padded up the slope to join her and Sorreltail on the border.

"Hello, there," she meowed. "How's the prey running with you?"

"Fine, thank you," Leafpaw replied. She flashed a warning glance at Sorreltail, thinking it would be as well not to mention the confrontation with WindClan they had just witnessed. "Is all well in RiverClan?"

Mistyfoot inclined her head. "Yes, everything's fine, except . . ." She paused and then went on: "Have you seen anything of Stormfur and Feathertail? They disappeared from our territory four dawns ago. No cat has seen them since."

"We tracked them as far as Fourtrees, but of course we couldn't search on other Clans' territories," Hawkfrost added, coming up in time to hear what his deputy was saying. The black warrior stayed where he was, keeping watch beside the riverbank.

Hawkfrost dipped his head courteously to Leafpaw and Sorreltail. He was a powerful tabby with a glossy dark pelt, and for a heartbeat Leafpaw thought he reminded her of some cat she had seen before—but no other cat in the forest had such icy, piercing blue eyes.

"What do you mean?" she asked. "Feathertail and Stormfur have left RiverClan?"

"Yes." Mistyfoot's eyes were troubled. "We thought they must have decided to go to ThunderClan to be with their father."

Leafpaw shook her head. "We haven't seen them."

"But we've lost cats too!" Sorreltail exclaimed, lashing her tail eagerly. "And . . . yes, that was four dawns ago."

"What?" Mistyfoot stared at her in disbelief. "Which cats?"

"Brambleclaw and Squirrelpaw," Leafpaw replied, wincing. She wished Sorreltail hadn't blurted that out; her instinct had been to keep their disappearance secret from other Clans, but there was no taking the words back now.

"Is something taking them away?" Mistyfoot spoke almost to herself. "Some predator?" She shuddered. "I remember those dogs. . . ."

"No, I'm sure that's not what has happened." Leafpaw wanted to reassure her without giving away the secret that only she knew. "If it was a fox or a badger, there would be traces. Scent, droppings . . . something."

The RiverClan deputy still looked doubtful, but Sorreltail's eyes brightened.

"If they all decided to leave the forest, perhaps they've gone together," she suggested.

Mistyfoot looked even more confused. "I know Feathertail and Stormfur sometimes felt the Clan still blamed them for having a father in RiverClan," she meowed. "And Brambleclaw has to bear the burden of being Tigerstar's son. But Squirrelpaw . . . What reason could there be for her to leave her home?"

*Only the fire-and-tiger prophecy,* Leafpaw thought, and then remembered that Squirrelpaw herself had no knowledge of it—only what must have seemed to be unfair criticism from their father. It was the prophecy in Brambleclaw's dream that had sent Squirrelpaw on her journey. But for now Leafpaw could say nothing about either prophecy.

"Perhaps other Clans have lost cats too," Hawkfrost meowed. "We should try to find out. They might know more than we do."

"True," Mistyfoot agreed. Casting a grim look back toward the bank where the WindClan cats had gathered to drink, she added, "It will be easy enough to ask WindClan. But no cat will be able to speak to ShadowClan until the Gathering."

"That's not long now," Leafpaw remarked.

"Are you sure it will be easy to speak with WindClan?" Sorreltail ventured boldly, as if she were challenging Mistyfoot to admit that WindClan still drank freely inside RiverClan borders.

Mistyfoot drew back a pace, suddenly taller and with eyes like cold fire. From anxiously sharing her worries with Leafpaw, she had become the RiverClan deputy again, guarding her Clan's weaknesses. "I suppose you saw what happened," she hissed. "Tallstar has broken the spirit of his agreement with Leopardstar. She allowed them to come down to the river only because they had no water in their own territory, and he knows it."

"We should drive them off!" Hawkfrost's voice was hard, and his pale blue eyes stared stonily in the direction where the WindClan cats had disappeared.

"You know Leopardstar has forbidden that." Mistyfoot's tone suggested she had gone over this argument before. "She says that she'll keep *her* word no matter what Tallstar does."

Hawkfrost bowed his head in agreement, but Leafpaw noticed that his claws flexed in and out as if he itched to rake them over the pelts of the cats who had invaded his Clan's territory. Forest-born or not, he was growing into a formidable warrior, she reflected, as exceptional in his way as his sister, Mothwing.

"Say hi to Mothwing for me," she mewed to him, and with a sudden thought darted back to the clumps of celandine. Grabbing up a few of the stems she had bitten off, she hurried back and dropped them at Hawkfrost's paws. "She might like to have those," she told him, "Cinderpelt uses it to help cats with weak eyes. I think it grows much better on our side of the border."

"Thank you," Hawkfrost replied with a nod of gratitude.

"We'd better be on our way," meowed Mistyfoot. "Leafpaw, tell your father about Stormfur and Feathertail, and ask him to let us know if he hears anything."

"Yes, Mistyfoot, I will."

Guilt swept over Leafpaw yet again as she watched the RiverClan patrol pad away upriver. She felt again the burden of being the only cat to know about both prophecies— one that had sent Brambleclaw and Squirrelpaw on a journey who knew where, and one that left Firestar convinced they would be involved in the destruction of his Clan—and yet her knowledge was not enough. StarClan had not chosen to tell her about the destiny of the forest, and Leafpaw did not feel that even the full moon, shining down on the next Gathering, would shed much light on her dark questions.

By the time Leafpaw and Sorreltail returned to camp, loaded with celandine, it was almost sunhigh.

"We'd better report to Firestar," Sorreltail meowed when they had taken the herbs to Cinderpelt. "He'll want to know about those missing RiverClan cats."

Leafpaw nodded and led the way to her father's den beneath the Highrock. The clearing was full of cats enjoying the last heat of early leaf-fall. Spiderpaw and Whitepaw were sprawled in the shade of the ferns that sheltered their den, while Cloudtail and Brightheart shared tongues in a patch of sunlight. Ferncloud was sitting outside the nursery with Dustpelt beside her, watching their kits as they played together.

A wave of sadness swept over Leafpaw. It was almost as if Brambleclaw and Squirrelpaw had never been part of ThunderClan, as if they had sunk out of sight as a drowning cat might sink in the river, the waters closing over its head.

The feeling ebbed a little when they reached Firestar's den and called out to him. Leafpaw heard his voice telling them to enter, and she brushed past the curtain of lichen to see him curled up in his nest; Graystripe was sitting next to him, and the anxiety in the eyes of both cats was enough to reassure Leafpaw that her sister and Brambleclaw had not been forgotten.

"We've brought news," Sorreltail meowed immediately, and poured out what Mistyfoot had told them about Feathertail and Stormfur going missing.

Firestar's and Graystripe's eyes narrowed, and the deputy sprang to his paws as if he wanted to dash out and look for his missing children right away.

"If a fox has taken them I'll track it down and flay its skin!" he snarled.

Firestar remained in his nest, but he unsheathed his claws as if he were sinking them into the pelt of whatever had stolen his daughter. "Surely the dogs can't have come back?" he muttered. "We couldn't have to deal with them more than once in a lifetime?"

"No, there's no sign of that," Leafpaw reassured him. "Feathertail and Stormfur must have gone with Brambleclaw and Squirrelpaw, and that . . . that suggests they had a reason for leaving." She tried desperately to think how much information she could give to the anxious fathers without revealing that she knew more than she was supposed to. So far she had kept her Moonstone vision of the traveling cats even from her mentor, Cinderpelt, but now she knew she would have to reveal it. She was not breaking her promise, she told herself; she would not betray anything of what Brambleclaw and Squirrelpaw had told her when they met in the forest.

"Firestar," she went on hesitantly, "you know how close I am to Squirrelpaw? Well, sometimes I can tell what she's doing, even when she's a long way away."

Firestar's eyes opened wide in amazement. "That's impossible!" He gasped. "I always knew you were close, but this . . ."

"It's true, I promise. When I went to the Moonstone, StarClan gave me a vision of her," Leafpaw went on. "She was safe, and there were other cats with her." She met her father's intense gaze, and saw how much he wanted to believe her. "Squirrelpaw is alive," she finished, "and the others must be with her. Four cats together will be safer than two."

Firestar blinked, bewildered. "May StarClan grant you're right."

Graystripe's amber eyes remained full of fear and uncertainty. "Even if that's true, why did they leave without telling us where they were going, or why?" he meowed. "If Stormfur and Feathertail had a problem, why didn't they come to me first?"

"We think the other Clans might have lost cats too," Sorreltail meowed. "We should ask them."

Firestar and Graystripe exchanged a glance. "Perhaps," mewed Firestar; Leafpaw could tell how hard he was struggling to sound decisive, to act like a Clan leader instead of a desperately worried father. "The next Gathering is only a few days away."

"StarClan keep them all safe!" Graystripe added fervently.

Leafpaw suspected that he had little faith in his prayer; he knew well enough the dangers that stalked outside the forest. As she left her father's den, she felt the burden of her knowledge weighing even more heavily on her. She was the only cat in the forest who had heard that there were two prophecies, and knew what each of them said.

*But I'm only an apprentice,* she told herself anxiously. *I know them by accident, not because our warrior ancestors chose to tell me themselves. What do StarClan expect me to do?*

Leafpaw found it hard to sleep that night, fidgeting in her bed of ferns while Silverpelt glittered coldly above her. She longed to know what was happening to the journeying cats, but she could think of no way to find out.

When she finally drifted into unconsciousness, she found herself in some dim place, racing panic-stricken among the trunks of shadowy trees.

"Squirrelpaw! Squirrelpaw!" She gasped.

She was answered only by the hoot of an owl and the bark of a fox. Death panted hard on her paws, drawing closer with every footfall, and for all her twisting and turning, Leafpaw knew that there was no escape.

# CHAPTER 19

*Brambleclaw raced panic-stricken among the* trees, bolting back and forth in a frantic effort to escape. Behind him he could hear the throaty bark of the dog that had leaped out from a thicket as he and his companions reached the wood. Glancing back, he saw the lean black shape crash through a clump of bracken, its tongue lolling. He could almost feel its sharp white teeth meeting in his pelt.

"StarClan help us!" Feathertail gasped as she dashed beside him.

They had fallen behind the other cats, though Brambleclaw heard a yowl of terror coming from somewhere just ahead.

"Dodge!" he called. "Try to lose it!"

The dog barked again, and from farther off Brambleclaw heard a Twoleg shouting. He lost sight of his pursuer, and he slowed down as a wave of relief swept over him; the creature must have gone back to its Twoleg.

Then he heard the dog's snuffling breath, and it shot out from behind a fallen tree trunk. For a heartbeat Brambleclaw stared into eyes like flames. Whirling around, he fled through the trees as the barking started up again.

Confused by fear, he remembered how Firestar and the other cats of ThunderClan had led the dog pack through the forest until they fell into the gorge and drowned. But how could he and his friends lead this dog away, here in unknown territory?

"Climb trees!" he yowled, hoping his friends could hear him above the fierce barking that sounded louder than ever.

He glanced upward as he ran, but every tree seemed to have a smooth trunk with no low-growing branches. He could not stop and search; the beast would be on him at once. Had it already caught one of the others? Was he about to find one of his companions terribly injured like Brightheart, or worse, dead?

His breath was rasping in his throat and his paws burned with every step; he knew he could not keep up this pace for much longer. Then a voice hissed at him from somewhere above his head. "Up here—quick!"

Brambleclaw skidded to a halt beside a tree that was covered with ivy. A pair of eyes gleamed down at him. In the same heartbeat the dog crashed through a tangle of briars behind him. With a terrified yowl, Brambleclaw launched himself upward, clawing frantically at the ivy stems. They gave way under his weight, and for a heart-stopping moment he swung helplessly; the dog leaped up and he heard the snap of its teeth and felt hot breath on his fur.

Then he managed to sink his claws into a stronger ivy stem and hauled himself upward again. Squirrelpaw appeared below, shot past the nose of the dog, and clawed her way up the tree, overtaking Brambleclaw to crouch shivering on a branch. Brambleclaw scrambled up beside her.

He spotted Stormfur and Tawnypelt clinging to another branch just above his head, and Crowpaw scrabbled his way up to join them from the other side of the trunk.

"Feathertail!" gasped Brambleclaw. "Where's Feathertail?"

The dog was on its hind legs at the bottom of the tree, less than a foxlength below him. Its claws tore at the ivy while it snarled furiously, drool spilling out of its jaws. The sound of the Twoleg shouting came again, but a long way off.

Then Brambleclaw noticed Feathertail crouching in the briars just behind the dog, staring out in terror. If she tried to run for the safety of the tree, the dog would cut her off. How long, Brambleclaw wondered, before it scented her?

Suddenly he heard Crowpaw spit furiously. "Fox dung! I've had enough of this." The WindClan apprentice hurled himself out of the tree, narrowly missing the dog, and hit the ground just beyond it. The dog spun around and gave chase, its paws scrabbling on the dry leaves. While it was distracted, Feathertail bolted out of the briars and across the clearing to make a desperate leap for a thin branch that swung alarmingly under her weight.

"Crowpaw!" Brambleclaw yowled.

The gray-black tom had vanished into the bushes. Brambleclaw could hear the dog crashing about, barking wildly, and the shouts of the Twoleg growing closer. Then Crowpaw appeared again, his belly close to the ground as he ran all-out for the tree. The dog was panting just behind him. Brambleclaw squeezed his eyes tight shut and opened them again in time to see Crowpaw take a flying jump and dig his claws into the ivy.

At the same moment the Twoleg lumbered into the clearing and made a dive for the dog's collar. He was red-faced and yelling furiously. The dog dodged to one side, but the Twoleg managed to grab it and clip a lead onto its collar. The dog's barks changed to whining as it was dragged away, clawing the grass and leaf mold as it struggled to return to its prey.

"Thank you, Crowpaw!" Feathertail gasped, still clinging to the swaying branch. "You saved my life!"

"Yes, you did," meowed Brambleclaw. "Well-done."

Crowpaw scrambled higher until he reached the branch beside Brambleclaw and Squirrelpaw. "Big brute," he muttered, looking embarrassed. "Tripped over its own paws."

Feathertail's blue eyes were fixed on him, huge as moons with shock. "It would have caught me for sure if you hadn't come to help me," she whispered.

As Brambleclaw's fear ebbed, he remembered for the first time the voice that had called him up into the tree. It wasn't one of the Clan cats. Looking up again, he saw a pair of eyes gleaming from the leaves a little way above his head. Then the leaves rustled and an unfamiliar cat emerged.

It was a tabby tom, old and plump with rumpled fur that looked as if he never bothered to groom himself. His movements were slow and careful as he clambered down the tree to join the six journeying cats.

"Well," he rasped. "You're a fine bunch, an' no mistake.

Don't you know that that dog runs loose every day, 'round about sunrise?"

"How would we know that?" Tawnypelt spat. "We've never been here before."

The tom blinked at her. "No need to get so snippy. You'll know another time, won't you? Get out o' the way then."

"There won't be another time," Stormfur meowed. "We're just passing through."

"Thank you for helping us," Brambleclaw added. "I was beginning to think we'd never escape."

The tabby ignored his thanks. "Just passin' through, eh?" he mewed. "I'll bet you've a story to tell. Why not stay awhile an' share it wi' me?" He stood up and braced himself, ready to jump down into the clearing.

"Down there?" Squirrelpaw sounded nervous. "What if that dog comes back?"

"It won't. It's gone home now. Come on."

The old cat scrambled down the ivy-covered trunk and ungracefully dropped the last foxlength to the ground. Looking up, he opened his jaws wide in a yawn. "Comin'?"

Brambleclaw leaped down after him; he wasn't going to let this elder, or kittypet, or whatever he was, show more bravery than warriors. His companions joined him, clustering around to gaze uncertainly at the stranger.

"Who are you?" Stormfur asked. "Are you a kittypet?"

The old tom looked blank. "Kittypet?"

"Living with Twolegs," Squirrelpaw mewed impatiently. "Twolegs?"

"Oh, let's go," Crowpaw's ears twitched in contempt. "There are bees in his brain. We won't get any sense out of him."

"Who're you callin' senseless, young fellow?" The tabby tom's voice was a deep rumble, and his claws extended to sink into the leaves under his paws.

"Sorry," Brambleclaw meowed hastily, with a glare at Crowpaw; the apprentice might have shown amazing courage, but that didn't make him any less annoying. Turning to the old cat, he began to explain. "Twolegs, like the one who came to fetch the dog."

"Oh, you're talkin' about Upwalkers. Why didn't you say so? No, I don't live with Upwalkers. Used to once, mind you. Those were the days!" He settled down at the foot of the tree, gazing into the distance as if he were looking back at the young cat he had once been. "A fire to sleep by, an' all the food I could eat."

Brambleclaw wasn't sure he liked the sound of that. Firestar always said that kittypet food was nowhere near as tasty as fresh-kill you caught yourself. As for sleeping beside a fire . . . Brambleclaw remembered the fire that had swept through the ThunderClan camp, and the very thought of it made his fur prickle.

"Talking of food," Crowpaw meowed loudly, "we need to get on and hunt. There should be prey somewhere among these trees. Here, you . . ." He stretched out a paw and prodded the old cat, who had drifted into a doze. "What's the prey like around here?"

The tabby opened one amber eye. "Young cats," he muttered.

"Always dashin' off. There's no need to catch your own squeakers in these parts. Not if you know where to go."

"Well, we don't." Squirrelpaw flicked her ears back irritably.

"Please, won't you tell us?" Feathertail asked the old cat. "We're strangers here, so we don't know the good places. We've been traveling a long way, and we're all very hungry."

Her gentle tone, and the pleading look she gave him from liquid blue eyes, seemed to win over the old cat. "I might show you," he replied, scratching himself vigorously behind the ear with one hind paw.

"That would be very kind of you," Stormfur added, coming to stand beside his sister.

The old cat's gaze traveled over them, coming to rest at last on Brambleclaw. "Six of you," he mewed. "That's a powerful lot to feed. Who are you, anyway? Why don't you have Upwalkers of your own?"

"We're warriors!" Brambleclaw explained. He introduced himself and his companions. "I suppose you must be a loner," he finished, "if you don't live with Twolegs—I mean Upwalkers." Trying to sound as polite as Feathertail, he added, "Won't you tell us your name?"

"Name? Don't rightly reckon I've got one. Upwalkers feed me, though I don't stay with them none. They call me different names—a cat can't be expected to remember them all."

"You must have had a name to begin with," Squirrelpaw insisted, rolling her eyes at Brambleclaw.

"Yes, what was your name when you lived with the . . . the Upwalker who had the fire?" Feathertail asked.

The old cat gave the other ear a good scratch. "Well, now . . . that was a long time ago." He let out a gusty sigh. "A long time and a good time. I caught more squeakers in that Upwalker den than you youngsters have seen in your whole lives."

"So why did you leave, if it was as good as all that?" Tawnypelt asked; Brambleclaw could see by her twitching tail that her patience was running out.

"My Upwalker died." The tabby shook his head as if he were trying to flick away a clinging burr. "No more food . . . no more strokin' by the fire, dozin' on his lap. . . . More Upwalkers came after that, an' set traps for me, but I was cunnin', see. I went away."

"But what was your name?" Squirrelpaw hissed at him through clenched teeth. "What did the Upwalker call you?"

"Name . . . oh, yes, my name. Purdy, that's right. He called me Purdy."

"At last!" Squirrelpaw muttered.

"We'll call you Purdy, then, shall we?" Brambleclaw meowed, batting Squirrelpaw's muzzle with the tip of his tail.

The old tabby heaved himself to his paws. "Suit yourselves. Now, do you want food or don't you?"

He padded off through the trees. Brambleclaw exchanged a doubtful glance with his friends. "Do you think we should trust him?"

"No!" Crowpaw replied at once. "He was a *kittypet*. Warriors can't trust kittypets."

Tawnypelt murmured agreement, but Feathertail meowed, "We're all so hungry, and we don't know these woods. Would it do any harm, just for once?"

"I'm starving!" added Squirrelpaw, her claws flexing impatiently.

"StarClan know we could do with some help," Stormfur mewed. "I can't say I like it, but so long as we keep our eyes open . . ."

"Okay, then," Brambleclaw decided. "We'll risk it."

He led the way, bounding quickly through the undergrowth to catch up to the old tom, who was ambling ahead as if he did not care whether they followed him or not. To Brambleclaw's surprise, Purdy didn't show them anywhere in the wood where they could catch prey. Instead he made straight for the far side, where a narrow strip of grass separated the last of the trees from a row of Twoleg nests. Purdy strolled confidently across the grass toward the nearest fence without even looking to see if there was danger.

"Hey!" Crowpaw halted on the edge of the wood. "Where's he taking us? I'm not going into a Twoleg nest!"

Brambleclaw halted too. For once he agreed with Crowpaw. "Purdy, wait!" he called. "We're warriors—we don't go into Upwalker places."

The old cat paused at the bottom of the fence and looked back, his face creased in amusement. "Scared, are you?"

Crowpaw took a single step forward, his legs stiff and his neck fur bristling. "Say that again!" he hissed.

To Brambleclaw's surprise, Purdy didn't flinch a single whisker, even though Brambleclaw would bet that Crowpaw could have ripped him apart.

"Touchy, ain't he?" the old cat mewed. "Don't you worry none, young fellow. There'll be no Upwalkers around just yet. And there's good food in their garden."

Brambleclaw looked at the others. "What do you think?"

"I think we should give it a try," meowed Stormfur. "We need food."

"Yes, let's just get *on*," Tawnypelt muttered.

Feathertail nodded eagerly and Squirrelpaw gave a little excited bounce. Only Crowpaw stayed apart, staring ahead without replying to Brambleclaw's question.

"Let's go, then," Brambleclaw meowed.

After a cautious glance from side to side he crossed the grass to join Purdy, and the rest of his companions followed, even Crowpaw, though Brambleclaw noticed he trailed behind with his gaze on the ground.

"Crowpaw knows about my saltwater dream," Feathertail murmured into Brambleclaw's ear. "He seemed in a good mood when he woke up, so I told him, before the dog started chasing us. I think he's upset."

"Well, he'll have to get over it." Brambleclaw's patience was running short; he had enough to worry about without making allowances for Crowpaw's wounded pride.

Feathertail shook her head doubtfully, but just then they caught up with Purdy, so she said no more.

When they were all together the old tabby pushed his way through a gap in the fence and led the way into the Twoleg garden. Brambleclaw's nose wrinkled at the unfamiliar smells: at least two Twolegs, the acrid reek of a monster, though to his relief that was stale, and a whole mixture of unfamiliar plant scents. Some of the plants had huge, shaggy flower heads that bent under their own weight; Squirrelpaw sniffed one, and jumped back in surprise as it shed a shower of petals over her fur.

Purdy padded across the grass and sat in the middle of it, waving his tail invitingly. Coming up beside him, Brambleclaw saw a pool of water edged with some hard Twoleg stuff. Pale flowers and green leaves floated on the water, and in the depths he spotted a flash of gold, so bright that he instinctively glanced upward to see if the sun had appeared, but all the sky was still covered with cloud.

"It's a fish!" Feathertail exclaimed. "A golden fish!"

"What? Fish aren't golden!" Crowpaw sounded irritable.

"No, but these are." Stormfur was sitting beside his sister, gazing into the water. "I've never seen anything like it. We don't get those in the river."

"Can you eat them?" Tawnypelt asked.

"Aye, there's good eatin' on one of those," Purdy told her.

"I'm going to try!" Squirrelpaw gave the water an experimental dab with her paw.

"Not like that!" meowed Stormfur. "You'll just disturb them and send them all to the bottom. Let me and Feathertail show you."

The two RiverClan cats sat poised by the edge of the pool, their gazes fixed on the water. Then Feathertail flashed out a paw. A bright golden fish flew into the air in an arc of glittering raindrops and fell on the bank, where it lay wriggling and flopping.

"Someone grab it, before it falls back in," Stormfur ordered.

Squirrelpaw, who was nearest, pounced on the fish and bit it behind the head. "It's good!" she announced, swallowing.

Stormfur had already caught another fish, and soon Feathertail caught a third, so that Tawnypelt and Brambleclaw could feed. Brambleclaw tasted his fish with some suspicion, not knowing what he expected, but the flesh was succulent, and he polished it off rapidly.

When Stormfur hooked out the next one, he patted it over to Crowpaw. "Come on . . . it's okay."

Crowpaw gave the fish a contemptuous look. "We should be on our way, not messing about with Twoleg stuff. I would never have come if I'd thought the journey to the sun-drown place—or wherever—would take so long. I'm missing out on warrior training with my mentor."

"I reckon you're getting some pretty good warrior training here," Stormfur pointed out.

"Come sit with me," Feathertail meowed persuasively, "and I'll teach you how we catch them."

"Teach me as well, please!" Squirrelpaw demanded eagerly.

Crowpaw glanced scornfully at the ThunderClan apprentice. He padded across to Feathertail, and sat beside her on the side of the pool.

"That's right," she meowed. "The trick is not to let your shadow fall on the water. When you see a fish, scoop it up as quick as you can, before it has time to swim away."

Crowpaw bent over the water, a paw half extended, and a moment later flashed it down into the pool. He scooped out a fish, but it turned in the air and fell back into the water, spattering Crowpaw with a shower of drops. Squirrelpaw let out a snicker and Brambleclaw glared at her.

"That was very good for a first try," Feathertail soothed the angry apprentice. "Try again."

But Crowpaw had backed away from the pool. He dipped his head and began licking the splashes of water from his fur, only to stop in disgust. "What sort of water is this? It's salty!"

"No, it's not," mewed Stormfur in surprise.

Whatever he was going to say was drowned in a crash and an angry Twoleg yell. Brambleclaw looked up to see a Twoleg standing in the open doorway of the nest, shouting. He gripped something in one hand and hurled it at the cats; it landed in among the shaggy flowers just beyond Purdy.

"Uh-oh," mewed the old tabby. "Time to go."

He lumbered back to the gap in the fence. Brambleclaw and Stormfur followed; Tawnypelt and Squirrelpaw streaked ahead to slip through the gap first, with Feathertail on their heels. Crowpaw came last; as he emerged from the garden and raced across the grass to the shelter of the trees, he was spitting fury.

"Why did you take us there?" he demanded, turning on Purdy. "We should never have trusted you. Did you want that Twoleg to catch us? The filthy fish weren't even worth it."

"Crowpaw, don't," Feathertail pleaded, dropping the fish she was carrying. "There's nothing wrong with the fish or the water."

"I tell you it tasted salty!" Crowpaw snapped.

Brambleclaw was about to intervene—they had wasted far too much time, first in fleeing from the dog and now in arguing—until he saw the glow in Feathertail's eyes.

"You know why it tasted salty to you and not the rest of us, don't you?" she meowed quietly, resting the tip of her tail on his flank. "It's your saltwater sign, Crowpaw. You've had it at last!"

The gray-black cat opened his mouth to reply, but nothing came out. He stared at the fish and then at Feathertail. "Are you sure?" he meowed, sounding astonished.

"Of course, you stupid furball," Feathertail purred. Brambleclaw thought that no other cat but Feathertail could call Crowpaw a stupid furball and get away unclawed. "Why else would water in a Twoleg pool taste salty? It's StarClan's sign that we're still on the right track."

Crowpaw blinked and let his fur lie flat along his spine.

"What's all this about signs and salt water?" Purdy growled.

"We're on a really important journey!" Squirrelpaw informed him excitedly. "StarClan sent us to find out something vital for our Clans."

"Journey . . . where from? What Clans?"

Brambleclaw sighed. Even though he wanted to keep going, he guessed the old tabby was lonely; it seemed unkind to abandon him without even telling him why they were there. He had saved them from the dog, after all, and then led them to the shining golden fish.

"Come here into the bracken," he meowed. "We won't be seen there, and then we can tell you all about it."

All the cats followed him; even Crowpaw didn't object. Stormfur and Feathertail shared the fish and Tawnypelt kept watch while Squirrelpaw poured out their story. Brambleclaw chipped in to correct her or explain when Purdy didn't understand.

"StarClan?" the old tom meowed with a doubtful look when Squirrelpaw told him about Brambleclaw's dream. "Talking to you in dreams? I never heard o' that before."

The young apprentice gaped at him, her green eyes filled with disbelief that there could be a cat who did not know about StarClan.

"Just carry on," Brambleclaw meowed to her, not willing to waste time in long explanations.

Squirrelpaw rolled her eyes at him, but went on without arguing. When she finished, the old loner was silent for a while—so long that Brambleclaw wondered if he had fallen asleep. Then he straightened up and opened his yellow eyes wide, with a fire in them that had not been there before. "I know about this sun-drown place," he meowed unexpectedly. "I've spoken to cats who've been there. It's not far from here."

"Where?" Squirrelpaw leaped to her paws. "How far?"

"Two, maybe three days' travel," Purdy replied. His eyes gleamed. "Tell you what, I'll come with you an' show you."

His expression faded to disappointment when the forest cats said nothing. At last, Crowpaw voiced what Brambleclaw was thinking. "No way. You won't be able to travel fast enough."

"And I don't remember inviting you," Tawnypelt muttered.

"But if he knows the right way . . ." Stormfur mewed. "Maybe we should let him come."

"He's bound to know the way through this Twolegplace," Feathertail added, twitching her tail toward the rows and rows of dull red Twoleg nests that blocked their view of the horizon.

That was true enough, Brambleclaw thought, remembering the trouble they had met in the last Twolegplace. If Purdy really did know the way to the sun-drown place it might be quicker to go with him, even if he couldn't move so fast. Perhaps he was the guide StarClan had sent in response to Brambleclaw's prayer. He seemed an unlikely savior, but he certainly had the courage of any forest cat.

"Okay," he meowed, realizing with a jolt of surprise that the other cats were looking at him as if they expected him to make the decision. "I think he should come."

## CHAPTER 20

*Purdy led the forest cats along* the edge of the wood. It was the day after their narrow escape from the dog, and Brambleclaw was still struggling with doubts about his decision to follow the old cat; he knew that Crowpaw and Tawnypelt were unhappy about it, too. But there seemed no other choice; more and more Twoleg nests filled the horizon, and clouds still covered the sky, so there was no sun to guide them to the sun-drown place.

"Is there any chance of more food?" he asked Purdy as they left the trees behind and began to cross a grassy space dotted with clumps of brightly colored flowers. "The fish yesterday weren't really enough, and Crowpaw didn't eat at all."

"Sure, I can take you to a place," Purdy replied with a hostile glance at Crowpaw, who had been the most outspoken in voicing his distrust of the old cat.

He led them to the other side of the grassy place, where there was yet another row of Twoleg nests. Brambleclaw watched uneasily as the old cat flattened his belly to the ground and heaved himself under a wooden gate, grunting with the effort and shaking himself vigorously on the other side.

"More Twolegs?" Crowpaw hissed. "I'm not going in there."

"Suit yourself," Purdy meowed, beginning to pad up the path to the door with his tail held straight up.

"We'd better all stay together," Brambleclaw murmured. "Remember what happened last time."

Crowpaw snorted but said nothing, and none of the other cats disagreed. One by one they squeezed under the gate and followed Purdy up the path. Crowpaw came last, casting wary glances behind him.

Purdy was waiting for them by the half-open door of the Twoleg nest. A harsh glow lit up the space inside it, which was full of strange shapes and scents that Brambleclaw had never encountered before.

"In there?" he mewed to Purdy. "You're expecting us to go into an Upwalker nest?"

Purdy twitched his tail impatiently. "That's where the food is. I know this place. I often come here."

"This is wasting time," Tawnypelt meowed. Brambleclaw thought his sister sounded scared; her claws were flexing anxiously on the hard stuff of the path. "We *can't* go in there. We're not kittypets. Eating kittypet food is against the warrior code."

"Oh, come on." Stormfur gave Tawnypelt's ear a friendly flick with his tail. "There's no harm in it. We're on a long journey, and if we can get food easily it saves time we would have to spend hunting—time we might need for something else. StarClan will understand."

Tawnypelt shook her head, still unconvinced, but Feathertail looked reassured by her brother's reasoning, and both RiverClan cats ventured cautiously inside.

"That's right," Purdy encouraged them. "There's the food, see, in bowls over there, all ready for us."

Brambleclaw's stomach growled; the fish he had eaten had been small, and it had been a long time ago. "Okay," he meowed. "I think Stormfur's right. Let's go, but make it quick."

Squirrelpaw didn't wait for his decision, bounding inside hard on Purdy's paws. Brambleclaw followed her, but Crowpaw and Tawnypelt stayed outside.

"We'll keep watch!" Tawnypelt called after him.

Stormfur and Feathertail were already crouched beside the bowls, gulping eagerly. Brambleclaw peered suspiciously at the food; it was hard, round pellets like rabbit droppings, but the scent that came from it told him it would be safe to eat.

Squirrelpaw thrust her muzzle into the other bowl; when she looked up her fur was plastered into spikes by something white, and her green eyes were glowing. "It's *good!*" she exclaimed. "Purdy, what is it?"

"Milk," Purdy replied. "A bit like the milk you suck from your mother."

"And kittypets drink this every day?" Squirrelpaw was astonished. "Wow! It's nearly worth being a kittypet." She plunged her muzzle back into the bowl.

Brambleclaw crouched beside her and lapped up a few drops of the white liquid. Squirrelpaw was right—it was good, rich and full-tasting with hardly any tang of Twolegs about it. He settled down and tucked in.

The first hint he had of trouble was the sound of a door

opening and a high-pitched Twoleg voice crying out above his head. Brambleclaw sprang to his paws in time to see a Twoleg kit run through the door and scoop up Feathertail in her arms.

Taken by surprise, Feathertail let out a startled yowl and began struggling, but the young Twoleg had her in a tight clasp. Stormfur stretched up with his forepaws, trying to reach his sister, but the Twoleg kit took no notice. Brambleclaw stared in dismay. *Feathertail!* He glanced around for Purdy, only to see the old cat padding calmly toward a full-grown Twoleg that stood in the doorway, waving his tail in welcome.

Then Crowpaw appeared from the garden, a black whirl wind with glaring amber eyes. "See?" he hissed at Brambleclaw. "This is your fault! You let that old mange bag bring us here."

Brambleclaw gaped at the accusation, but Crowpaw did not wait for an answer. He spun around to face the Twoleg kit, lips drawn back in a snarl. "Let her go, or I'll claw you to shreds!" he spat.

The little Twoleg, happily stroking Feathertail with loud squeaking noises, hadn't noticed Crowpaw, nor understood his threat. The black apprentice was ready to spring when Squirrelpaw slipped in front of him. "Wait, mouse-brain! It's only a kit. Do it this way."

She padded up to the Twoleg. Raising her green eyes pleadingly, she let out a purr and rubbed herself against the Twoleg's legs.

"Good idea!" Stormfur exclaimed, and crowded up to the

Twoleg kit on the other side, purring.

The little Twoleg's eyes gleamed. It let out a cry of delight and bent down to stroke Squirrelpaw; at the same instant Feathertail, feeling the grip on her slacken, managed to wriggle free and leap to the ground.

"Let's go!" Brambleclaw yowled.

The forest cats shot out of the door and streaked down the path to the gate. As Brambleclaw squeezed underneath he heard the little Twoleg yowl loudly but he did not stop to listen. "This way!" he shouted, heading for a clump of shrubs.

As he dived under the low-hanging, glossy-leaved branches, he realized to his relief that all his companions were with him. A moment later, with a lot of puffing and blowing and scrabbling, Purdy joined them.

"Get out of here!" Crowpaw spat at the old tom. "It was you who took us in there, to be caught by Twolegs." With a pointed glance at Brambleclaw he added, "If you had listened to me, it wouldn't have happened."

Purdy twitched an ear, and showed no signs of leaving. "I don't know what you're worried about. They're decent Upwalkers. They wouldn't hurt a cat none."

"Just keep her prisoner," Tawnypelt growled. "That Twoleg kit obviously wanted to turn Feathertail into a kittypet."

"I wasn't in any danger," Feathertail pointed out. "I could have escaped by myself, except I didn't want to claw the little Twoleg." She blinked gratefully at the ThunderClan apprentice. "But Squirrelpaw had the best idea."

Squirrelpaw ducked her head, looking embarrassed. "If

ever *any* of you tell the cats back home that I purred at a Twoleg," she mewed through gritted teeth, "I'll turn you into crowfood, and that's a promise."

In spite of Crowpaw's protests, the journeying cats trekked on with Purdy as their guide. All day the old tabby led them along hard Twoleg paths that made their paws burn, where they had to slink along in the shelter of walls or dart across Thunderpaths under the noses of monsters roaring down on them.

By the end of the day Brambleclaw was exhausted, finding it hard to put one paw in front of the others. His companions were no better. Squirrelpaw was limping and Crowpaw's tail drooped; Brambleclaw remembered that the black-pelted apprentice still hadn't eaten, and he wondered if there would be any prey to be found so deep in Twoleg territory.

"Purdy!" he called, forcing himself to quicken his pace and catch up with the old cat. "Is there anywhere safe we can spend the night? Anywhere we can find food—not kittypet food," he added. "We need somewhere to hunt."

Purdy flopped down in the angle where two Thunderpaths met, and raised one hind paw to scratch his ear. "Don't know about prey," he rasped. "There's a place we can spend the night just up ahead."

"How far?" Tawnypelt growled. "My paws are dropping off."

"Not far." Purdy heaved himself to his paws again; Brambleclaw had to admit the old cat was showing more stamina than he would have expected on the seemingly endless journey. "Not far at all."

As Brambleclaw braced himself to set off again, he spotted a faint reddish gleam falling on the hard surface of the Thunderpath. His head whipped around and he stared in horror. The clouds were clearing away on the horizon, and now, in the gap between two of the Twoleg nests, he could see the setting sun. It was behind them. They had been traveling in completely the wrong direction!

"Purdy!" His voice was a strangled yowl. "Look!"

The old cat blinked at the red light in the sky. "Fine weather tomorrow, I shouldn't wonder."

"Fine weather!" Crowpaw hissed. "He's been leading us wrong all day."

Squirrelpaw sank down on the hard ground and put her head on her paws.

"We're supposed to be going *toward* the sunset," Brambleclaw pointed out. "Purdy, do you *really* know how to find the sun-drown place?"

"'Course I do," Purdy defended himself, his rumpled fur beginning to bristle. "It's just . . . well, goin' through Upwalker places, you get turned around on yourself now and then."

"He doesn't know," Tawnypelt mewed flatly.

"Of course he doesn't," Crowpaw scoffed. "He couldn't find his own tail. Let's leave him here and carry on by ourselves."

Another monster roared by; Stormfur, who had been standing nearest the edge of the Thunderpath, jumped back as a shower of grit spattered his fur.

"Look," he meowed, "I agree that Purdy's leading us the

wrong way. But we can't go off on our own now. We'd never get out of this Twolegplace."

Feathertail nodded glumly, padding over to stand beside her brother and lick the grit off his fur.

Brambleclaw knew they were right; he forced down frustration at the thought of how much time they were wasting.

"Okay," he meowed. "Purdy, show us this place where we can sleep. Everything will look better in the morning."

Ignoring a contemptuous noise from Crowpaw, he set out once again in the pawsteps of the old tabby.

By the time they reached Purdy's sleeping place, the sky was almost completely dark, but their path was lit up with a harsh glare from Twoleg lights like small, dirty suns. The old tabby led them to a stretch of shrubs and grass, surrounded by a spiky fence with gaps between the posts where a cat could easily slip through. There was shelter, water in shallow puddles, and even the scent of prey.

"There!" Purdy meowed, twitching his whiskers with satisfaction. "This isn't so bad, is it?"

It wasn't bad at all, Brambleclaw decided, wondering whether Purdy had really meant to lead them here, or if finding the place was just a lucky accident. Tired though they were, they hunted at once; the mice they caught were scrawny and reeked of Twolegplace, but they tasted like the juiciest voles to the hungry forest cats.

Squirrelpaw polished hers off, looked around for more, and sighed. "What wouldn't I give for a bowl of kittypet milk! I'm *joking*," she added, as Crowpaw curled his lip at her. "Lighten up, will you?"

Crowpaw turned his back, too exhausted for a real quarrel.

To Brambleclaw's relief, it was not long before all his companions settled down to sleep. He curled up under some low-growing branches, where he could almost imagine himself back in the warriors' den. Gazing through the gaps between the leaves, he looked up at the sky, but the harsh Twoleg lights cut off the glitter of Silverpelt. StarClan seemed very far away.

The next day they struggled on under Purdy's directions. Brambleclaw felt as if he had been plodding along for the length of an elder's life, at the base of tall Twoleg walls that were as steep as the cliff at the sun-drown place. By now he was pretty much convinced that the old tabby was ambling along at random, not caring if they were going the right way or not. But the forest cats had no hope of finding their own way out of the Twolegplace. Cloud covered the sun again, so there was no help there, and now and again rain fell in a cold spatter.

"We'll never get out of this." Tawnypelt echoed Brambleclaw's thoughts as they lined up to cross another Thunderpath.

"You might as well stop complaining," Stormfur retorted. "There's nothing we can do about it."

Brambleclaw was surprised to hear such a hostile response from the easygoing RiverClan warrior. But they were all still tired, even after the night's sleep, and hope was trickling away like water falling onto sand. As Tawnypelt glared, her neck fur bristling, he stepped in front of her. "Take it easy, both of you," he meowed.

He broke off when Stormfur whipped around and pelted across the Thunderpath, almost straight under the paws of an approaching monster. Feathertail let out a distressed mew and sprang after him.

"And don't take stupid risks!" Brambleclaw yelled after them.

The RiverClan warriors ignored him. Shrugging, Brambleclaw turned to Squirrelpaw, who was crouching beside him at the edge of the Thunderpath, watching for her chance to cross. "I'll tell you when it's safe to go," he told her.

"I can do it!" Squirrelpaw spat. "Stop trying to sound like my father." She leaped out onto the hard surface of the Thunderpath; fortunately no monsters were in sight.

Brambleclaw raced behind her, catching up as she reached the other side. He bent over her so they stood nose-to-nose, and his words came out in a hiss of fury. "If you ever do something so stupid again, you'll wish I *was* your father! I'll be tougher with you than he ever was."

"I wish you were my father *now!*" she retorted. "Firestar would know which way to go."

There was nothing Brambleclaw could say to that. She was right—the heroic ThunderClan leader would never have made such a mess of this journey. Why had StarClan chosen him, *why?*

He turned to the old tabby, who was strolling across the Thunderpath as if he had all the time in the world. "Purdy, how much farther is it to the edge of this Twolegplace?"

"Oh, not far, not far at all." Purdy let out an amused purr. "You youngsters are too impatient."

A faint growl came from Crowpaw's throat, and he took a step toward their guide. "At least age hasn't cracked our wits," he snapped. "Get a move on!"

Purdy blinked at him. "All in good time." He stood still, scenting the air, and then turned decisively alongside the Thunderpath. "This way."

"He hasn't got the faintest idea," Crowpaw snarled, but he still followed. As with all of the forest cats, it was no longer a question of faith or courage. They just didn't have any choice.

The day seemed to drag on forever, and when the light began to fade again they were limping painfully beside a tall Twoleg fence. Brambleclaw thought the skin on his pads must have been worn off with so much walking on stone; he longed for the soothing coolness of growing things under his paws.

He opened his mouth to ask Purdy to find them another place to stop, only to realize that he could taste a sharp, unfamiliar smell on the air. He paused, trying to identify it; at the same moment Tawnypelt came hurrying up to him.

"Brambleclaw, have you noticed that smell? It's like the carrionplace, on the edge of ShadowClan territory. We'd better watch out. There'll be rats."

Brambleclaw nodded. Now that his sister had reminded him, he could clearly detect the scent of rat among the other foul reeks of Twoleg rubbish. Glancing back the way he had come, he saw that the rest of his companions were spread out behind, worn out by fear and uncertainty and the hard slog of their journey.

"Hurry up!" he called. "Keep together!"

A dry chittering sound interrupted him. Whirling around, he saw three huge rats squeezing under the fence to stand in his path, their naked tails curled high over their backs. Their eyes glinted in their evil, wedge-shaped faces, and he could just make out the gleam of their sharp front teeth.

In a heartbeat, the leading rat sprang at him; Brambleclaw leaped back and felt its teeth snap a hairbreadth from his leg. He swung a paw and raked his claws down the side of the rat's head. It fell back, squealing, but at once another one took its place. More appeared from the other side of the fence, streaming onto the path like a vicious, squealing river. Brambleclaw caught a glimpse of Tawnypelt snarling fiercely as a rat sank its teeth into her shoulder. Then two more of them struck him and he went down under a writhing mass of bodies.

At first he could hardly get his breath. The disgusting stink of the rats filled his nostrils, choking him. He kicked out with his hind paws and felt his claws sink into fur and flesh. A rat squealed and the weight on him vanished, letting him scramble to his paws again to slash at another of the vile creatures as its teeth met in his ear.

Just beside him Squirrelpaw was writhing underneath a rat almost as big as she was; before Brambleclaw could make a move to help her she threw it off and hurled herself at it, ears flattened and jaws parted in a furious yowl. The rat fled; Squirrelpaw let it go and turned to aim her claws at another that was clinging onto Feathertail's back, sending streams of bright red blood running from its sharp claws.

Brambleclaw threw himself back into the battle beside Crowpaw, who was being dragged along the ground with his teeth embedded in a rat's leg. Brambleclaw dispatched the rat with a single blow of his paw, and spun to meet the next attacker. Stormfur and Feathertail were fighting side by side at the base of the fence, and Tawnypelt, one shoulder bleeding heavily, shook a rat by its tail before dropping it and biting hard at its throat. Purdy had come back too, wading into the mass of rats and tossing them aside with one powerful forepaw.

As quickly as it had begun, the fight was over. The surviving rats retreated through the hole in the fence; Crowpaw aimed a blow at the last of them as its tail vanished.

Brambleclaw was left gasping for breath, feeling a sharp sting in his tail and one hind leg, as he gazed at the remaining rats strewn across the ground, some of them still feebly twitching. *Fresh-kill*, he thought dully, but he could not summon the energy to gather the bodies together or to eat. The rest of his companions huddled around him, gazing at each other with huge eyes, all their quarrels forgotten in their shared fear.

"Purdy," Brambleclaw mewed exhaustedly. "We've got to rest. What about over there?"

He pointed with his tail to a gap in the wall on the other side of the Thunderpath from the carrionplace where the rats were. Beyond, everything was dark. He could pick up the scent of Twolegs, but it was stale.

Purdy blinked. "Sure, that'll do."

This time it was Brambleclaw who led the way across the Thunderpath. Every cat was so worn out that if a monster had appeared it could have flattened them all, but StarClan watched over them and everything was quiet. Crowpaw, Stormfur, and Feathertail dragged rats across with them, while Squirrelpaw lent her shoulder to help support Tawnypelt, who was limping badly and left a trail of blood drops behind her.

Through the gap in the wall there was a dark enclosed area behind a dead-looking Twoleg nest. Rough stones were stuck out of the ground; puddles of greasy water had gathered among them. Crowpaw bent his head to drink and grunted in disgust, but did not have the strength to complain out loud.

There was nothing to use as bedding. The cats huddled together in one corner, except for Squirrelpaw, who went nosing around the wall and came back with cobwebs plastered over one paw, which she pressed onto Tawnypelt's wound.

"I wish I could remember the herb Leafpaw uses for rat bites," she meowed.

"No herbs here anyway," Tawnypelt murmured, wincing. "Thanks, Squirrelpaw, that really helps."

"We'd better keep watch," Brambleclaw announced. "Those rats might be back. I'll go first," he added, worried that some cat would start protesting. "The rest of you get some sleep, but if you've got any bites, give them a good lick first."

All his companions, even Crowpaw, obeyed without question. Brambleclaw guessed that they were so frightened, they were just glad to have some cat tell them what to do.

He padded back to the gap in the wall and sat in shadow,

gazing out across the Thunderpath to the place where the rats had appeared. Everything was quiet, leaving Brambleclaw nothing to do but worry about how the journey had gone so disastrously wrong. Most of all he worried about Tawnypelt. They all had scratches from the battle with the rats, but his sister's was the only deep bite; it looked nasty, and he knew that of all bites, those from a rat were feared most by his Clan mates. How would they cope if the bite became infected, or if her leg stiffened so that Tawnypelt couldn't go on?

A whisper of movement beside him made him jump, until he saw that it was Squirrelpaw. Her ginger fur stood on end and blood was oozing from a scratch on her nose, but her eyes were still bright. Brambleclaw braced himself for criticism or some clever remark, but when she spoke her voice was quiet. "Tawnypelt's asleep."

"Good," Brambleclaw meowed. "You . . . you fought well today. Dustpelt would have been proud of you, if he could have seen." He let out a long sigh, full of weariness and uncertainty.

To his surprise, Squirrelpaw pushed her nose comfortingly into his fur. "Don't worry," she mewed. "We'll be fine. StarClan are watching over us."

Breathing in her soft, warm scent, Brambleclaw wished that he could believe her.

# CHAPTER 21

❧

*Leafpaw jumped up from her nest* in the ferns outside Cinderpelt's den. The sun was just rising, its rays glittering on drops of water that trembled on each fern frond and blade of grass. There was a chill in the air, reminding Leafpaw that leaf-fall would give way to leaf-bare before many moons.

At first she was not sure what had awakened her. There was no sound except for the gentle sigh of wind in the tree-tops and the distant murmur of the warriors rousing in the main clearing. Cinderpelt had not called her, yet Leafpaw's fur prickled with the certainty that there was something she had to do.

Almost of their own accord her paws took her to the mouth of Cinderpelt's den. Peering into the cleft in the rock, she meowed softly, "Cinderpelt, are you awake?"

"I am now." The medicine cat's voice was sleepy. "What's the matter? ShadowClan attacking? StarClan walking among us?"

"No, Cinderpelt." Leafpaw shuffled her paws. "I just wanted to check if we have any burdock root."

"Burdock root?" Leafpaw heard her mentor scramble to her paws, and a heartbeat later Cinderpelt poked her head out of the den. "What do you want that for? Come on, Leafpaw, what do we use burdock root for?"

"Rat bites, Cinderpelt," Leafpaw meowed. She sat down and wrapped her tail around her paws, trying to calm her heart, which was pounding as if she'd just run all the way from Fourtrees. "Especially if they're infected."

"That's right." Cinderpelt slipped out of the den and made a quick tour of the clearing, prodding the clumps of fern with one paw. "No, just as I thought. No rats here," she pronounced at last.

"I know there aren't any rats," Leafpaw mewed helplessly. "I just needed to check that we have burdock root, that's all."

Cinderpelt's eyes narrowed. "Have you been dreaming?"

"No, I—" Leafpaw broke off. "Actually, I think perhaps I have, but I don't know what it means. I can't even remember what the dream was about."

Cinderpelt's blue eyes considered her calmly for several heartbeats. "This may be a sign from StarClan," she meowed at last.

"Then can you tell me what it means?" Leafpaw begged. *"Please!"*

To her dismay Cinderpelt shook her head. "The sign—if it is a sign—is yours," she explained. "You know that StarClan never speak to us in plain words. Their messages come in little things . . . the prickling of fur, a tugging in our paws—"

"The feeling that something's right—or wrong," Leafpaw put in.

"Exactly." Cinderpelt nodded. "Part of being a medicine

cat is learning to read those messages by instinct . . . and we both know how hard it can be to make a leap of faith. That's what you have to do now."

"I'm not sure I know how," Leafpaw confessed, scraping the ground with one forepaw. "Suppose I get the meaning wrong?"

"Do you think I'm never wrong?" Cinderpelt's gaze suddenly grew intense. "You must trust your own judgment. Believe me, Leafpaw, one day you will make a wonderful medicine cat—perhaps even as good as Spottedleaf."

Leafpaw's eyes flew open. She had heard many stories of the gifted young medicine cat who had been killed not long after Firestar had joined ThunderClan. She had never in her wildest dreams thought that she might be compared with her. "Cinderpelt, you can't mean that!"

"Of course I mean it," Cinderpelt mewed dryly. "I don't talk for the pleasure of hearing my own voice. As for burdock, you'll find it growing on the edge of the training hollow. Why don't you go and dig up a few roots—so we'll have plenty, just in case."

As Leafpaw trotted out of the camp, she tried to remember what she had dreamed about. But nothing came into her mind except for a picture of dark Twoleg nests and harsh light shining on a Thunderpath. She wondered if the dream had really been a sign from StarClan; instead, she had a sense that Squirrelpaw was trying to tell her something, though the strength of their link had dwindled with distance. Leafpaw had not seen her sister and the other journeying cats in her

dream, but somehow she became convinced that Squirrelpaw
had been bitten by a rat.

*If only I'd gone with her,* she thought helplessly. *They need a medicine cat. Oh, Squirrelpaw, where are you?*

In the sandy hollow, Mousefur and Thornclaw were training their apprentices. Leafpaw paused for a few moments to
watch, but somehow she could not summon up much interest.
She felt as if the sunlight were draining all her energy away, so
that she could hardly manage to put one paw in front of the
others.

The tall stems of the burdock were easy to find. Leafpaw
burrowed under the dark, sharp-scented leaves to dig up the
roots. When she had scraped off most of the clinging earth,
she carried them back to Cinderpelt's den and laid them in a
neat pile beside the other herbs.

Tonight was the Gathering, she remembered. When
Cinderpelt had first told her she would be going she had been
excited, especially at the thought of seeing Mothwing again.
Now she did not feel she had enough strength for the journey to Fourtrees. She would have given up every Gathering
from now until she went to join StarClan, if only she could
have been sure that her sister was safe.

By the time the ThunderClan cats reached the Gathering,
Leafpaw felt better. She had snatched a brief nap after sunhigh, her nose filled with the scent of burdock clinging to her
fur, and woken with energy in her paws again.

As she emerged from the bushes in the clearing at Fourtrees, she saw Mothwing pushing her way toward her.

"Hi, there," Leafpaw meowed. "How are you getting on?"

Mothwing paused. "Fine, I think, but there's so much to learn! And there are times I don't feel any closer to StarClan than before I went to Mothermouth."

Leafpaw let out a wry meow. "We all feel that. I think every medicine cat in the forest has felt it at some time."

Mothwing's huge amber eyes were confused. "But I thought I'd be wise now that I'm a medicine cat. I thought I'd walk closely with StarClan and always know the answer to everything."

She looked so dejected that Leafpaw leaned over and gave her ear a comforting lick. "One day perhaps you will. We walk closer to StarClan every day." When Mothwing still looked uneasy she added, "Mothwing, is there something in particular bothering you?"

Mothwing started. "Oh, no," she replied, shaking her broad golden head. "Nothing at all, only—"

Leafpaw never found out what she was going to say. A loud yowling drowned out Mothwing's voice as Tallstar, on the top of the Great Rock, called for silence. Leopardstar stood beside him, while Firestar and Blackstar, the leader of ShadowClan, sat a little way behind.

Leopardstar was the first of the leaders to speak. "Tallstar," she meowed, "rain has fallen many times on the forest since the last Gathering. Do the streams run freely again in Wind-Clan territory?"

Tallstar inclined his head toward her. "They do, Leopardstar."

"Then I take back the permission I gave to you and your Clan to enter RiverClan territory to drink. From now on, my warriors will drive out any WindClan cats we find across our borders."

She said nothing about the way that WindClan had gone on visiting the river even when they no longer needed to, but her voice was sharp, and Leafpaw could see the displeasure she was not expressing in words.

Tallstar faced the RiverClan leader, unblinking. "Leopardstar, WindClan thanks you for your help and will not abuse your trust."

The RiverClan leader gave him a sharp little nod and stepped back. Suddenly there was a disturbance among the cats in the clearing, and a sleek tabby cat with massive shoulders rose to his paws. It was Mothwing's brother, Hawkfrost.

"With your permission, Leopardstar, I would like to speak," he meowed.

Leafpaw was surprised; young warriors did not usually speak at Gatherings.

"Well?" Leopardstar mewed.

Hawkfrost hesitated, scuffling the ground in front of him with one paw in apparent shyness, though Leafpaw noticed that his ice-blue eyes flicked from side to side as if making sure that every cat was watching him. "I'm not sure I should say this, but . . . well, when WindClan came to the river, they didn't just drink. I've seen them stealing fish."

"What?" Tallstar sprang to the edge of the rock and crouched there as if he were about to pounce on the RiverClan warrior. "How dare you! No WindClan cats have stolen prey!"

Leafpaw knew that was a lie; she remembered Squirrelpaw telling her about catching a WindClan patrol on Thunder-Clan territory with a stolen vole.

"Did any other cats see this?" Leopardstar asked Hawkfrost.

"I don't think so." Hawkfrost sounded apologetic. "I was on my own at the time."

Leopardstar's gaze raked the clearing, but no cat spoke. Leafpaw wondered if she should say anything, but she had not seen the theft for herself; Squirrelpaw and Brambleclaw were long gone, and Dustpelt, who had also seen it, had not come to this Gathering. She kept silent.

Tallstar turned to the RiverClan leader. "I swear by StarClan that WindClan have taken nothing but water from the river. Are you going to condemn us on the word of one warrior?"

Leopardstar's neck fur bristled. "Are you saying that my warrior is lying?"

"Are you calling my Clan thieves?" Tallstar's lips drew back in a snarl, his teeth bared and his claws unsheathed.

Yowls of protest broke out in the clearing from both RiverClan and WindClan cats. Leafpaw watched the warriors turn on each other, spitting challenges. She felt her fur stand on end, suddenly terrified that the sacred truce of the Gathering would be broken.

"Did Hawkfrost *have* to start this?" she murmured, half to herself.

"What should he do?" Mothwing's voice was sharp as she

defended her brother. "Keep quiet and let WindClan get away with it? Every cat in RiverClan knows that for a couple of mousetails those cats would steal the pelt off your back." Her amber eyes blazed and she sprang to her paws as if she were ready to join in a fight the moment it started.

A furious hiss came from her mentor, Mudfur, reminding her that medicine cats were meant to keep peace, and Mothwing shot him a glance, half-angry, half-ashamed.

"Wait!" The single word carried clearly across the hollow. Leafpaw saw that Firestar had come forward to the edge of the rock. "StarClan is angry—look up at the moon!"

With every other cat, Leafpaw gazed upward. The full moon floated above the trees; not far away a single cloud was being driven toward it, even though there was barely a breath of wind in the clearing. She shivered. If StarClan were angry enough to cover the moon, the Gathering would have to break up.

The warriors crouched down, their hostility fading to fear.

Firestar's voice rang out again. "Leopardstar, Tallstar, will you lead your Clans into battle on the word of one warrior? Hawkfrost, is it possible that you were mistaken in what you saw?"

Hawkfrost paused for a moment, his eyes narrowing to slits as he stared at the ThunderClan leader. "I believe what I said," he replied at last, "but I suppose it's possible I got it wrong. I might have been dazzled by the sun on the water, or something."

"Then let there be friendship between RiverClan and

WindClan," Firestar meowed. "Tallstar has already promised not to come down to the river again."

"And I'll keep my promise," Tallstar spat. "But you should teach your young warriors to show a bit of respect, Leopard-star."

"Don't tell me what to do!" Leopardstar was still angry, but Leafpaw recognized that the threat of battle was over. Above their heads the cloud was carried away from the moon, as though StarClan's anger were fading.

"Remember how good life is in the forest just now," Firestar urged both leaders. "Prey is plentiful, and the streams are full again. We are all well prepared for leaf-fall and leaf-bare. There is no need for us to invade one another's territories." He flashed a glance at Blackstar, who had been sitting with a knowing look on his face, as though he were enjoying the disagreement between the other Clans. "That doesn't mean my borders are not well guarded," he added pointedly.

"And so are RiverClan's," Leopardstar hissed, but she took a pace back, as if acknowledging that the dispute was over.

Tallstar moved away, too, leaving Firestar at the front of the rock. Leafpaw knew what was coming; her father paused before he began to speak, and she guessed that he was choosing his words with care. He would not want the other Clans to think that he had driven out his own cats.

"A quarter moon ago," he began, "the warrior Brambleclaw and Squirrelpaw, an apprentice, left ThunderClan. We do not know where they have gone, but we have reason to believe that they did not go alone." Turning to the other leaders, he went on. "Have any of your warriors gone missing?"

Leopardstar replied willingly enough; Leafpaw guessed that Mistyfoot had told her she had already passed on the news about Stormfur and Feathertail. "Two warriors left RiverClan—Stormfur and Feathertail—just before the half-moon. At first we assumed they had crossed the river to live in your territory, Firestar. Since they have connections in ThunderClan"—she spoke with icy disapproval of her warriors' half-Clan heritage—"we can assume they have all gone together."

There was a pause; then Tallstar cleared his throat and mewed quietly, "WindClan has lost an apprentice, Crowpaw. It would have been about the same time." He added, "I thought a fox or a badger might have gotten him, but it looks as if he might be with your lot."

A murmur of uneasiness broke out in the clearing. Some cat called out, "How do you know? Maybe there's something in the forest picking us off one by one."

The murmur grew louder, and a cat on the edge of the throng let out a wail of terror. Leafpaw could see cats exchanging fearful glances or springing to their paws as if they were ready to flee from the clearing.

"What about the dogs?" another voice yowled. "Maybe the dogs have come back!"

Firestar paced to the edge of the Highrock and looked down. For a moment he caught Leafpaw's eye. She shivered; surely he wasn't going to talk about her link with Squirrelpaw in front of the whole Gathering?

She relaxed as her father began to speak. "We wondered about predators too," he meowed. "But there are none of the signs we would expect to see in the forest—and believe me, ThunderClan would know if the dogs were back. We are sure these cats left of their own accord."

His calm voice seemed to reassure his listeners; the cats who had sprung up sat down again, though many of them still looked uneasy.

"What about ShadowClan?" Firestar turned to Blackstar. "Have you lost cats too?"

The ShadowClan leader hesitated; it was always the nature of that Clan to be secretive, as if information were as precious as prey.

"Tawnypelt," he meowed at last. "I assumed she had gone back to ThunderClan to be with her brother."

Murmurs filled the clearing, as the cats tried to make sense of what they had just learned.

"That's at least one cat from every Clan!" Mothwing exclaimed. "What does it mean?" Sounding frustrated, she added, "Why hasn't StarClan shown this to me?"

Leafpaw longed to tell her friend what Squirrelpaw and Brambleclaw had told her before they left. She wondered if Cinderpelt would mention the omen she saw in the burning bracken, that fire and tiger would join together, somehow connected to trouble for the whole forest. But when she spotted the medicine cat, crouched beside Littlecloud at the base of the Highrock, her head was lowered and she did not speak.

"What do you suggest we do, Firestar?" Tallstar asked.

"There's not much we can do," Leopardstar interrupted before Firestar could reply. "They're gone. They could be anywhere."

Tallstar looked troubled. "I don't understand why they had to go all together like that, but they must have had some idea in their heads. I'd swear Crowpaw was loyal to his Clan."

Firestar nodded. "They are all loyal cats." Leafpaw knew he must be thinking of his quarrels with Brambleclaw and Squirrelpaw before they left, and his worries about the prophecy.

"There must be something we can do," Tallstar asserted. "We can't just pretend they never existed."

"Your concern honors you, Tallstar," Firestar meowed. "But I agree with Leopardstar. There's nothing we can do. They are all in the paws of StarClan. And may StarClan grant that one day soon they will come back safely."

Blackstar, who had made no suggestions so far, added derisively, "Hope is easy, but it catches no prey. If you ask me, we've seen the last of them."

From somewhere behind Leafpaw some cat muttered, "He's right. It's dangerous out there."

Leafpaw felt as though a huge talon were squeezing her heart. Her fears for Squirrelpaw flooded over her again, and she remembered her dream about the rat bites. *Squirrelpaw,* she murmured to herself, *there must be something I can do to help you.*

She found it hard to listen as Blackstar reported more

Twoleg activity around the Thunderpath, even harder when it seemed that the new monsters were all gathered around a boggy piece of ground where the cats never went.

*What does it matter?* she thought distractedly. *Who cares what Twolegs do?*

When the meeting was brought to a close she said good-bye to Mothwing and hurried to find Cinderpelt. An idea had come to her; she was eager to get back to camp and try it out.

On the way back to the ThunderClan camp she made herself keep to Cinderpelt's slower pace, until the two medicine cats were walking alone, behind the others.

"Cats from all four Clans have disappeared, have they?" Cinderpelt mused. She paused briefly to gaze up at the full moon, now sinking below the trees. "Leafpaw, you're worried about Squirrelpaw, aren't you? Do you know anything about where she is now?"

The direct question startled Leafpaw, and for a couple of heartbeats she did not know how to reply.

"Come on, Leafpaw." Cinderpelt narrowed her eyes. "Don't try to tell me you know *nothing*."

Leafpaw stopped and faced her mentor, grateful for the chance to tell the truth. "I know that she's alive, and that she's with the other cats who have left. But I don't know where they are, or what they're doing. They're very far away, I think— farther than any of the forest cats have gone before."

Cinderpelt nodded; Leafpaw wondered if StarClan had told her anything about the journey, but if they had the medicine cat said nothing.

"You might tell your father that," she meowed. "It will help reassure him."

"Yes, I will."

They reached the ravine at last; Leafpaw's paws felt weary as she followed her mentor down the gorse tunnel and into the camp.

"Cinderpelt," she meowed, "will it do me any harm to eat some of the burdock root?"

"It might give you a bellyache if you eat too much," Cinderpelt replied. "Why?"

"Just an idea I had." *If I can tell what Squirrelpaw is thinking,* she added to herself, *maybe she can pick up something from me.* She almost felt that she was stupid to hope she could reach her sister across such great distances, but she knew she had to try.

Warmth glimmered in Cinderpelt's eyes, and she did not press her apprentice to say more. Before she went to her nest in the ferns, Leafpaw bit hard into one of the burdock roots stored in the den, and settled down to sleep with the bitter mouthful in her jaws.

*Burdock root. Burdock root,* she whispered. *Squirrelpaw, can you hear me? Burdock root for rat bites.*

CHAPTER 22

Brambleclaw crouched in the bushes and watched the full moon suspended in the dark blue sky. Back at Fourtrees, the Clans would have met for their Gathering. The thought of the clearing thronged with cats, of gossip exchanged and stories told, made him feel lonelier than ever.

For another endless day they had struggled through the Twolegplace, along Thunderpaths, through fences, over walls. At least they had left the worst of the hard ground behind them; now the Thunderpaths were edged with grass, and gardens surrounded the Twoleg nests. They had found shelter for the night beneath some shrubs, and had even managed to hunt. Yet the sharp teeth of his anxiety kept Brambleclaw awake.

He still did not know if they were going the right way. Purdy led them on confidently, but the twisting route he took among the Twoleg nests took no account of the sun, and Brambleclaw felt as if the sun-drown place were as far away as it had ever been.

"I think we're farther away than ever." Crowpaw had scornfully echoed his thoughts before he settled down to sleep.

Worst of all were his worries about Tawnypelt's shoulder.

Though his sister was too proud to admit she was in pain, by the time they stopped for the night she could barely walk. The rat bite had stopped bleeding, but her shoulder was swollen and the flesh where her fur had been torn away was red and puffy. Brambleclaw didn't need to be a medicine cat to know that the bite was infected. Squirrelpaw and Feathertail had taken turns licking the wound while Tawnypelt slipped into an uneasy, shallow sleep, but every cat knew that it would take more than that to heal her.

Brambleclaw jumped at a scrabbling sound close by in the bushes, then relaxed when Stormfur appeared and crouched down beside him.

"I'll watch for a bit if you like," the gray warrior meowed.

"Thanks." Brambleclaw arched his back and drove his claws into the ground in a stretch. "I'm not sure I can sleep, though."

"Try," Stormfur advised him. "You'll need your strength for tomorrow."

"I know." With another glance at the moon, he added, "I wish we were all safely back at Fourtrees."

To his surprise Stormfur blinked at him sympathetically. "We will be soon. Don't worry. StarClan are with us here just as much as if we were at the Gathering with the rest of our Clans."

Brambleclaw let out a sigh. Somehow, tangled as they were in Twolegplace, it was hard to imagine the starry warriors weaving among them. With a last look at the moon, he curled up and closed his eyes, and at last managed to sink into sleep.

※    ※    ※

The barking of a dog woke him. He sprang up, quivering, only to realize with relief that it was too distant to be a threat; there was no dog scent close by. A gray light filtered through the bushes, and the leaves stirred in a chill breeze with a damp tang to it, as if rain was not far off.

Brambleclaw's companions were sleeping around him, all except Stormfur, who was not in sight. Brambleclaw braced himself, preparing to wake them and get them moving again, when Crowpaw lifted his head and scrambled to his paws, shaking the leaf mold off his pelt.

"Listen, Brambleclaw," he meowed, sounding less aggressive than usual. "We've *got* to get out of here today. Things would be better if we could find a forest, or even farmland. We might need to stop for a bit to let Tawnypelt rest, and we can't do that in the middle of all these Twolegs."

Brambleclaw hoped he hid his surprise at how reasonable the younger cat sounded, especially at how concerned he was for Tawnypelt. "You're right," he agreed. "But I'm not sure. We've no choice but to trust Purdy to get us out of here."

"It's a pity we ever let him come with us," Crowpaw growled. He padded across to where Purdy was sleeping, an untidy heap of tabby fur, snoring and twitching. Crowpaw prodded him hard in the ribs with one paw. "Wake up!"

"Hey? Wha'?" Purdy blinked and then heaved himself up until he was sitting. "What's all the hurry?"

"We need to get moving." Crowpaw's abrasive tone was back. "Or had you forgotten?"

Leaving him to get some sense out of Purdy, too tired and anxious to go over and soothe the festering quarrel, Brambleclaw went to wake the others. He left Tawnypelt until last, bending over to sniff her wound and examine it closely.

"It's no better," Feathertail murmured at his shoulder. "I'm not sure she'll be able to go far today."

As she spoke, Tawnypelt opened her eyes. "Brambleclaw? Is it time to go?" She struggled to sit up, but Brambleclaw could see that her leg would barely support her.

"Lie still for a bit," Feathertail told her. "Let me give that bite another lick."

She crouched down and her tongue rasped in a comforting rhythm over the swollen flesh. Tawnypelt let her head drop onto her paws again. As Brambleclaw watched, Stormfur reappeared with a mouse in his jaws, which he dropped close to Tawnypelt's muzzle.

"There you are," he mewed. "Fresh-kill."

Tawnypelt blinked up at him. "Oh, Stormfur . . . thank you. But I should catch my own."

Brambleclaw's belly clenched with pity. No cat had ever looked less able to hunt.

Stormfur just touched her ear with his nose. "You eat that one," he murmured. "You need to keep up your strength. I can catch more later."

With a little nod of gratitude, Tawnypelt began to eat. Ignoring the argument that was developing between Purdy and Crowpaw, Brambleclaw went to see what Squirrelpaw was doing.

The ginger apprentice was sitting up in the nest of leaves she had made the night before. She was muttering something under her breath, and she kept passing her tongue over her lips as if she could taste something foul.

"What's the matter?" Brambleclaw asked. Trying to joke, he added, "Have you been eating your own fur?"

For once Squirrelpaw did not react. "No," she replied, still licking her lips. "It's just this funny taste. I keep thinking I should remember what it is."

"Not salt, I hope?" Brambleclaw suggested lightly. He had never thought he would miss Squirrelpaw's smart remarks, but this seriousness made him anxious.

"No . . . something else. Just let me think about it, and I'll remember in a bit. Something tells me it might be important."

They set off again, with Purdy in the lead. The night's sleep seemed to have helped Tawnypelt, and she limped along valiantly, managing to keep up with Purdy's ambling pace. Brambleclaw kept an eye on her, determined to stop for a rest if he thought his sister needed it.

The old tabby led them through more Twoleg gardens and out onto a narrow Thunderpath bordered on one side by a wooden fence and on the other by a high wall. Two or three monsters crouched at the edge of the Thunderpath, their huge eyes gleaming. Brambleclaw eyed them suspiciously as he and his companions passed, ready to flee if they roared into life.

The Thunderpath bent sharply to one side; Purdy rounded the corner and Brambleclaw saw Feathertail halt and stare disbelievingly in front of her.

"No!" she spat with uncharacteristic fury. "That's too much! We can't go that way, you furball!"

As if in answer, a dog started barking on the other side of the wall. Brambleclaw glanced around in alarm, but he could see no way for the dog to reach them. Anxiously he bounded forward, and when he reached Feathertail he saw what had upset her. A few foxlengths in front of them the Thunderpath ended abruptly in a high wall, blocking the path ahead with the same dull red stone that had surrounded them for days. They couldn't go any farther that way. Every muscle in Brambleclaw's body shrieked in protest at the thought of having to retrace their steps.

Purdy had stopped to look back, an injured expression on his face. "There's no call to be like that, now."

"You have no idea where we are, do you?" Feathertail demanded. She had flattened herself against the hard surface of the ground; Brambleclaw wasn't sure whether she was trying to hide, or preparing to attack their hopeless guide. And if she did, would he stop her? "We've got an injured cat with us. We can't spend all day traipsing after you up and down this . . . this vile place!"

"Steady." Crowpaw came up and bent over Feathertail, rasping his tongue over her ear. "Just ignore the old fool. We'll make a plan to get out of here by ourselves."

Feathertail bared her teeth at him. "How can we? We

don't know where we are."

Behind the wall the dog was going crazy, letting out a flurry of high-pitched barks. Brambleclaw tensed, ready to run if it found a way out of its garden. Behind him, Stormfur bounded around the corner, checked his pace as he realized the dog was no immediate danger, and went over to his sister. A moment later Squirrelpaw arrived with Tawnypelt.

"What's going on?" asked the ThunderClan apprentice. "Where's Purdy?"

Brambleclaw realized that the old cat had vanished. He wasn't sure whether to feel relieved or angry.

"Good riddance," growled Crowpaw.

The words had hardly left his mouth when Purdy's head reappeared, poking through a gap beside the wall that Brambleclaw had not noticed until now.

"Well?" the old cat meowed. "You comin' or not?"

He withdrew again; Brambleclaw padded over to the broken fence panel and looked out. He was ready for yet more Twoleg nests, and gaped in astonishment. Across a narrow, dusty track was a grass-covered slope dotted with clumps of gorse, and beyond that—trees! Trees as far as Brambleclaw could see, with not a Twoleg nest in sight.

"What is it?" Squirrelpaw called impatiently from behind him.

"A forest!" Brambleclaw's voice squeaked like a kit. "A real forest at last. Come on, all of you."

He slid through the gap to stand beside Purdy. The old tabby was looking at him with a knowing gleam in his eye.

"Satisfied now?" he purred. "You wanted out; I've brought you out."

"Er . . . yes. Thanks, Purdy, this is great."

"Not so much of the 'stupid furball' now, hey?" Purdy asked, with a meaningful look at Crowpaw as the WindClan apprentice slipped through the gap.

Brambleclaw and Crowpaw exchanged a glance. Brambleclaw suspected that Purdy had been as surprised as the rest of them to find the way out of the Twolegplace, but the old cat would never admit it. Anyway, it didn't matter now. Twolegplace was behind them, and they could start looking for the sun-drown place again.

They crossed the track and began to climb the slope. Brambleclaw reveled in the feel of fresh grass on his pads, and the forest scents wafting toward him on the faint breeze. When they stood underneath the trees, it was almost like coming home.

"This is more like it!" Stormfur meowed, gazing around at the clumps of bracken and the long, cool grass. "I vote we stay here for the rest of today and tonight. Tawnypelt can get a good sleep, and the rest of us can hunt."

Brambleclaw bit back a protest; his compulsion to make for the sun-drown place was growing stronger as time slipped away, but he knew they would make better progress if they stopped to recover their strength.

The other cats murmured agreement, except for Tawnypelt. "You don't have to stop for me."

"It's not just for you, mouse-brain." Squirrelpaw pushed

her nose affectionately into the ShadowClan cat's fur. "We all need to rest and eat."

Slowly the cats began to move deeper into the wood, clustered together and alert for danger as they looked for a good place to rest. Brambleclaw stopped every few paces to taste the air, but he could not scent fox, or badger, or other cats— nothing that was likely to give them trouble. But the air was full of prey-scent; his mouth began to water at the thought of sinking his teeth into a plump mouse, or better still, a rabbit.

Before long, they came to a spot where the ground fell away toward a thin trickle of water beneath dense hawthorn bushes.

"Couldn't be better," Crowpaw meowed. "There's water and shelter, and if there are predators about they won't find it easy to sneak up on us."

Tawnypelt, who was limping badly again, half slid, half scrambled down the slope and dragged herself into a mossy nest between two twisted roots. Her green eyes were clouded with pain and exhaustion. Feathertail settled down beside her and began to lick her wound again. Purdy flopped down on her other side and immediately curled up and went to sleep.

"Right, you three stay here," Crowpaw mewed, "and the rest of us will hunt."

Brambleclaw opened his mouth to challenge him for ordering everyone else around, then decided it wasn't worth it. Besides, it made a nice change not to be expected to make all the decisions for once. Instead, he padded over to Squirrelpaw. "Fancy hunting with me?" he asked.

Squirrelpaw just nodded, as if half her mind were on something else. She followed Brambleclaw up the stream, and they were hardly out of sight of their temporary camp when Brambleclaw spotted a mouse scuffling among the grass near the water's edge. In one smooth movement he dropped into the hunter's crouch and sprang, killing his prey with a swift blow. Turning to show Squirrelpaw, he saw her standing with her head lifted and her jaws parted to drink in the forest scents.

"Squirrelpaw, are you okay?"

The apprentice jumped. "What? Oh, yes, fine, thanks. There's something I can't quite . . ." Her voice trailed off and she licked her lips again.

Guessing that he wouldn't get any more sense out of her, Brambleclaw scraped earth over his fresh-kill to keep it safe until he came to collect it, and padded farther into the wood. The whole place was rich in prey, and they hardly seemed to know what a predator was. It was one of the easiest hunts he had ever known.

Squirrelpaw helped, but it was clear her mind wasn't on the task. Usually she was a skillful hunter, but today she let a blackbird escape by hesitating too long, and completely missed a squirrel that was nibbling a nut barely a foxlength away.

Then as Brambleclaw was stealthily creeping up on a rabbit, she cried out, "That's it! Over there!"

At once the rabbit shot upright in the grass, and a heartbeat later all Brambleclaw could see of it was its white tail bobbing up and down as it fled.

"Hey!" he exclaimed indignantly. "What did you do that for?"

Squirrelpaw wasn't listening. She had darted down toward the waterside, where clumps of tall plants with dark green leaves were growing. As Brambleclaw stared, mystified, she began to scrape vigorously at the base of the stems.

"Squirrelpaw, what are you doing?" he asked.

The apprentice paused long enough to give him a glance from green eyes that glowed with triumph. "Burdock!" She panted, attacking the stems again. "It's what Tawnypelt needs for her rat bite. Help me to dig up the roots."

"How do you know?" Brambleclaw asked as he began to dig.

"You know that taste I told you about? I've been trying to think of it all morning. Leafpaw must have mentioned it when she was saying good-bye to us."

Brambleclaw paused and looked at her. Leafpaw had certainly told them about several herbs that she thought they might need, but he couldn't remember burdock root being one of them. Then he shrugged and dug harder. There was no other way that Squirrelpaw could have found out about it.

Once they had dug up three or four of the roots, Squirrelpaw pushed them into the water to wash off the earth and then gripped them in her teeth to carry them back to the camp. Brambleclaw followed more slowly, collecting as much of their prey as he could carry.

When he reached their resting place again he found that Squirrelpaw had already chewed up some of the root and was gently pressing the pulp onto Tawnypelt's injured shoulder. The ShadowClan warrior lay still, watching, but as the juice from the root seeped into her wound she relaxed and let out a long sigh.

"That's better," she mewed. "It's going numb. I can't feel the pain anymore."

"That's brilliant," Brambleclaw meowed.

"I think you must be a secret medicine cat," Tawnypelt said to Squirrelpaw, settling herself more comfortably into the moss. "Perhaps you're carrying a bit of your sister's spirit." Blinking drowsily, she sank back into sleep.

Squirrelpaw was watching Tawnypelt with shining eyes, and Brambleclaw felt his fur prickle. Had Leafpaw really mentioned the burdock root back in the forest, or was there something more mysterious going on between her and her sister?

He went back into the wood to collect the rest of the prey. By the time he returned, Stormfur and Crowpaw had also brought back a good catch. For the first time in many days, they were able to eat as much as they wanted. Purdy woke up and gulped down the fresh-kill enthusiastically, as if he found it much tastier than the kittypet food he was used to.

They all slept well. When he woke, Brambleclaw saw that the clouds had vanished and sunlight was angling through the trees, bathing the forest in a reddish glow. Springing up, he climbed as high as he could above the stream and managed to find a gap in the trees so that he could see where the sun was going down.

"That's the path we have to take." Stormfur scrambled up the slope to stand beside him, and his voice was as calm and determined as if he had shared the visions himself. "That's where we will find what midnight tells us."

Brambleclaw's paws itched to race toward the setting sun, as if he knew for certain that Bluestar was waiting there to tell him exactly how he could save the forest. But he knew that it was more sensible to stick to their original plan and spend the night in the wood. Carefully noting the direction they needed to travel, he went back to his friends beside the stream.

Tawnypelt was tearing ravenously into a rabbit. She paused to nod a greeting at Brambleclaw as he appeared. "I'm famished," she admitted. "And my shoulder feels much better. What did you say that was you put on it, Squirrelpaw?"

"Burdock root." Brambleclaw noticed that Squirrelpaw did not try to explain how she knew that burdock root was the right remedy for the infected bite. Perhaps she was wondering about it, too.

She began chewing up another of the roots, and when Tawnypelt had finished eating she applied more of it to her wound. Brambleclaw noticed that the swelling had gone down and the angry red color had faded. He breathed silent thanks to StarClan—and to Leafpaw—for his sister's recovery.

By the time they set out the next morning, after another good meal, Tawnypelt looked almost like her old self. She was barely limping at all and her eyes were bright again.

Long before sunhigh they came to the edge of the forest.

Ahead of them was open country for as far as they could see. The ground rose and fell in a series of gentle slopes. Wind rippled over short, springy grass interspersed with creeping trefoil and wild thyme. It looked to be easy going, and the air had a fresh tang.

"Like home!" Crowpaw murmured, obviously remembering the open moorland of WindClan.

Unlike the WindClan apprentice, Brambleclaw was reluctant to leave the trees behind. The shelter of the canopy had been comforting. But the food and rest had given them all new strength, and he hoped that at last they were coming to the end of their journey.

To his surprise, Purdy said good-bye to them before they left the trees. "I don't feel right under the open sky," he confessed, echoing Brambleclaw's own thoughts. "I guess I've had too many Upwalkers chasing me. I like to be somewhere I can hide. Besides, you don't need me anymore. StarClan, whatever they might be, won't be waiting for *me* at midnight," he added with a glint in his eye.

"Maybe not," meowed Brambleclaw. "Thanks for everything, anyway. We'll miss you." Surprisingly he realized that was true; he had come to feel something like affection for the exasperating old cat. "If you're ever in our forest, you'll be welcome to visit ThunderClan."

As he finished speaking, he couldn't help hearing Crowpaw mew under his breath to Tawnypelt, "Your brother might miss him, but I won't!"

Brambleclaw curled his lip in warning at the WindClan cat,

but Purdy hadn't caught the apprentice's muttered words. "I'll wait here two or three days for you," he promised. "In case you need help to find your way back."

Brambleclaw glanced at Crowpaw in time to see him rolling his eyes at Feathertail, who just shrugged.

"Always supposin' you come back of course," Purdy went on as he padded away with his tail high. "You wouldn't catch me so close to the sun-drown place. Shouldn't wonder if you all end up drowned."

"That's right," Squirrelpaw muttered into Brambleclaw's ear. "Way to keep our hopes up!"

But by the end of that day, even Brambleclaw's hopes were fading. The heat of the sun had drained his energy, and with no water on these rolling uplands his mouth felt like the floor of the sandy training hollow. His companions were no better off, plodding along with their heads down and tails drooping. Tawnypelt was limping again; though she didn't want any cat to examine her wound, Brambleclaw could see the swelling had returned, and wondered how much longer she could keep going. There was no more burdock root here.

Straight in front of them, the sun was sinking in a blaze of scarlet fire, tongues of flame spreading halfway across the sky.

"At least we're heading the right way," Feathertail murmured.

"Yes, but how far do we still have to go?" Brambleclaw had tried not to share his doubts, but his anxiety was becoming too much for him. "The sun-drown place could be days away."

"I always said this was a mouse-brained idea," Crowpaw remarked, though he sounded too exhausted to be aggressive.

"Well, how long do we carry on?" asked Stormfur. As all the other cats turned to look at him, he went on: "If we don't find the place, sooner or later we have to decide . . . do we give up or keep trying?"

Brambleclaw knew he was right. At some point they might have to admit defeat. But what would that mean for their Clans, to ignore the will of StarClan and go home with the journey unfinished?

Then Squirrelpaw, who had been facing into the wind to drink in the scents it carried, spun around to face the others, her eyes blazing with excitement.

"Brambleclaw!" She gasped. "I can smell salt!"

# CHAPTER 23
❧

*Brambleclaw stared at the apprentice for* a moment before opening his mouth and tasting the air for himself. Squirrelpaw was right. The salt tang was unmistakable, carrying him right back to his dream, and the bitter taste of the water that had surged around him.

"It *is* salt!" he meowed. "We must be close. Come on!"

He raced into the wind with the sun dazzling his eyes. A swift glance behind showed that his companions were following. Even Tawnypelt was managing to hobble faster. Brambleclaw felt new strength pouring into his limbs, as if he could go on running forever until he soared into the fiery sky like one of the white birds that wheeled and screamed above them.

Instead, he came to a skidding, terrified halt on the edge of a huge cliff. Steep sandy slopes fell away barely a mouse-length in front of his paws. Waves crashed at the bottom, and stretching out ahead of him was a heaving expanse of blue-green water. The sun was sinking into it on the horizon, its flames so bright that Brambleclaw had to narrow his eyes against them. The orange fire burned a path like blood across the water, almost reaching the foot of the cliff.

For a few moments no cat could do anything but stare. Then Brambleclaw shook himself. "We've got to hurry," he meowed. "We have to find the cave with teeth before it gets dark."

"And then wait for midnight," Feathertail added.

Brambleclaw glanced from side to side, but he couldn't see anything to tell him which way to go. Choosing a direction at random, he led the way along the cliff top. From time to time they stopped and peered over the edge to look for the cave. Brambleclaw dug his claws firmly into the tough grass; it was too easy to imagine slipping over and falling, falling, falling into the hungry waves.

Gradually the land sloped down until the water was only the height of a tree below them. The cliff top jutted out so they could not see the bottom, and the almost sheer surface was deeply scored with ancient runnels of rain. As the cliff grew less steep, the cats scrabbled a little way down and made their way along closer to the water, sometimes even within reach of a salty burst of wave. Clefts, riven by ancient streams, split the rock, sometimes so wide that the cats had to leap over them, and the grass frequently gave way to hollows where a few twisted shrubs clung to the scant soil.

"There are plenty of places to shelter for the night if we don't find the cave," Stormfur pointed out.

Brambleclaw was beginning to think they might need to find somewhere to stop. The sun had sunk beneath the water by now, though great orange flares still streaked the sky. The breeze was growing colder. Tawnypelt at least could lie down, he thought, while the rest of them went on searching.

His sister had fallen a little way behind. Brambleclaw was just bounding back to her, skirting the edge of one of the clefts, when his paws slipped and he found himself sliding helplessly into the hollow. He scrabbled at the loose soil but it gave way under his claws, showering him with dirt. He kept on sliding; in the shadows he could not see the bottom and he let out a yowl of alarm.

"Brambleclaw!" Stormfur leaped into the hollow beside him and tried to sink his claws into Brambleclaw's shoulder, but Brambleclaw felt more of the soil give way and they both slid downward more rapidly than before. Soil spattered over Brambleclaw's face, stinging his eyes and choking him. From somewhere above he heard an earsplitting yowl and Squirrelpaw launched herself practically on top of him.

"No—go back!" he choked out, getting a mouthful of soil.

Then even the shifting soil vanished and there was nothing beneath him at all; he fell, howling, for a few terrified heartbeats and landed with a thump on damp pebbles.

For a moment he lay stunned. A booming echo thundered in his ears, and he felt as if the whole world were spinning around. Then he opened his eyes and stared in horror as he saw the shape of a massive gaping mouth with teeth closing on him, outlined against the red evening sky. He tried to scramble up, but a sudden rush of water swept him off his paws. His yowl of terror was cut off abruptly as water swirled into his mouth, with the terrifying salt taste of his dream.

Brambleclaw flailed with all his strength but the waves

hurled him mercilessly toward the teeth and then tossed him back again, far under the cliff. He did not know where he was or which way he should try to swim. Water filled his eyes and ears, roaring around him. He gasped for breath, only to swallow more of the salt water.

His frantic struggles were growing weaker, and the cold, stifling waves were closing over his head when he felt a sharp pain in one shoulder. Suddenly the pressure on his fur vanished and he could breathe again. Coughing up water, he turned his head and saw Squirrelpaw's eyes blazing at him, her teeth fastened firmly in his fur.

"No!" He gasped. "You can't—you'll drown. . . ."

Squirrelpaw could not reply without letting go of him. Her only response was to kick out strongly with all four paws. Brambleclaw felt pebbles shifting underneath his feet, and then the waves washed them back toward the teeth.

Summoning the last scrap of his strength he thrashed at the water, trying to drive himself and Squirrelpaw away from those spiky rocks. The water surged and lifted them up; he got a brief glimpse of sodden dark gray fur—Stormfur—beside him, before the waves sent them crashing down on hard ground.

The breath driven out of him, Brambleclaw scrabbled among the rolling pebbles while the shallow, sucking water threatened to drag him back again. Squirrelpaw, still gripping his shoulder, pulled him up, and he felt another cat give him a shove from behind. At last he collapsed on solid rock and lay still, letting the world drift away.

A paw prodding against his flank roused him.

"Brambleclaw?" It was Squirrelpaw, sounding desperately anxious. "Brambleclaw, are you all right?"

Brambleclaw opened his mouth and let out a moan. His fur was soaked and he was ice-cold. He felt too exhausted to move; every muscle shrieked with pain, and his stomach felt distended from all the water he had swallowed. But at least he was alive.

He managed to raise his head. "I'm fine," he rasped.

"Oh, Brambleclaw, I thought you were dead!"

As his vision cleared he could make out Squirrelpaw bending over him. He could not remember ever seeing her look so upset, not even when her father had been angry with her back in the forest. The sight of her troubled eyes urged him to make an effort: he sat up, and instantly vomited up several mouthfuls of salt water.

"I'm not dead." He coughed. "Thanks to you. You were great, Squirrelpaw."

"She took a huge risk." That was Stormfur's voice; the gray warrior was standing over Brambleclaw. With his fur plastered to his body he looked much smaller than Brambleclaw was used to. He sounded disapproving, and yet there was a glow in his eyes as he looked at Squirrelpaw. "But it was a very brave thing she did."

"And a stupid one." With a start of surprise Brambleclaw realized that Tawnypelt was there as well, standing close by with water washing around her paws and her eyes narrowed in anger. "What if you'd both drowned?"

"Well, we didn't," Squirrelpaw flashed at her.

"I could have helped."

"With that infected bite?" Stormfur pressed his muzzle briefly against Tawnypelt's flank. "StarClan know how you managed to get down here at all."

"I fell, like the rest of you." Tawnypelt's voice was wry, and she relaxed a little as she looked at Squirrelpaw. "I'm sorry," she meowed. "You *were* brave. It's just that I'm finding it hard being injured and not able to help. Like you, I . . . I thought we'd lost Brambleclaw for good."

By now Brambleclaw was beginning to feel better, enough to look around and recognize the cave of his dream. He was *inside* it. The gaping mouth with its ring of teeth was at one end. Water washed through it in a strange, ceaseless rhythm, crashing in with a roar and then hissing out again, rolling the pebbles over the floor as it went. The rock walls were smooth and rounded. The ground sloped upward to the back of the cave, which was lost in shadows; the only light came through the mouth and from a small hole high in the roof, where Feathertail and Crowpaw were peering anxiously down.

"Are you all right?" Feathertail called.

"I'm fine." Brambleclaw rose shakily to his paws. "I think we've found what we were looking for."

"Hold on, we're coming down," meowed Crowpaw.

Brambleclaw almost called out an order to stay where they were—which Crowpaw would certainly have disobeyed—but when he looked more closely he could see a series of ledges and clefts in the rock wall where it would be possible to climb safely down and then to get out again. Feathertail and Crow-paw picked their way down carefully until they reached the cave floor and stood looking around, blinking.

"Do we have to stay here until midnight?" Squirrelpaw asked, raising her head from licking her damp chest fur. Her voice echoed strangely around the walls.

"I suppose—" Brambleclaw began, then stopped, his muscles tensing.

From the darkness at the back of the cave came a heavy scratching noise. A powerful, rank scent reached his nostrils. A shadow moved, not wholly black, but patched with white. Then lumbering into the dim light came a shape that was terrifyingly familiar: one of the deadliest enemies of the forest cats.

*A badger!*

CHAPTER 24

*Brambleclaw glanced wildly over his shoulder,* but there was nowhere to flee except into the water; the difficult climb back to the hole in the cave roof would take too long. Guilt crashed over him with the cold force of the waves that had almost drowned him. All his visions, all his certainty, had led his companions to this dreadful place, where they would find no knowledge, no vision from StarClan, only a pointless and horrible death. What use were faith and courage now, when they were trapped like rabbits in a hole?

Crowpaw had flattened himself to the ground and was creeping forward with his teeth bared in a snarl. Stormfur was edging around the badger to attack it from the side. Despairingly Brambleclaw knew that they were heading to meet their death. Even all six of them, weak and starving as they were and worn out by their travels and the struggle in the water, could not hope to defeat a badger. Caught as they were by the choking waves, it would not be long before the blunt claws and snapping jaws picked them off one by one.

The badger had paused on the edge of the shadows that filled the back of the cave. Its powerful shoulders were hunched and its claws scraped on rock. Its head swung to and fro, the white stripe glimmering, as if it were deciding which of them to attack first.

Then it spoke.

"Midnight has come."

Brambleclaw's mouth fell open, and for a moment he felt as if the ground had given way beneath him again. That a badger could speak, could say words he understood, words that actually meant something . . . He stared in disbelief, his heart pounding.

"*I am Midnight.*" The badger's voice was deep and rasping, like the sound of the pebbles turning under the waves. "With you I must speak."

"Mouse dung!" Crowpaw spat. The WindClan apprentice was still crouched ready to spring. "Make one move and you'll have my claws in your eyes."

"No, Crowpaw, wait—"

The badger's throaty laughter interrupted Brambleclaw. "Fierce, is he not? StarClan have chosen well. But there will be no clawing this day. Here is talk, not fight."

Brambleclaw and his companions uncertainly looked at each other, their tails bristling. Crowpaw put words to what they were all thinking. "Are we going to trust it?"

"What else can we do?" Feathertail responded, blinking.

Brambleclaw weighed up the badger again. It was smaller than the one he had seen at Snakerocks—probably a female— but no less dangerous for that. Believing what she said went against everything he had been taught as a kit. Yet so far she had made no move to attack them; he even thought that he could make out a gleam of humor in her eyes.

He glanced back at his friends. Crowpaw, Stormfur, and Feathertail might have managed to fight well, but he and Squirrelpaw were exhausted from their near-drowning, while Tawnypelt had sunk down onto the floor of the cave with her injured shoulder held awkwardly, and hardly seemed to be conscious.

"Come," the badger rasped. "All night we cannot wait."

Brambleclaw knew for certain that this was no ordinary badger. Never before had he heard of a badger who could speak in a language that cats understood—still less one that spoke of StarClan, as if she knew more of their wishes than any cat alive.

"Feathertail's right," he hissed. "What choice do we have? She could have turned us all into crowfood by now. This must be what Bluestar meant in my dream when she told me to listen to midnight. She didn't mean a *time* at all." Turning to the badger, he asked out loud, "You are Midnight? And you have a message for us from StarClan?"

The badger nodded. "Midnight am I called. And it was shown to me that here I would meet with you . . . though four were numbered to me, not six."

"Then we'll listen to what you have to say," Brambleclaw told her. "You're right; four were chosen, but six have come, and all deserve to be here."

"But make one wrong move . . ." Crowpaw threatened.

"Oh, shut up, mouse-brain!" Squirrelpaw growled. "Can't

you see, this is what we came here to find? 'Listen to what midnight tells us.' *This* is Midnight."

Crowpaw glared at her through the gathering darkness, but did not reply.

Midnight turned with the single word, "Follow," and headed for the back of the cave. Brambleclaw could just make out the dark opening of a tunnel. Taking a deep breath, he meowed, "Okay, let's do it."

Stormfur took the lead, with Crowpaw just behind him; Brambleclaw hoped that the apprentice would stop looking for a fight long enough to hear what the badger had to say. Feathertail gently nudged Tawnypelt to her paws and lent her shoulder for support as she staggered into the tunnel. Brambleclaw exchanged a glance with Squirrelpaw and was surprised to see that in spite of her wet, exhausted state her eyes were sparkling with excitement.

"What a story we'll have to tell when we get home!" she meowed, getting up and trotting into the tunnel after Feathertail.

Brambleclaw brought up the rear, with a final glance over his shoulder at the rocky teeth that framed the mouth of the cave and the waves that still surged back and forth. The last crimson rays of the drowned sun still stained the sky; in a single heartbeat Brambleclaw seemed to see an endless river of blood pouring down upon him, filling his ears with the screams of dying cats.

"Brambleclaw?" Squirrelpaw's voice cut through the terrified sounds. "Are you coming?"

The vision was gone; Brambleclaw found himself back in the wave-filled cave to see that the color was rapidly fading from the sky and a single warrior of StarClan shone down on him. Shivering, he followed his friends and Midnight.

The tunnel sloped upward. Brambleclaw could see nothing in the pitch darkness, but he felt sandy soil beneath his paws, rather than pebbles or rock. As well as the wary cat-scent of his friends, there was a powerful reek of badger.

Then he came out into another cave. Fresher air moved against his fur, and at the far end a hole led into the open. A faint silvery gleam filtered through it, telling Brambleclaw that outside, the moon was crossing the sky. By its light he saw that this cave had been dug out of the earth, with twisting roots entangled in the roof and the floor covered with a thick layer of bracken. Feathertail was already helping Tawnypelt to make a nest among the soft fronds, and settled down beside her to lick her wound again.

"You have injury?" Midnight asked the ShadowClan warrior. "What gave it?"

"It's a rat bite," Tawnypelt replied through gritted teeth.

The badger made a spitting noise. "Is bad. Wait." She vanished into the shadows at one side of the cave and returned a moment later with a root clamped in her jaws.

"Burdock root!" Squirrelpaw exclaimed, with a triumphant glance at Brambleclaw. "You use it too?"

"Good for bite, good for infected paw, good for all sores." The badger chomped up the root and laid the pulp on Tawnypelt's wound, just as Squirrelpaw had done in the wood.

"Now," she went on when she had finished, "is time for talk."

She waited until all the cats had settled themselves among the bracken. Brambleclaw felt his excitement rising. He was only just beginning to realize that they had reached the end of their journey. They had found the place where StarClan had sent them, and now they were about to hear what Midnight had to tell them.

"How is it you can speak to us?" he asked curiously.

"I have traveled far, and many tongues have learned," Midnight told him. "Tongues of other cats, who speak not same as you. Of fox and rabbit also." She grunted. "They speak not of interest. Fox talk is all of kill. Rabbit has thistledown for brain."

Squirrelpaw let out a *mrrow* of laughter. Brambleclaw could see that her fur lay flat again and her ears were pricked. "So what do you want to tell us?" she meowed.

"Much, in good time," replied the badger. "But first, tell me of your journey. How came you from your tribes?"

Stormfur looked puzzled. "Tribes?"

Midnight shook her head irritably. "My brain thistledown also. Forget which sort of cats here. You say Clans, not?"

"That's right," meowed Brambleclaw. He nudged away the uneasy thought that there were other cats like them, not loners, who lived in Clans known as tribes. They had not seen them on their journey—they probably lived far in a different direction.

With the others to help him, he began the story of their journey, from the first dreams that four of them had shared, to his own dream of the sun-drown place and the decision to leave the forest. Midnight listened intently, with a low chuckle as the cats told her of their misadventures with Purdy, and an understanding nod when they described how they had all, in the end, received their own saltwater sign.

"So here we are," Brambleclaw finished. "We are ready to know what StarClan's message is."

"And why we had to come here to find out," Crowpaw added. "Why couldn't StarClan have told us what we needed to know back in the forest?"

His tone was still hostile, as if he had not accepted that Midnight was not a threat, but that didn't seem to bother the badger. Feathertail flicked her tail out in a calming gesture, and at her touch the WindClan apprentice relaxed a little.

"Think, small warrior," Midnight replied to his question. "When you set out, you were four. Six with friends who would not stay behind. Now you are one." Her voice grew deeper and seemed to Brambleclaw to be full of foreboding as she went on, "In days coming now, all Clans must be one. If not, trouble destroy you."

Brambleclaw felt icy claws rake down his spine. The shudder that ran through him had nothing to do with his sodden fur. "What *is* the trouble?" he whispered.

Midnight hesitated, her deep, dark gaze resting on each cat in turn. "You must leave the forest," she growled at last. "All cats must leave."

"What?" Stormfur leaped to his paws. "That's mouse-brained! There have always been cats in the forest."

The badger heaved a long sigh. "No longer."

"But why?" Feathertail asked, anxiously kneading her paws on the bed of bracken.

"Twolegs." Midnight sighed again. "Always is Twolegs. Soon they come with machines . . . monsters is your word, not? Trees will they uproot, rocks break, the earth itself tear apart. No place left for cats. You stay, monsters tear you too, or you starve with no prey."

There was silence in the moonlit cave. Brambleclaw struggled with the dreadful vision the badger had summoned. He imagined Twoleg monsters—huge shining things in bright unnatural colors, roaring through his beloved camp. He could almost hear again the screams he had heard in the cave with teeth, though now they were the terrified cries of his Clan mates as they fled. Everything in him strained against what he had heard, yet he could not tell Midnight that he did not believe her. Every word she had spoken was filled with truth.

"How do you know all this?" Stormfur meowed quietly; there was no challenge in his voice, only a desperate need for an explanation.

"It happened to my sett, many seasons ago. I have seen all before; I can see what will come now. Just as the stars speak to you, they talk to me also. All that you need to know is written there. Is not hard to read, once you know."

"No more Sunningrocks?" Squirrelpaw mewed in a small voice; she sounded as scared as a kit without its mother. "No more training hollow? No more Fourtrees?"

Midnight shook her head, her eyes tiny bright berries in the shadows.

"But *why* would the Twolegs do that?" Brambleclaw demanded. "What harm have we ever done them?"

"Is no harm," Midnight replied. "Twolegs hardly know you there. They do it for build new Thunderpath—go here, there, more faster."

"It won't happen." Crowpaw stood up with a fierce gleam in his eyes, as if he were ready to take on the whole race of Twolegs single-pawed. "StarClan won't allow it."

"StarClan cannot stop it."

Crowpaw opened his mouth to protest again, but nothing came out. He looked utterly bewildered to think of a disaster that was beyond the power of StarClan to stop.

"Then why did they bring us here?" mewed a faint voice. Tawnypelt had raised her head from her nest of ferns to fix her gaze on Midnight. "Are we supposed to go home and watch our Clans being destroyed?"

"No, indeed, injured warrior." The badger's voice was suddenly gentle. "For hope is given to you. Hope you shall bring. You must lead your Clans away from the forest and find new home."

"Just like that?" Crowpaw let out a snort of disgust. "I'm supposed to go to my Clan leader and say, 'Sorry, Tallstar, we've all got to leave'? He would claw my ears off, if he didn't die laughing first."

Midnight's reply rumbled from deep in her chest. "When you reach home I think you will find that even your Clan leaders will listen."

Terror seized Brambleclaw. What more had the badger seen in the stars? When they returned to the forest, would they find that the destruction had already begun?

He sprang to his paws. "We must go now!"

"No, no." Midnight shook her head from side to side. "Time is for rest tonight. Hunt in moonlight. Eat well. Let injured friend sleep. Tomorrow is better for travel."

Brambleclaw glanced at his friends and nodded reluctantly. "That makes sense."

"But you haven't told us where to go," Feathertail pointed out, her blue eyes full of trouble. "Where can we find another forest where all the Clans can live in peace?"

"Fear not. You will find, far from Twolegplaces, where is peace. Hills, oak woods for shelter, running streams."

"But how?" Brambleclaw persisted. "Will you come with us and show us?"

"No," Midnight rasped. "Much have I traveled, but no longer. Now enough is this cave, roar of sea, wind in grasses. But you will not be without a guide. When return, stand on Great Rock when Silverpelt shines above. A dying warrior the way will show."

Fear clutched harder at Brambleclaw. Midnight's words sounded more like a threat than a promise. "One of us will die?" he whispered.

"I did not say. Do so, and you will see."

Evidently the badger was not prepared to say more, if indeed she knew. Brambleclaw did not doubt her wisdom, but he realized that not everything had been revealed to her. His breath grew shaky as he caught a glimpse of other powers beyond StarClan—perhaps a power so great that the whole blaze of Silverpelt was no more than the dazzle of moonlight on water.

"Okay," he meowed, letting out a long breath. "Thank you, Midnight. We'll do as you say."

"And now we'd better hunt," added Stormfur.

Dipping his head in deep respect to the badger, he padded past her up the tunnel and out into the night. Crowpaw and Feathertail followed him.

"Squirrelpaw, you stay with Tawnypelt," Brambleclaw mewed. "Rest and get your fur dry."

To his surprise, Squirrelpaw agreed without question, even giving his ear a quick lick before settling down in the bracken beside his sister. Brambleclaw watched them for a moment, realizing how much they meant to him—even the pesky ginger apprentice whom he had tried so hard to leave behind. Stormfur and Feathertail, too, were true friends, and even Crowpaw had become an ally he would want beside him in any battle.

"You were right," he meowed thoughtfully to Midnight. "We have become one."

The badger nodded gravely. "In days to come, you need each other." She pronounced the words with all the force of a prophecy from StarClan. "Your journey not end here, small warrior. It only just begin."

# EPILOGUE

The long grass beside the Thunderpath parted and Firestar prowled into the open, the weakening leaf-fall sun shining on his flame-colored pelt. Beside him Graystripe sniffed suspiciously at the air.

"Great StarClan, it smells foul today!" he exclaimed.

Cloudtail and Sandstorm padded up to join them, and Leafpaw, the last member of the patrol, turned away from the clump of marigold she was examining. Cloudtail let out a snort of disgust. "Every time I come up here, it takes me all day to get the reek out of my fur," he complained.

Sandstorm rolled her eyes but said nothing.

"You know, there's something strange about today," Firestar meowed, glancing up and down the Thunderpath. "There aren't any monsters in sight, but the smell's worse than ever."

"And I can hear something," Leafpaw added, her ears pricked.

The wind carried a deep-toned roaring sound toward the group of cats, faint with distance but growing gradually louder.

Cloudtail turned to his Clan leader with a puzzled look in

his blue eyes. "What's that? I've never heard . . ." His voice trailed off and he stood gaping.

Over a rise in the Thunderpath came the biggest monster any of the cats had seen in their lives. Sunlight dazzled off its gleaming body, and its shape rippled in the heat rising from the surface of the Thunderpath. Its throaty roaring grew and grew until it seemed to fill the whole forest.

It came slowly, followed by another and yet another. Twolegs swarmed over them like ticks, yowling at each other, their words all but drowned by the roar of the monsters.

Then as the leading monster drew abreast of the five watching cats, the unthinkable happened. Instead of going past it swerved, crunched over the narrow strip of grass that edged the Thunderpath, and headed straight for them.

"What's going on?" Graystripe gasped as Firestar howled, "Scatter!"

He dived for cover into a clump of bracken while his deputy fled deeper into the forest and turned to stare out from underneath a thornbush. Cloudtail shot up the nearest tree and crouched in the fork between two branches, gazing down. Sandstorm headed into a narrow gully with a trickle of water at the bottom, pausing to look back only when she reached the other side, her fur bristling in mingled shock and anger. Leafpaw followed her, and flattened herself in the long grass.

The monster barreled forward on huge black paws that crushed everything in its path. As all five cats watched, frozen with horror, it rammed its shoulder up against an ash tree; the tree shook under the impact, and then, with a shriek like all the prey in the forest dying at once, its roots tore out of the earth.

The tree crashed to the ground. The monster rolled on.

The destruction of the forest had begun.

KEEP WATCH FOR

THE NEW PROPHECY

BOOK 2:

# MOONRISE

*As the questing cats journey through* the harsh mountains, they encounter a tribe of wild cats who have their own set of warrior ancestors . . . and their own mysterious prophecy to fulfill. Stormfur can't understand their fascination with him, but he senses that they are hiding a deadly secret.